THE DOUBLE DUCHESS

ANNA HARRINGTON

NYLA Publishing

121 W 27th St., Suite 1201, New York, NY 10001

http://www.nyliterary.com

PRAISE FOR ANNA HARRINGTON'S BOOKS

"As steamy as it is sweet as it is luscious. My favorite kind of historical!" —Grace Burrowes, *New York Times* bestselling author, for *Dukes Are Forever*

"A touching and tempestuous romance, with all the ingredients Regency fans adore." — Gaelen Foley, *New York Times* bestselling author, for *Dukes Are Forever*

"Harrington has created a richly woven novel, complete with romance, a touch of mystery, and wounded, believable characters." —*Publishers Weekly* for *Along Came a Rogue*

"Thoroughly entertaining...seduction and adventure take center stage." —*BookPage* for *Along Came a Rogue*

Dedicated to my darling Mel

A very special thank you to
Sara Kortenray, Head of Charity
Greenwich Hospital, London
for her help in researching this story

PROLOGUE

Fort St George, India
October, 1813

Lieutenant Maxwell Thorpe stared at the letter in his hand, for once oblivious to the hot rains that poured endlessly over the white stone fort. The candle lighting the small writing desk in the quarters he shared with five other junior officers sputtered as a drop of water dripped through the ceiling and onto the flame.

... to notify you that I will be asking for her hand in marriage.

A burning clawed at his gut, helped along in no small part by the now-empty bottle of whiskey sitting on the desk, one last swallow of the stuff in the glass beside it.

She will become a respected woman of rank and fortune within the Collins family, protected by my brother, Duke of Winchester. I will offer a generous settlement that will erase her father's debts. She will never want for anything.

Hell... that's what this was. He had seen torment and suffering on the battlefields. Had endured weather that killed lesser men.

Had once even been in such physical pain that he'd wished for death. None of that compared to the agony that pulsed through him now.

So I ask you, as one gentleman to another, to let her have the life she deserves.

Slowly, he set it down and picked up a second letter. This one had arrived the same day as the first, dated nearly two months ago. Two months that he'd lived thinking that his fate was still his own, his future his to claim. In reality, his heart had been killed then, but the damnable thing only now knew to break.

... a terrible position. Papa wants me to marry Lord George Collins. He sees that as the salvation for our family's future. But I want only you for a husband, my love. Please come home—come home and help me.

With grim determination, he tossed back the last swallow of whiskey, then reached for the inkpot and paper. She would think him a bastard for this. But let her place the blame on him, let her hate him to the end of her days. Small price to pay for the life that he could never give her otherwise. Scribbling quickly before he changed his mind—

My dearest Belinda, I cannot return to England. My life is in the army here. I want you to forget me...

CHAPTER 1

Brighton, England
July, 1823

Belinda stared across the meeting table toward Maxwell Thorpe and bit out, "You are a heartless monster."

The monster himself said nothing. He silently continued to gaze at her with brown eyes that had always reminded her of melted chocolate, with a face that most women would have said was handsome enough to give sweet dreams but which had brought her nightmares.

Around them, the other members of the board of the Royal Hospital who had arrived in time for this meeting shifted awkwardly in their chairs. The tips of Mr. Peterson's ears turned red, and Lord Daubney was downright shocked. But when had she ever cared what Society gentlemen thought of her?

And she certainly couldn't care less what the monster at the head of the table thought. Maxwell Thorpe had lost that right a very long time ago.

Colonel Woodhouse leaned forward. "Your Grace, if you would consider—"

She slid a narrowed gaze at him, silencing him with a look. Nor did she care what opinions the colonel—or any actively commissioned officer, *especially* the one leading the meeting— held about this matter. Those same officers were now conspiring to shut down the Royal Hospital, home to more than sixty military pensioners, and she refused to let that happen.

"Of course *you* support him, Colonel." Her calm words belied her anger. "I'm certain the orders came down from the highest level in the War Office, and a good soldier never questions his orders. Not even when it destroys the home of elderly men who have lost the best years of their lives—and several dozen eyes and limbs between them—protecting England."

That silenced the colonel. He leaned back in his chair and busied himself by shuffling through the papers in front of him.

It silenced all protests from the other board members as well. *Good.* They needed to know that she was resolute in carrying out the remaining few months of her late husband's three-year tenure on the board. Once a new board was seated, she'd lose the influence she held as a voting member. But until then, she planned to fight to keep those men in the only home they had left, and the one they deserved.

"As I explained," Maxwell interjected, "the army needs another training facility in the south of England, and because the garrison barracks are already located here, Brighton is the most logical choice."

"Very well." She kept her hands folded demurely in her lap, not once reaching for the tea tray that the flustered aide-de-camp had hurried to ready and bring into the room, once his surprise had worn off at a woman arriving unannounced for the meeting. The widow of a duke, no less. One who spoke her mind on military matters and held her own against peers and His Majesty's officers. "Then, by all means, you should build one."

And leave the Royal Hospital and its pensioners alone. The unspoken challenge hung in the air between them.

She'd received word only yesterday about this called meeting of the board and the War Office's plans, which had taken her completely by surprise. And she certainly hadn't expected that the man who was leading the meeting, as special War Office liaison to the board, was the same one who had once shattered her heart.

Now, apparently, he was also set on turning pensioners out of their home, just so soldiers could learn to more effectively wage war.

But he had another think coming if he thought he could come sweeping in and so easily close the hospital.

She flashed a saccharine smile. "Other properties are available where the academy can be constructed."

"Unfortunately, that's not feasible." Maxwell's answer was calm, although she was certain he wanted to throttle her for raising objections to his plans. "We need the academy to be operational within six months, which means we need these existing buildings."

"Without regard to the men whom the army no longer has any use for?" She held up the list of pensioners' names. "What's to become of them?"

"They're not being kicked out into the cold, Your Grace." His forced smile proved that she was wearing on his patience. *Good.* "They'll be relocated to other hospitals, including Chelsea."

"But their home isn't Chelsea. It's Brighton."

"They will adapt to their new home, wherever it is." His hard expression told her that he was through attempting to win her over by persuasion. So did the way he leaned back in his chair, reminding her of a tiger studying his prey. Right before it pounced. "His Majesty's soldiers are all loyal men who are used to doing what's needed of them."

"Are they? My experience tells me differently."

His eyes glinted at that private cut, the only outward reaction that her arrow had hit home. But she'd noticed. After all, there was a time when she'd noticed everything about this man.

"With respect, Your Grace," Mr. Peterson interjected, perhaps fearing the two of them would come to blows if someone didn't intercede, "your experience with the military is limited. I'm certain Brigadier Thorpe is doing what's best for both the pensioners and the cadets."

"While my experience with the military might be limited"—she leveled her gaze on Maxwell to make certain he understood that she'd neither forgotten nor forgiven how he'd used her for his own advancement all those years ago—"my experience with *military officers* is not. In addition to serving on this board in my late husband's stead and being the hospital's leading patroness, I am also a patroness for the Royal Hospital Chelsea and the Greenwich Hospital."

As the Duchess of Winchester, she wielded a great deal of influence, and her role here couldn't be dismissed out of hand. That was the greatest gift that her late husband, George, had ever given her—the power of a duchess, along with a dower that ensured she'd be able to give financially to whatever charities she favored. Winchester had known since the day he married her that her heart lay with her charity work. He'd probably laugh to know that she was using his old position on the board to put a thorn in Maxwell Thorpe's side.

She straightened her shoulders to become as imposing as her twenty-eight years could be. "Gentlemen, need I remind you that those pensioners are here because they have no money and no families to look after them? It is up to us to defend them."

"And it is up to His Majesty's active army and navy to defend *all* of England," Maxwell countered. "Sandhurst has proven a grand success, and the War Office believes—and I concur—that more academies are needed. Of course, we want to work with the board, not against it, to ensure a smooth transition."

In other words, the War Office was going ahead with the academy whether the board liked it or not.

"And if the board refuses?" she pressed.

The men all looked at her as if she'd sprouted a second head. After all, they'd have to be mad to go against the War Office's wishes.

Except for Maxwell, in whom she saw a flash of admiration for her tenacity.

Perhaps, though, it wasn't admiration at all but simply acknowledgment of an adversary. If so, he had no idea how stalwart an opponent she could be.

Colonel Woodhouse gently cleared his throat. "I believe, Your Grace, that the board agrees with Brigadier Thorpe."

"Does it? By my count, only a third of the board is present." Eleven men—and one lone widow—sat on the board, but because of the rushed nature of this meeting, only four of them were present. "Do we really want to expose ourselves and the War Office to the hostilities that might ensue if sixty pensioners are expelled from their home based upon the agreement of only one-third of the board?"

The men exchanged troubled looks. Only Max's inscrutable expression remained unchanged, as if he'd expected a fight from her all along.

"What are your terms, Your Grace?" he asked. The same words, she noted, that generals used when negotiating surrender.

The question was... which one of them did he think was surrendering?

"That we hold a formal vote by the entire board in a fortnight. Delaying the decision will give the others the opportunity to weigh in or send their proxies."

And give her time to sway them all to vote against the academy.

Woodhouse's patience snapped. "This is absurd!" He dismissingly waved a hand at her. "To let this woman—"

"*Colonel.*" The force of that word reverberated through the room as Maxwell rose from his chair. "You forget yourself."

Woodhouse snapped his mouth shut, but his nostrils flared. "Yes, Brigadier."

"Apologize to Her Grace."

Woodhouse hesitated. "Sir?"

"Apologize."

Clenching his jaw, Woodhouse was anything but apologetic as he ground out, "My apologies, Your Grace."

Well, that was a surprise—Maxwell coming to her defense. Yet Belinda regally inclined her head to coolly accept the apology.

"Her Grace has a valid point."

That surprised her even more. Did Maxwell truly mean it, or was he simply flattering her in an attempt to appease? Especially since he remained standing at the head of the table in a posture of pure command.

"Of course, the War Office can petition Parliament to claim the property if it likes," he explained. "But the secretary would prefer the cooperation of both the board and the town, and avoiding rancor will be more pleasant for everyone."

For everyone... For King George, he meant.

While the War Office might very well have the influence to take over the property, the soldiers—and King George himself—

would find Brighton a very inhospitable place if the board voted against them. She'd use that to her advantage and personally appeal to His Majesty on behalf of the pensioners, if she had to.

"So we'll adjourn for today and take up the discussion again when the other board members arrive." He closed his portfolio. "But if they are not all here within the fortnight, we proceed without them. Lord Palmerston wants a new academy established by Christmastide."

Belinda forced her shoulders not to sink. A fortnight would barely be enough time for the others to travel to Brighton, let alone for her to sway them to her side.

But she would have to. Somehow.

"Gentlemen and Your Grace." Maxwell nodded at the room at large, then at Belinda. "Thank you for your time."

He moved toward the door, where he spoke to each man in turn as they left. But when Belinda rose from her seat, the devil closed the door instead of following the men from the room, shutting them inside together.

With his curly black hair highlighted against the red of his uniform and his broad shoulders accentuated by the cut of his jacket, he leaned a hip against the closed door in a posture so rakishly alluring that her belly knotted. That was one undeniable facet of Maxwell Thorpe—the sight of him had always taken her breath away.

Apparently, some things never changed.

"It's been a long time, Belinda."

She trembled at his audacity to use her given name. When she'd stepped into this room, she'd thought she was seeing a ghost. But she wasn't fortunate enough to simply be haunted. Oh, no. He was blood and flesh… and oh, what flesh. Even now her fingertips ached with the sudden memory of how it had felt to touch him, the soft warmth of his skin, the hardness of his muscles. Only the faint lines at the corners of his eyes and mouth gave proof that he'd aged beyond the image of him she still carried in her mind from the last time she saw him.

"How have you been?"

Ha! As if he cared. "I was perfectly fine until you came along."

His eyes gleamed at the sharpness behind her comment. As if he'd also expected *that*.

Not daring to challenge her, he said sincerely, "It's good to know that you're still dedicated to helping the pensioners. Your kind heart has always been your very best trait."

At that unexpected compliment, she fought to keep her well-studied composure in place. The *very* last thing she'd allow was for him to see how much he still affected her. And most likely always would. "It's easy to be kind... to those who deserve it."

Instead of rising to the bait, he returned to the table and reached to pour a cup of tea from the tray, putting in milk and sugar. Then he held it out to her. A peace offering.

Her irritation spiked that he would remember how she took her tea. But then, didn't she remember every detail about him, right down to the small scar at his right brow?

He murmured, "You're also just as beautiful as I remember."

Damn her heart for stuttering! And double-damn the dark emotion that squeezed her chest around it like an iron fist, because she knew better than to fall for his charms. She'd learned the hard way how little his word was worth.

Ignoring the offered tea, she stepped past him to the buffet cabinet to withdraw a bottle of port that was kept there for after the board meetings when the men finished their business. She filled a tea cup and offered it to him.

For a moment, they held each other's gaze. Two adversaries now on even ground, both filled with such determination that tension pulsed between them.

"If you're attempting to flatter me into conceding," she warned, "it won't work."

He accepted the cup, then lifted it to his nose to draw in the port's sweet scent. "I would never dare to presume such a thing."

And *she* was certain that he'd dared to presume a great deal more about her in the past. A presumption that had made her beg her father to ask favors from his friends in order to give Maxwell a high-profile post in India where he could more easily distinguish himself.

Oh, she'd been so naïve!

He offered the tea again. This time, she accepted it... only to set it down, unwanted.

"Why are you doing this?" She folded her arms over her chest. There was no need for pleasantries between them.

The small tea cup in his hand served to remind her of how large and solid he was. Ten years ago, he'd been a young man just beginning to fill out his frame. Now he was a man in his prime. Every inch of him displayed the powerful officer he'd become. "As I told you, your cooperation makes establishing the academy easier."

"I mean the orders from the War Office that brought you here." *And back into my life.* "Why are you closing the hospital and putting those men out of their home?"

"Because we need a training academy."

"You already have Sandhurst."

"It isn't enough."

He set down the cup and stepped up to the large map of the world that decorated the wall. Red pushpin flags were scattered across it, one flag for each place the pensioners had served.

A frown creased his brow as he studied the map. "Do you have any idea how limited training was during the wars with France? The army needed men on the battlefield immediately, with no

time for instruction except for a cursory overview of how to use
their guns and bayonets. We had good generals with solid battle
plans, but the lower-ranking officers and foot soldiers didn't
know enough to carry them out. Our men were little more than
cannon fodder. We won only because of sheer numbers and our
cavalry. Two years." His voice grew distant as he touched one of
the flags in the mass of those pressed into the Iberian Peninsula.
"Two years of the worst bloodshed in British military history…"
He flicked the flag with the tip of his finger. "How much of that
carnage could have been avoided if they'd had better training?
How many wives and children could we have kept from
mourning their dead?"

His hand dropped to his side.

In the silence between them, Belinda shivered. He'd been
wounded himself in the fighting in Spain, before her father
arranged for him to be posted in India. The summer she'd
met him.

"If I have the chance to save men's lives—even if just a handful
—I'm going to take it." Then he turned away from the map, and
the vulnerability she saw in him vanished. He was once more a
brigadier, straight-spined and impassive. Once more the man sent
to close the hospital. "No respectable officer would refuse that."

Her chest tightened with empathy, but the pensioners needed
to be defended. "At the cost of men in their golden years who have
sacrificed all for their country, including the loss of limbs?"

He picked up his port and swirled it gently. "Wouldn't it be
better to have an academy to instruct soldiers so they don't lose
limbs in the first place?"

Damn him! He was twisting everything around, refusing to see
the situation from the perspective of the pensioners. But then,
hadn't he always gotten his way? Hadn't what he wanted always
come first, no matter whom he hurt in the process?

She arched an imperious brow. "What do you gain from this?"

A haunted expression came over him, one as dark as the port in the white bone cup.

"The knowledge that there will be fewer widows and orphans."

She was no fool and refused to let that arrow pierce her. His answer was meant solely to pull at her heartstrings… and dodge her question. "What do *you* gain from this, Maxwell?"

He took a slow sip of port before answering, "The War Office thought I would be the best officer to present the plans to the board. They knew I'd been a patient at the hospital once myself."

She inhaled sharply. The *very* last thing she needed was that reminder of how they'd met. He'd been wounded and was recuperating at the hospital, while she'd been doing charity work there as a way to fill the long, dull days that summer. Her father had insisted that the family spend their season here in Brighton, where there was nothing for a young lady her age to do except volunteer. Only later did she discover that her father was on the verge of being thrust into debtors' prison and needed to ask favors of several men who had followed the Prince Regent down from London to keep the creditors at bay. She hadn't discovered until season's end that Papa was already ill. Or until the following year how much the medical expenses had added to the debt, sending her family into financial ruin.

She pushed away the flood of memories. *All* in the past. She had to focus on the present. "And a promotion for you, perhaps? I imagine it would be advantageous for your career to found a school that rivals Sandhurst."

"Perhaps." He set down the port. "But that's not my prime motivation."

"Forgive me if I don't believe you." She reached a hand to the table to steady herself as ten years of hurt and anger rose inside her. The old bitterness returned in force. "I have firsthand knowledge of how you advance your career."

She felt him stiffen, as surely as she felt the tension filling the air around them.

With the ghosts of the past rising between them, she expected him to deny it. To defend himself and claim that he'd not used her all those years ago, only to abandon her once he'd no longer needed her. To strike out and attack—

Instead, his eyes softened as he took a slow step toward her.

Her heart skipped, the foolish thing momentarily forgetting what he'd done to her. But then, hadn't it always loved him, even when he didn't deserve it? Didn't it even now remember the kind and caring man he'd been before he left for India, and how they'd healed each other that summer—her with his physical wounds, him with her heartbreak over her father?

Oh, he'd changed, certainly, both in appearance and in demeanor. But she could still see in him the only man she'd ever loved. Which was why she didn't slap his hand away when he raised it to caress his knuckles across her cheek.

She gasped at the touch, pained by it.

"And what do you gain from this, Belinda?" His deep voice seeped into her, warming her as thoroughly as his hand against her cheek. "Why fight so hard when you know that the pensioners will be taken care of?"

"Split up and shipped off to other hospitals, you mean?" She'd wanted to sound determined and strong. Instead, her voice emerged as a whisper. "This place is their home, and those men have no other family but the men living with them. To force them apart…"

The knot of emotion in her throat choked her.

He reached for her hand and gave her fingers a soothing squeeze. "Why?"

She trembled, then cursed herself that he might be able to feel it. That he might dare to believe he still possessed even an ounce of influence over her. It certainly wasn't a yearning for the old days. It was anger and pain... memories of how she'd placed her trust in him, only to have it destroyed. She'd *never* make that mistake again.

"An act of decency." Her answer was a blatant challenge. "In your world of war, surely you can appreciate that."

Then she stepped out of his reach. He didn't deserve to know the real reason or to lessen his guilt about the past by attempting to console her now. They had a long fight ahead of them over the hospital, and she had no intention of making one second of that any easier on him.

"I won't give up this fight." She snatched up his tea cup of port and finished it in one swallow.

Something unreadable sparked in his eyes, and he quietly confessed, "I'd be disappointed if you did."

CHAPTER 2

*T*wenty minutes later, Max strode into the Honors Club with determination. Good Lord, how he needed a drink!

When he'd first approached the War Office about creating the new academy, he'd known that winning the board's support wouldn't be easy. Neither was seeing Belinda again, even after all these years. But he hadn't realized until he saw the fire in her green eyes exactly how difficult his task would be.

Or how much he still loved her.

"Cognac," he ordered the attendant behind the bar, who nodded and promptly set to pouring a glass.

He squelched a tired sigh. He was getting too old to fight battles like this.

At thirty-two, he certainly wasn't young anymore, and the years spent distinguishing himself in the army had left more scars than he wanted to admit. But he'd made a good life for himself, rising from lieutenant to brigadier, one hard-won promotion at a time. From the youngest son of a minor baron to a man who commanded legions.

But those days were done. He was tired of foreign posts and wanted to return to England. He'd grown sick of sending men to their deaths and wanted instead to train them to survive the carnage and destruction that battle brought. When he couldn't bear to write one more letter home to yet another widow, informing her of her husband's death, he knew he needed a new purpose. This academy would give him exactly that.

He hadn't been exaggerating when he said that the governing board's support would make the transition easier for everyone. Peace had lasted long enough that the British people were no longer willing to accept without question such a decision by the military.

And Belinda, Duchess of Winchester, held the balance of that decision in her delicate little hands. The same woman who had healed him all those years ago and made him believe in the possibility of a future that was more than simple survival. A future that had purpose, wonder, goals… a home.

The same woman he'd so brutally hurt. Fate was surely laughing at him.

No difference that he'd rejected her for her own good—he would go to his grave letting her think the worst of him in that. What mattered now was that her trust in his character would be an enormous part of the board's decision, and in that, she believed he'd failed her.

Worse. Based on her comments today, she believed he'd used her.

He could have asked to be replaced in this mission. *Should* have asked for that, in fact, when he'd discovered that Belinda was serving out her late husband's term on the board. But the academy was his idea, one he needed to follow through to the end.

He'd also needed to see Belinda again, the way that thirsty men needed water to live.

"Brigadier!" a fellow officer called out and stepped up to the bar, with a half-dozen others following.

They announced their greetings as they pressed in around him. A few slapped him on the back.

"Thorpe! Good seeing you here."

"We were wondering when you'd stop by."

"Can't keep a soldier away from his brothers-in-arms, eh?"

Max's lips curled wistfully. Perhaps not, but he wasn't here for military brotherhood. He was here in search of drink and solace.

"Heard you were back in England." Another officer slapped him on the back. "When I heard that, I knew you were putting yourself up for a new position."

He grimaced. Rumors were more reliable than military intelligence these days. "I am."

"Ha!" The officer nodded toward two young captains in their group. "Told you that Thorpe was here to pursue that new post in Africa."

"No," another soldier interjected from behind Max's shoulder. "The brigadier's returning to India, aren't you?"

He hesitated to answer. But what could it hurt to share his plans? They'd all find out as soon as the board members started spreading news of the meeting. "I *am* interested in a new position. But not in India or Africa. I'm pursuing a much more dangerous location, gentlemen."

Curious murmurs surrounded him, along with bewildered frowns.

He accepted the glass of brandy from the attendant and raised it high. "Brighton!"

Laughter exploded from the soldiers. They all thought he was bamming them.

"The army needs a new academy, and the Royal Hospital is

being converted into one." He took a long swallow. "I'm here to carry it out."

That sobered the group. They stared at him as if he'd just admitted to attempting to kill the king.

After several awkward moments while it became clear that Maxwell was serious, the senior officer commented, "I'd heard rumors that they were seeking battle-tried officers to train cadets."

"Not rumors. They are."

"Is that truly to be your next move, Thorpe? Retiring to the seaside like some old woman past her prime?" One of the captains didn't bother with holding out his glass to the attendant for a refill but took the bottle from the bar and began topping off glasses himself. He pointed the bottle at Max and jokingly asked, "Earning your commission by putting young lords through their paces on their bellies?"

Before he could answer that he was here only to establish the academy, not run it, the senior officer interjected, "Bollocks! He won't retire to the seaside if he's offered the African post. It's the perfect place for a career army man on the verge of becoming a major-general, which is assured."

"Far from assured." The *only* thing he was certain of at that moment was his need for Belinda's understanding. Professionally and personally. He'd had no choice before but to let her hate him. He'd not do it again.

"An *academy*?" a lieutenant who had served briefly with Max on a short stint in Egypt repeated with disdain, as if he hadn't heard properly. "Don't need no fancy academy to train officers. Those cadets are just a bunch o' coxcombs who'll piss their britches the first time a ball whizzes by 'em!"

More laughter rose from the group, but Max only sipped his cognac, saying nothing.

"A good soldier cuts his teeth on th' battlefield," one of the weathered officers explained. "Not on books in some academy lecture hall. Thorpe knows that, don't ye, Brigadier? That's how ye did it, an' a fine officer ye became, too."

Another soldier shook his head, tapping his glass against the older officer's chest to impress his point. "Can't study battle strategy while the artillery's targeting your arse."

Max hid his smile behind the rim of his glass.

"What's your game, Thorpe? Truly—you'd give up a good post to teach a bunch of dandies how to march in line and point their muskets at the enemy?"

It was so much more than that. None of the soldiers here would understand, even if he tried to explain it. But someday they would, when they'd had enough of the slaughter of battle themselves, when they were ready to return home.

"Actually, I've always liked the idea of academies, even though I chose a different path. I'm all for anything that can make for better soldiers on the battlefield, especially if the training they receive comes from officers who have been through the fire." He leveled his gaze on the older officer. "And it's damned hard to cut your teeth on battle when the wars are over and there's none to be fought."

Laughter went up from the group of men, until Max raised his glass in a toast.

"But we should all pray to God that our memories of war are long, even in times of peace," he added somberly, quashing the men's amusement. "Lest we forget the hell of it and rush too easily back into the fray."

The men soberly raised their glasses with his to drink to fallen comrades and a continuation of peace. One of them murmured, "Hear, hear."

The men moved away, now that the novelty of having Max

among them had worn off, to return to their card games and cigars.

He set down his empty glass and gestured for a refill, grateful to finally have the peaceful drink he'd sought when he entered the club. And a moment to himself to contemplate what to do next about Belinda. If he didn't complete his orders, his military career would be over. There would be no more promotions, no more command posts. He'd be lucky not to be sent to some godforsaken post in northern Canada.

But if he succeeded, he'd never win Belinda's forgiveness.

Either way he was damned.

The attendant placed the glass in front of him. Just as Max raised the drink, a large hand slapped him on the back, causing him to nearly spill the brandy.

Oliver Graham grinned at him. "Heard you and Colonel Woodhouse just had a set-to."

"I was a dashing hero, I'll have you know." He took a gasping swallow and welcomed the burn down his throat. Thank God Graham was in Brighton this summer. The way things were going, he could certainly use an ally. "I was defending a woman's honor."

"So that's what they're calling it these days." Graham signaled for a drink. "And here I thought you'd simply struck out at a man for daring to criticize the woman you once loved, then shut the two of you together into a small room." He paused. "Alone."

Max grimaced. Apparently, rumors were faster than military intelligence, as well.

"Were you hoping to hold her captive until she declared her undying devotion to your cause?" Graham joked.

"Holding her captive is on tomorrow's agenda." He was only half teasing. If tying up Belinda until she agreed to champion him to the board would have worked, he'd have done it right there in the hospital.

Graham's amusement sobered. "I take it that your meeting didn't go well."

"As well as can be expected."

"That badly, huh?"

In answer, Max tossed back the brandy and signaled for another.

Graham was one of his oldest and most trusted friends, and fate had tossed them together in Brighton this summer. But even after years apart, they'd fallen back into their fast friendship. Graham was one of a handful of men in the world whom he trusted unquestioningly with his life, and the only one who knew the real reason why he'd broken off with Belinda. He knew he could count on his advice. And when his advice failed, he could count on Graham's silence to let him wallow in misery in peace.

Graham arched a brow. "Well?"

Usually.

"Circumstances weren't the best." Max rubbed at the knot in his nape. "I surprised her by being the officer in charge."

Surprised? Hardly. He'd downright stunned her. The look of wounding that had gripped her beautiful face when she'd walked into the room and seen him had torn his breath away. So had the hatred that immediately replaced it.

He hadn't reacted much better, staring at her throughout the meeting like a smitten pup. He simply wasn't prepared for his visceral reaction to seeing her again. One that had come like a punch to his gut when he saw her face, those sparkling green eyes, and that auburn hair that was even softer than it looked. And the way he'd chastised Woodhouse—*Christ.* He'd have to seek out the colonel to offer his apologies.

But seeing her again changed nothing. "I have no intention of giving up trying to win her support." The academy was too important.

"What about winning her over in other ways?"

His gaze snapped to his friend. Surely he didn't mean… "Pardon?"

"You haven't heard?" Graham eyed him warily. "Pomperly's arrived in Brighton."

A rush of jealousy burned through him at the mention of the duke, followed by an unreasonable flash of hatred that Pomperly would dare try to claim her—

Then he felt like a damned fool.

Good God. Less than an hour in Belinda's presence, and he was already losing his mind.

What did it matter to him if rumors were flowing through London like the Thames that the Duke of Pomperly had determined to marry Belinda? So many rumors, in fact, that all of Society believed just that would happen, so confident in it that the gossips had begun to call her the Double Duchess. What difference did it make to him whom she chose to let into her life… or into her heart?

Still, he couldn't stop his hand from shaking as he raised the glass to take a bracing swallow.

"So if you want to pursue her yourself, then—"

"No." He said that with more force than he'd intended. But good God, he wasn't here because of *her*. He was here exactly for the reason he'd given her—to turn his experience into saving men's lives rather than leading them to their deaths. To think he'd come here wanting anything else was preposterous. "It's no concern of mine who courts her."

And yet, he was shaken by seeing her again, hearing her voice, and breathing in the sweet lavender scent of her… by seeing firsthand that she still possessed the same fiery spirit and kindness of heart that had made him fall in love with her. Just as he couldn't help experiencing again the old jealousies and desires he'd once felt over her. He wouldn't be a warm-blooded man if he didn't, even if he had no intention of acting upon them.

"Seems to me you've been given a second chance," Graham said thoughtfully. "You might consider taking it."

He laughed, although in truth he didn't find the suggestion at all amusing. "All I want is her vote."

"Are you certain?"

"Absolutely." A damned lie. He wasn't certain at all.

He'd loved her once, he couldn't deny that. And ten years ago, he'd convinced himself that he loved her enough to let her go, just as he'd convinced himself that a life in the army was all he needed. He'd had to, in order to keep getting out of bed in the mornings once she was gone. In order to simply keep breathing. He'd hoped that eventually, with the passage of enough time and distance, he could purge her from his heart the way he'd purged her from his life.

He'd been a damned fool to ever think that.

BELINDA SLUMPED DOWN ONTO THE BENCH IN THE TOWN HOUSE'S garden and hung her head.

Maxwell Thorpe... *good God.*

Of all the places to encounter him again, of all the ways she'd always imagined in her mind for how they'd meet after all these years, if ever—*this* certainly wasn't it. She'd planned to pretend not to recognize him at all at first, then give a well-practiced look of bored disdain, followed by a haughty sniff and a toss of her head, then casually pass him by as if he meant nothing to her...

actions she'd replayed countless times in her mind. Not one of which had involved a fight over elderly pensioners.

She bit back a groan. Only Maxwell would reappear in her life at this very moment and completely invert it, now that she'd finally found her footing after Winchester's death nearly three years ago.

But then, hadn't he always taken her off guard?

She sucked in a pained breath as the memories rushed over her like a tidal wave. The day she'd met him, when her eighteen-year-old eyes had never seen a more handsome man, even wounded and covered with bandages... Their first dance at the assembly rooms, first picnic in the park, first stroll... Their first kiss, when she could never have imagined a more magical moment. Until he'd said he loved her and wanted to marry her. And *that* had been simply perfect. Because she'd never expected to find love.

To say that her prospects for marriage had been limited would have been a grand overstatement of how bleak they'd actually been.

Bleak? *Black*, more like.

Despite empty flattery from gentlemen about how beautiful and brilliant she was, those compliments never turned into courtship. Not once those same gentlemen discovered that she had no dowry because her father had made bad business decisions and stumbled far into debt. She'd been destined for spinsterhood.

Until she met Maxwell.

The biting irony was that she'd met him right here in Brighton, recuperating in the very hospital he now wanted to destroy. He'd been wounded during his first engagement on the Peninsula, by the slice of a French bayonet across his chest that nearly killed him. He'd needed doctors' care and a place to heal before he could return to his post.

Love had been immediate for both of them, she'd been so certain of that then. Both had helped heal the other, with Maxwell accepting her help in mending his physical wounds and Belinda relying upon his strength and resolve when she learned that her father was dying. When she was with Maxwell, she'd felt healed, whole... loved. They'd given each other hope for a brighter future, one with a happy home and loving family. Together. But fate had had other plans, and less than one year later, their future was over.

Maxwell Pennington Thorpe... Heavens, what *was* she going to do?

Because the problem wasn't speaking her mind and telling him what she thought of him and his plans. Oh, she'd done a fine job of that!

No. The problem was that even now, despite the hell he'd put her through, a part of her still loved him. And always would.

"There you are!" Eugenia swept through the open French doors of the town house into the garden. Diana followed closely behind.

When the three of them had decided to share the town house this season, escaping London for the seaside with her two oldest and dearest friends had seemed like a godsend. The perfect way to put distance between her and the Duke of Pomperly until he found another woman to cast his attentions upon.

Now it felt as if she'd been tossed from the pan into the fire.

A distraught expression marred Diana's pretty face. "I just heard—*Maxwell Thorpe?* How are you holding up?"

She forced a smile. "I'm fine. There's nothing to worry about."

But the two joined her at the bench, with Diana reassuringly clasping her hand. Her throat tightened with emotion at their concern.

"Truly. He's here only for military business." When the two

women exchanged dubious looks, Belinda reminded them, "I deal with military officers all the time. I know how to hold my own against them."

Neither woman replied to that. They'd been friends since their school days, and they knew each other well enough to spot when one was dissembling. Or, in this case, outright lying.

Then Eugenia arched a brow in silent recrimination.

Belinda sighed and, biting her lip, admitted quietly, "There *is* more to the story."

"I knew it!" Diana clapped her hands, then turned toward Genie. "I told you that something was amiss. That Maxwell Thorpe just *happened* to be in Brighton at the same time as she is. That he just *happened* to be there when she needed to be rescued from Colonel Woodhouse—"

"I did *not* need to be rescued," she ground out in aggravation, then felt immediately guilty over poor Colonel Woodhouse and the spurious stories being spread about him already. Apparently, the Brighton rumor mill was operating at breakneck speed. And as inaccurately as ever.

"Oh, I think we *all* need to be rescued by tall, dark, and handsome men in uniform," Genie drawled.

"Especially when we don't," Diana finished with a smile.

Belinda rolled her eyes. "And do we need to surrender as well?"

Genie's smile faltered. "He said that? That he wanted you to…"

"Surrender?" Diana whispered breathlessly.

"Of a sort."

She stood and stepped a few feet away, presumably to study a bloom on the rosebush, but more because she simply couldn't sit still. Her heart pounded too hard, her breath came too ragged. Maxwell's unexpected arrival had flustered her, and it wasn't just the confusion and anger that set her trembling. Because he'd looked good. *Very* good. The years had matured him into a man who was very much confident in himself, one used to getting what he wanted.

She straightened her spine with as much courage as she could muster. "Maxwell is here in Brighton to close the hospital."

Shock flashed across their faces, yet they listened silently as she told them about the meeting. Both were remorseful when she explained what really happened with Colonel Woodhouse, and neither reacted at all to Maxwell's caress of her cheek... because she conveniently forgot to tell them.

"He's truly going to do that?" Diana paled, her hand going to her throat. "Turn the hospital into an academy?"

She grimaced. "If I cannot find a way to stop him."

"Then he's just as terrible as before, isn't he?" Genie's question was a statement.

More like sisters than friends, they both knew what had happened between her and Maxwell. They'd been at her side during those wonderful months when he'd said that he wanted to marry her—only an understanding, not a formal agreement. But at the time, she'd thought that had been for the best. After all, he'd been at the start of his career and off on a bad foot at that. Or rather, on a bayoneted chest. It might have been years before he rose in the ranks high enough to provide a home for her and the children she'd dreamed of having, but she had been willing to wait... sort of. Because she'd gone to her father, to ask Papa to use his influence to help Maxwell with his career. It had worked, and he was assigned to Fort St George in India, where he would be able to quickly distinguish himself while staying out of the fray of the wars.

Maxwell had been away less than a year when her father's debts became so out of hand that creditors began beating at the door, when Papa's illness grew worse and death became a certainty. In desperation, she'd written to him, begging him to come home and help her... only for him to reply that his future lay with the army. In India.

But out of the ashes of that love came salvation for her family, if not for her heart. Lord George Collins offered for her, and she married him. He saved her family from ruin, taking them in after Papa's death and paying off their debts, and eventually, he made her a duchess when his brother died. Overall, it was as good a Society marriage as could be hoped. Winchester was kind and generous, dedicated to his position in Parliament and to his family... but she never loved him, not the way she once loved Maxwell.

Inhaling a jerking breath, Belinda answered, "It appears so."

"I don't mean to defend him," Diana said delicately, "but he does have a good point about the soldiers needing better training."

He did, drat him. "But at the expense of the pensioners' home?"

"Perhaps you could talk with him," Genie interjected. "Convince him that the hospital isn't at all the kind of facility that cadets in training need."

"Yes!" Diana's face lit up at the possibility. "Surely he's receptive to reason."

"He's a brigadier who will most likely be promoted to major-general in recompense for starting this new academy." She shook her head. "I don't think logic matters."

"But he wasn't always a brigadier," Genie reminded her.

Belinda knew that well. Despite the agony he'd caused her, she still hadn't been able to bring herself to let go of him completely in the intervening years. She'd followed him as best she could through newspaper reports and shared acquaintances, knowing every place he'd been stationed since leaving England... first at Fort St George, then stints in Egypt and Nassau, before heading back to the Continent to help restore Europe after the wars and ensure the peace. Just as she knew every heroic act he'd committed to save his men in battle, every promotion he'd received that raised him from lieutenant to brigadier. She couldn't help herself. He was an addiction she couldn't quit.

Yet he'd picked now to reappear, when she was least prepared for him. How had she managed to keep from screaming from the searing pain at the sight of him? No idea. But she would *never* let him know how much he'd wounded her. Or that the reason she clung so fiercely to the pensioners and worked tirelessly on their behalf, both here and in London, was because they reminded her of that summer when she was in love and happy... before everything turned black.

"He loved you once, I'm certain of it," Genie assured her.

Belinda was far less certain.

"Perhaps he still holds a soft spot in his heart for you and will listen."

Her shoulders sagged wearily. "He chose the army over me—"

"Ten years ago," Diana reminded her.

"And is even more firmly entrenched in the ranks now."

Nothing that she'd seen in him today proved otherwise. Yet her foolish heart held out hope... and her past experience quashed it.

She shook her head. "What guarantee do I have that he'll listen?"

Her two friends pondered that for a moment. Then Diana conceded, "None, I suppose."

That was the crux of it. He'd shattered her heart ten years ago, brutally breaking her trust. If he wounded her a second time, how would she survive it?

"I'm not certain you have a choice but to try," Diana said somberly. "And quickly."

A dark smile tugged at her lips. "Knowing Maxwell, I'm certain he's already prepared for siege warfare."

"Unfortunately, you don't have time for a siege."

No. She had less than a fortnight. "I'll just have to—"

"His Grace has arrived in Brighton."

Cold dread shivered through her at that quiet announcement.

"Pomperly?" she breathed, barely louder than a whisper. The earth tilted beneath her as aggravation added to the confusion and frustration already swirling inside her.

Genie confirmed that with a nod. "The Duke of Pomposity."

Belinda rolled her eyes. She disliked that nickname. Yet she also had to admit that, in his case, it certainly fit.

Oh, Pomperly meant well, she supposed. But a more arrogant man she'd yet to meet, which was saying a lot, considering she knew King George. And one she had no intention of letting court her.

With a snap of its stem, she plucked one of the roses from its bush. "I'll rebuff him in Brighton as I did in London."

Her friends didn't seem at all confident about that. But *she* was certain of it. Pomperly might have missed the hint in London that she held no interest in becoming his new duchess, loathing the nickname, the Double Duchess, that the gossips had given her. As if marrying the man was an absolute certainty. But while he might believe that she'd make an excellent wife for him, *she* had other intentions. She'd refused to receive him at her town home whenever he called, just as she'd refused every request he made to dance with her at balls, to sit beside her at soirees, to join him in his box at Vauxhall… She'd returned every gift he'd sent her, including two doves. The most inappropriate—and ironic—gift of courtship she'd ever seen. Did he think that symbolized what their marriage would be like… her imprisonment in a gilded cage?

The fact that he'd chased after her to Brighton changed nothing. "I'll refuse his overtures here just as I did in Mayfair."

"He already stopped by the town house while you were with Maxwell," Diana informed her.

She grumbled, "I wasn't *with* Maxwell." At least not the way Diana had implied.

Genie pulled a note from her pelisse pocket. "He left this for you. An invitation to dinner at the Pavilion."

"Then I'll refuse him." Her rejection was surely routine for him by now. Soon, he might just give up completely and—

"You cannot."

Just watch me. She smiled confidently. "A lady always has the opportunity to forgo a soiree." Especially a duchess.

"Not when the king is in attendance."

Her stomach sank. "No," she whispered, "not with the king."

Their slender shoulders sagging, the three of them seemed to deflate in unison, all falling into contemplative silence. They were all part of the *ton*, all knew what an invitation to the palace meant. A command appearance. She nearly laughed at the irony. Thrust inside a gilded cage after all—one that resembled an Asian pleasure palace.

Then her stomach plummeted right through the floor as the full realization of what this meant fell over her. "Not when Pomperly sits on the board."

And not when she desperately needed every vote she could get.

Her friends were right. There was no way out of the dinner, no way to keep from having to attend on Pomperly's arm.

"Unless..." The two looked at her hopefully as a desperate thought struck her—"Maxwell."

That made their brows shoot up.

With a smile like the cat who'd gotten into the cream, she

plucked the petals from the rose. "I cannot very well accompany Pomperly if I've already agreed to attend on the arm of another, now can I?" The petals fell to the ground, one by one. " As one of the highest-ranking officers in Brighton, the brigadier has surely been invited."

Oh, it was turning into a perfect idea!

Almost.

It would mean having to be in close proximity to Maxwell all evening, to tolerate the ghosts of past heartbreaks and pretend that nothing was wrong between them.

But she would suffer through it. After all, what was one evening in his presence compared to the torment of the past decade?

"I'll simply make certain that I arrive as Maxwell's guest."

Somehow.

Her friends exchanged unconvinced looks, before Diana asked, "But why would the brigadier agree?"

Because he has no choice. "He wants my support with the academy, so he'll do whatever he can to win my favor."

"Are you certain about this plan?" Genie asked.

She tossed away the bare stem. "Absolutely."

Maxwell Thorpe might be the devil himself, but if he thought he could once more take her soul and cast her into hell without a fight, oh, he had another think coming!

CHAPTER 3

*M*axwell waited on the far end of the promenade the next afternoon, where he'd sent word for Belinda to meet him, and tugged at his jacket sleeves. Good Lord, he was nervous! He hadn't been this much on edge since the last time he'd charged into battle. But then, this *was* Belinda. Little difference between her and the French.

Both had good reason to shoot him.

She'd surprised the devil out of him by asking to speak with him, but it wouldn't be to simply reiterate that she thought him a monster and that she had no intention of supporting the academy. That could have been put into the message itself, with no need to see him face-to-face. Most likely, she planned to attempt to cajole him to her side and, when that failed, toss him onto the first ship bound for Australia.

Still, the best defense was a good offense, and an experienced soldier never gave his opponent time to regroup. Which was why he'd told her to meet him at the edge of the town, right where the cliffs began to rise from the sea. And why he'd called in every favor he had with the men in the barracks to arrange the surprise waiting for her.

As if out of a dream, her lithe figure appeared on the promenade.

She walked toward him, with the skirts of her ivory dress stirring around her legs in the sea breeze and her bonnet shielding her face from the sun, and his pulse spiked. Old desires—and dreams—died hard.

Dear God, she was beautiful, and not because of how she looked. Oh, she was pretty, certainly, but not classically. Not with that pert little nose that turned up slightly at the tip, those green eyes that were too big for her face, and that auburn hair that couldn't decide if it wanted to be red or brown and never stayed in its pins.

No, it was her soul that radiated beauty and commanded a man's attention. While other women were content to follow, Belinda led with her heart. Always had. Indeed, he'd fallen in love with her because of it.

And it was her kind heart that once again had them at odds.

She stopped in front of him. When her eyes met his, an electric jolt sped through him so intensely that he lost his breath.

"My apologies for being late." The ribbons from her bonnet fluttered in the sea breeze, and she tucked them inside her jacket. "I dropped off a basket of sweet rolls at the hospital. It took longer than expected."

"No apologies necessary." His gaze languidly drifted over her. He felt like a blind man given back his sight, and he couldn't stop staring. "You look lovely."

"Maxwell, please don't." A faint blush pinked her cheeks, but he couldn't have said whether from pleasure at the compliment or aggravation. At that moment, he didn't particularly care which.

"You'd rather I'd lie and say the exact opposite?" When he

reached for her hand, she didn't pull away. Perhaps she didn't think him a complete monster after all. "Very well. You're the most hideous woman I've ever met, and every time I'm near you, I want to flee."

She laughed at the absurdity of his words. But the urge to kiss her was simply too great to resist, and he turned over her hand to place a tender kiss against her palm.

Her laughter died. She stiffened, as if waiting for him to wound her again.

Her reaction eviscerated him. But he hid the pain by forcing a grin and adding, "I want nothing more than to put as much distance between us as possible."

"You do, do you?" Suspicion thickened her voice.

"Absolutely." He pressed his advantage by looping her arm around his and leading her down the steps to the rocky beach below. Her sweet scent of lavender filled his senses. "I cannot think of anything I'd rather do less than spend hours in your company."

"Then it's a good thing that we'll only have to suffer a brief conversation this afternoon."

He stopped short. When she slipped her arm free and walked on ahead a few paces, he stared after her. Did the little vixen mean that as part of their teasing in opposites, or was she serious?

Once again, Belinda had him on his toes. No wonder dukes fought for the privilege of courting her. There was never a dull moment in her company.

He caught up with her and took her arm, guiding her along the beach. "This way."

"Where are we going?" She blinked against the late afternoon sun as it sank toward the horizon. "I was hoping we could talk."

"We will. But first, just a short walk along the beach." When she hesitated, he purposely misread her reaction and assured her, "Don't worry. The tide won't be in for several more hours."

"It isn't the tide that I'm worried about," she muttered.

His lips crooked into a half grin. "Worried that I'll tie you down and hold you captive until you see reason and support the academy?"

"I think you'd enjoy it."

A sharp pang of yearning reverberated shamelessly inside him at her unwitting innuendo. When they'd courted before, he'd never been anything more than a gentleman with her, no matter how much he'd longed to lay her down and strip her dress away. With his teeth.

He cleared his throat, but it didn't keep a husky rasp from his voice. "A man has to do what a man has to do."

She slid him a dubious sideways glance. "Including ropes and sailors' knots?"

"I'd never use sailors' knots against you."

"Well, thank good—"

"I'm a soldier," he continued, deadpan. "We use irons."

Halting in her steps, she jerked her arm away. The hard look that she narrowed on him could have cut glass.

He chuckled at how easily she'd risen to the bait, how much he'd always liked stirring the fire inside her. Ignoring her irritated but surprisingly adorable sniff at his teasing, he once more took her arm.

He led her farther down the cliff face, until they were out of sight of the town and on an isolated stretch of beach fronted by tiny coves and other indentations carved into the soft limestone rock. Until they were alone.

"Perhaps we should stop and talk now," she suggested, the nervousness visible in her.

"Perhaps we should explore what's just beyond that next cliff."

Whatever it was that she wanted to say to him would keep until she saw the surprise. It was mercenary, he'd admit that, and done more than just to gain her favor with the board—he also did it simply because he wanted time alone with her. "There's a stretch of sandy beach there that I think you'll appreciate."

She arched an unconvinced brow. "And *I* think you're simply hoping to get me alone so you can charm me into supporting the academy."

"You've given me no choice. When diplomacy fails, a good soldier attacks."

He sensed immediately that he'd said the wrong thing, despite his joking tone. The *very* worst thing because she stiffened, turning instantly cold.

"I don't need reminders of your military career, Maxwell," she said into the wind, turning her face away as if she couldn't bear to look at him. "I'm well aware of exactly how dedicated a soldier you are."

Damnation. He should have known better. "Then how about a reminder that I'm more than just a soldier? I'm out of uniform. Hadn't you noticed?"

"Oh, I noticed." Yet she slightly turned her head back toward him in a surreptitious glance.

He stopped her and tugged her around to face him. "Take a good look, Belinda." She startled slightly at his order. "A good, *long* look."

For a moment, her bright eyes never left his as she stubbornly refused to do as he asked.

Then, as if unable to resist, she slowly lowered her gaze, trailing it over him, from the neckcloth his man had taken great pains to knot to perfection, to the tan cashmere jacket and brown and white diamond-pattern waistcoat beneath. He was certain she'd stop her perusal there, but the audacious woman continued on, her eyes drinking in the cut of his brown trousers all the way down to his boots.

When she began a languid return up the length of him, he nearly groaned at the torture that her heated look spiraled through him.

A stray curl had escaped the confines of her bonnet, and using it as an excuse to touch her, he reached to tuck it back into place.

"See?" He opportunistically caressed her cheek as he pulled his hand away, then thrilled at the soft shiver that sped through her. "This afternoon, I'm simply a civilian. Don't think of me as a soldier."

"I don't think I can," she admitted. Ignoring the affectionate touch he'd just taken, she busied herself with securing the ends of the ribbons that once more danced in the breeze. But she couldn't hide the shaking of her hands. "I've only ever known you as a soldier."

Feeling as if he were plunging right over the cliffs above them, he corrected, "You knew me as a man, Belinda."

"I thought I did." Her breathless voice was so soft that it was almost lost beneath the noise of the wind and waves. "I was wrong."

"You knew me better than anyone."

"No." She gave up on securing the ribbons and tossed them away in irritation. "The man I knew would *never* have abandoned me."

He didn't attempt to lessen the wounding those words sliced into him, knowing he deserved it. Instead, he deepened the punishing pain by confirming her worst thoughts of him. "The man you knew would have done exactly that."

And did.

When she opened her mouth to reply, he cut her off. "The past is over." And nothing that he wanted to discuss with her. "We're different people now, with different responsibilities and concerns, and there's no point in arguing about the past when nothing can be done to change it."

She arched a piqued brow. "When we're so able to argue about the future, you mean?"

"When I'd rather not argue with you at all." Solemnly, all teasing gone, he held out his hand in invitation to continue their walk. "You once trusted me. Give me the chance to earn back that trust."

She hesitated.

"Please."

For a long moment, she didn't move. Then she gave a jerking nod.

Not letting himself think about the racing of his heartbeat when her hand slipped into his, he guided her carefully over the rocks as they gave way to sand just beyond the rounded front of the cliff face towering above them. Overhead, in the last light of sunset, gulls cried out against the din of the rolling waves striking far across the wide stretch of beach exposed by the outgoing tide.

"What was it that you called me in yesterday's meeting?" Although he knew very well. Despite not allowing it to show, he'd been pierced by the accusation. "A monster?"

Remorse flashed over her face, yet the stubborn woman didn't apologize. But he hadn't expected her to.

"I'm not a monster, Belinda. I'm simply trying to save as many lives as possible." He stopped, turning so that he blocked her view into the narrow cove behind him. "Give me the opportunity to convince you that I have only the best interests of everyone at heart. That's all I'm asking for. Just the chance to be heard."

He stepped aside to reveal the surprise waiting for her.

∽

BELINDA GASPED. "A PICNIC?"

She blinked at the sight, unable for a moment to believe her eyes. No, she was wrong—this was so much more than a picnic. This was... oh, this was simply magical!

A sailcloth lay spread across the patch of powdery white sand, anchored in place against the wind on all four corners by large brass lanterns whose flames danced in the sea breeze, their oil giving off a spicy scent. Scattered across the cloth were several dishes covered with lids so that she couldn't see what they contained, along with several pillows in jewel-tone satins and a long and narrow Turkish rug edging the side of the sailcloth. A small fire of driftwood flickered on the rocks a few feet away.

All like something out of *The Arabian Nights...* exotic and romantic, complete with red rose petals scattered across the white cloth.

"How..." She was too stunned to finish. Thank goodness that amazement covered her face, because it hid the confused thrill pulsating through her that Maxwell had gone to all this trouble for her.

"With the aid of the men at the barracks." He led her to the rug and helped her to gracefully lower herself. "Do you like it?"

She loved it. And yet... "I won't support the academy, if that's what this is about."

He repeated pointedly, matching her own stubbornness, "Do you like it?"

"It's tolerable," she grudgingly admitted.

Quirking a knowing smile, he placed one of the pillows behind her so she could recline. Then he sat beside her.

She gestured at the spread. "Why go to all this trouble?"

"Because you're right. I want your support." He reached to pour her a glass of wine. "I'm not above being the type of man who charms his way into a woman's affections."

At that, she couldn't prevent a little laugh. *Charming*. He was definitely that, all right. But she knew the truth. That he didn't have to charm his way back into her affections because he'd never completely left them, despite everything. Which was what had always bothered her most... How could a man whom she'd known well enough to love with all her heart fool her so well?

He held out the glass to her. "Surely you don't begrudge a man the opportunity to use every weapon at his disposal?"

"I suppose that would depend upon how the weapon was wielded," she clarified, accepting the wine.

His eyes shone knowingly. "And who was doing the wielding?"

She pressed her lips tightly together. *Drat him*. She couldn't properly answer that without digging herself deeper. The devil knew it, too. He was nothing if not razor-sharp, always had been. His mind had been one of the things she'd loved best about him. That and his understanding of how much her charity work meant to her, how much purpose she found in helping others.

Yet she wasn't a dolt herself. "Since when does a picnic count as a weapon?"

"Wait until you've had my cooking." He winked at her.

Her breath hitched. She stared at him, speechless. She couldn't have replied right then even if she'd known what to say.

He stretched out casually across the length of the rug behind her, propping himself up on one elbow. He reached to pluck a grape from the cluster lying on a platter in front of them. "You always liked picnics, and I thought this might be a good way for us to catch up on what our lives have been like since we last spoke."

Not wanting to reopen old wounds, she waved a hand toward the spread. "You spent your life lounging with Scheherazade by lantern light?"

"Actually, when I wasn't being shot at, I spent my summers mostly laboring in the hot sun, the rainy seasons fighting off mosquitoes, and my nights sleeping in cramped barracks with thirty other men." He blew out a long-suffering sigh and popped the grape into his mouth. "Every last one of whom snored loudly enough to shake the rafters."

When she laughed, he plucked a second grape and held it up to her lips.

Her belly pinched. Fearing that he was offering far more than a mere grape, she raised her wineglass to her lips like a shield. "If you think a picnic can sway me, you're mistaken."

"Not a picnic. I told you. A chance to get to know each other again."

In one last desperate attempt to cling to her pride, she sat up and busied herself with uncovering the dishes, each more exotic than the one before. Focusing all of her attention on a bowl of yellow rice, she mumbled, "I think we know each other well enough already."

"Not nearly well enough."

His low voice sent a warm tingle spiraling through her, which did nothing to put her at ease and everything to cause her hand to tremor as she lifted the lid on a plate of red chicken.

"I want you to know the man I've become, so you can understand why I'm set on opening the academy. Perhaps we can find common ground."

She wasn't certain she wanted to know him any better. "That depends." She sat back, her fingers tightening around her wineglass. "What do you want to know about me?"

"Nothing."

"*Nothing?*" she squeaked out. *That* pricked at her pride.

Mischief sparkled in his eyes, as if he could see right through her and knew exactly how much his comment baited her. Then he took the glass out of her hand, set it aside, and raised the grape once more to her lips.

She hesitated, then opened her mouth to let him place it on her tongue. She simply couldn't resist. Being with him like this felt too familiar to deny. Too *right.*

"I don't need to know about you," he explained, suddenly solemn, "because I made a point of always knowing what your life was like, what you were doing, all the charities you were involved with. No matter how far I traveled, I was never able to put you behind me."

Instead of lowering his hand, he audaciously stroked his thumb over her bottom lip. She shivered, but she couldn't tell which was making her head spin more—the deep, husky purr of his voice or the way he caressed her mouth, as if pondering whether he wanted to kiss her. Or devour her.

Then he dropped his hand so suddenly that she nearly whimpered at the loss of his touch. He reached for a plate and began to spoon out small bites of the various dishes. "But there is one thing I still need to know."

She inhaled a deep breath to steady herself. "Which is?"

"Why are you so concerned about the pensioners?" He held out the plate to her, as casually as if they were friends lunching on the green in Hyde Park instead of adversaries on a secluded stretch of beach. "They'll be taken care of, I promise you. They'll have good homes, perhaps even in Chelsea or Greenwich."

She took the plate and held it awkwardly. For one desperate moment, she wanted to tell him, in case it made a difference in keeping the men here in their home. But how could she share the awful truth? That it was the pensioners who comforted her and gave her strength and understanding when he'd abandoned her, choosing the army over her. That she was right here in Brighton when she received word that her father had died, helping in the hospital. Over the years, being a hospital patroness gave her a feeling of closeness to both of the men she'd lost, a connection she hadn't yet been able to relinquish. The pensioners had helped her survive when the darkness had closed in upon her. Now it was her turn to protect them and help them survive, just as they'd helped her.

How could she ever make him understand all that? *If* he even deserved to know in the first place.

She set the plate down, untouched, and threw his question back at him. "Why are you so concerned about training cadets? Surely they can learn battle tactics and leadership better on the field than in classrooms and on parade grounds."

His face hardened with a small deepening in the lines at the corners of his eyes. "Because I'm fed up with a system in which promising young men never have the chance to reach their full potential or demonstrate what they're capable of becoming. If we can enroll more cadets, then we can train better officers, and everyone has the opportunity to rise in the ranks as high as their competence and skills allow." He turned away from her, squinting into the sun that was sinking in a blood-red ball toward the horizon. "And perhaps more men can return alive from the battlefield."

She bit her lip. All good points. But… "Once they return, don't they deserve to be taken care of? To be given a permanent home and not be shuffled about from place to place whenever the army decides it no longer wants them around? What does that say to the men who risk their lives for England?"

"That once a soldier, always a soldier."

She leaned toward him, unwilling to let him dismiss her concerns so easily. "They have every right—"

"The real question," he interrupted, countering her offensive with one of his own, "is why you asked to meet me this afternoon." He rested his forearm across his bent knee, his hand clenching lightly into a fist as if to keep himself from reaching for her. "Obviously, it wasn't to tell me that you haven't changed your mind."

Guilt sparked inside her. When she'd schemed to avoid Pomperly, she'd still believed Maxwell to be the horrible, selfish blackguard who'd used her and cast her away, who deserved to be used in kind. But now, knowing how much it meant to him to have proper training for the soldiers, he seemed far less of a monster.

"Because I need you," she answered grudgingly.

He chuckled, a low sound that rumbled into her. "Why do I think it's not the way a man wants to be needed by a woman?"

Oh, that devil! Her face flushed hot. "That is *not* what I meant, and you know it!"

Without a repentant bone in his body, he stroked his knuckles across her cheek. "Pity."

Stunned, she clutched at the rug beneath her, desperate to hold on to anything as the world rocked around her. He couldn't *possibly* mean... could he?

Then the reality of their past crashed over her. What a fool she was! To let herself think it, even for a fleeting heartbeat—no. She doubted he held a single affection toward her. Even the trouble of this picnic wasn't for her but to try to persuade her to his side.

She pushed his hand away to hide her mortification that the devil could affect her even now. And to quash an unexpected pang of sadness that she didn't have the same effect on him. "There's a dinner at the Pavilion with His Majesty." She busied her empty hands by pulling at the yarns in the rug beneath her. "The Duke of Pomperly has invited me to be his guest. But I prefer not to attend with him."

"Then refuse." His blunt response startled her. So did the suddenly sharp edge to his voice. With any other man, she would have claimed he was jealous.

"I cannot refuse an invitation to dine with the king, even if it comes from a man whom I'd rather avoid." Nor could she afford to offend a board member. "But I *can* refuse if I'm already attending the dinner with someone else."

"Who?"

Guilt at using him to avoid Pomperly added to the knot sitting in her belly like a lead ball, and she bit her bottom lip. "You."

"I see," he drawled, his face inscrutable.

"You're a brigadier, one of the highest-ranking officers in Brighton," she rushed out. "Surely you'll receive an invitation or can wrangle one. Or *I* can contact the Pavilion and request that you be put on the guest list. So I thought—I thought that you'd—" Now that the scheme was hatched, the words poured from her as she attempted to find purchase in her persuasion. And failing. Because he returned her gaze with an unreadable expression, with no indication if he were sympathetic to her situation. Or simply thought her mad.

She fell silent, realizing with embarrassment that her explanation was paltry justification for using him.

He covered her hand with his, stilling her nervous fingers against the rug. "I'll accompany you."

She blinked. "You will?"

"But not to spite Pomperly." Masculine pride underpinned his voice. "I'll do it on two conditions."

She felt as if she were negotiating terms of surrender with the enemy. "Which are?"

"I'll escort you to the dinner if you agree to accompany me to the barracks to meet the soldiers."

Suspicion prickled at the backs of her knees. "Why?"

"Just to talk to them." His deep voice curled softly around her, nearly lost beneath the sound of the rolling waves breaking against the shore. "To find out what their lives in the army have been like."

Without agreeing, she asked a bit breathlessly, very aware of the warmth of his hand still covering hers, "And your second condition?"

"That you want to spend the evening with me because you want to be with me."

Clinging to what little pride she had left, she lifted her chin with an imperious sniff, but succeeded only in drawing a grin from him. Oh, that infuriating devil!

"Why would I want to spend the evening with you?" she asked, determined to pretend that he wasn't affecting her when he was actually shaking her to her core.

He smiled with arrogant charm. "Because you like me."

"Ha!" Her indignation flared at that. But blast it, she couldn't bring herself to pull her hand from his. "I don't like you."

His eyes gleamed. "A great deal."

"A very little," she shot back. Then she grumbled, "And less with each passing moment."

With a quirk of his brow, he lifted her hand to his lips to place a kiss to her palm. She managed to fight down the tremble that threatened to sweep through her. But when he slid his mouth down to her wrist, her pulse spiked tellingly against his lips, and he smiled.

"A great deal," he repeated in a rakish murmur.

He slipped a hand behind her nape and tugged her gently toward him before her confused mind had the chance to realize what was happening so she could stop him. Then his lips found hers, and stopping him was the *very* last thing she wanted to do.

Closing her eyes against the agonizing flood of bittersweet memories that his tender kiss unlocked, she placed her hand against his chest for something solid to cling to as the world around her fell away completely. His heart pounded beneath her fingertips, an echo to her own racing pulse, and she knew she was lost. The achingly sweet kiss tasted of the past, of love and promise... of *home.*

When he shifted back, breaking the kiss, the loss of contact was so powerful that a whimper rose on her lips.

He stared at her wide-eyed, as if he couldn't believe that he'd kissed her, with a bewildered expression that she was certain mirrored her own. But for all the confusion that kiss created, the pull of it had been irresistible.

"Maxwell," she whispered, her right hand rising to touch her lips. She could still feel the heat and strength of his kiss, like a shadow of the love they'd once shared. A ghost pain of the life together that fate denied them.

"Forgive me." He reached to once again gently take her hand, this time covering it with both of his. And this time, she couldn't hold back the trembling.

"Of course." But her voice sounded strained, as if every lie she was telling herself was audible in it. "It was only a kiss." Oh, it was so much more than that! "It was nothing." It was simply breathtaking. "We both got caught up in old memories and feelings and..." And something inside her had desperately wanted that kiss. "It won't happen again." Even now she yearned to be taken back into his arms, kissed breathless, and told that everything was going to be all right, as if the past had never happened—

But the past couldn't be changed. She was a fool to wish that it could.

"It was only a kiss... nothing," she repeated. This time, she meant every word.

"No." He gave her fingers a tender squeeze. "I meant about what happened ten years ago."

That small touch of affection raced up her arm and landed

warmly in her breast. Heavens, she desperately needed an anchor! But the soothing caress of his fingers over the backs of hers only increased the spinning inside her head. So did that stunning declaration.

"Forgive me, Belinda." The hard set of his jaw told her how difficult this was for him. "I made what I thought was the best decision at the time."

One that ended up nearly destroying her. She pulled her hand away and pressed her fist to her chest to physically hold back the pain of old wounds that were once more bleeding as if still fresh.

"Why should I forgive?" Somehow, she kept her voice even. She wanted to scream!

"Because I'm not the man I was before."

Oh, *that* was certainly true. She could see the changes in him with her own eyes. Age had mellowed his brashness, and maturity had dulled the impulsive edge she so clearly remembered in the young man he'd once been.

But was he truly repentant for what he'd done, or was he simply playing her for a fool... again?

As if reading her doubts, he slowly pulled at her bonnet ribbons, untying them with a gentle tug. She inhaled sharply at the far-too familiar gesture but couldn't find the resolve to push his hands away.

"Say that you'll forgive me," he cajoled, removing the bonnet and setting it aside.

Then he reached up to her hair and scandalously pulled loose the pins holding her chignon. Spurred on by the sea breeze, her hair spilled free, stirring in the wind around her shoulders.

He stilled as his eyes drank her in. Not moving, not touching, only looking... yet the heated intensity in him coiled a powerful longing deep inside her.

Somehow finding the strength to keep her wits about her, she rasped out in a breathless whisper, "I don't want your apology."

"Good. Because I'm not giving one."

Surprise darted through her, and her lips parted. Taking her reaction as an invitation, he brushed his thumb over her bottom lip. His eyes softened as he focused on the caress, as if touching her like this was the most important thing in the world.

"I've made a lifetime of mistakes," he admitted, remorse roughening his voice, "and I've learned that apologies are meaningless. I would never demean you by offering one." She stiffened beneath his touch, so stunned that for a moment she forgot to breathe. "An apology, no matter how sincere, can never make up for the pain I caused you. And for *that*, I am truly sorry."

Fresh anguish sliced into her heart, and she flinched at the pain, so fierce it was visceral. There was a time when she would have given anything to hear those words from him. But that was ten years ago—a different lifetime. Hearing them now brought only torment at the reminder of all they'd lost.

He stared at her so intensely that the little hairs on her arms stood on end. As if he had so much more he wanted to confess. But he said nothing and instead dared to comb his fingers through her hair.

Her heart skipped. In that missed beat, she saw everything her life could have been with him, the family and home they could have made, the dreams and hopes they could have shared—

Then it was gone in a flash of brutal reality.

The pain was vicious. Because her heart knew the truth… that Maxwell didn't regret what he'd done. What he regretted was that fate had brought them together again while she still blamed him, when he needed her on his side in the fight over the academy. When he once more needed her help to advance his career.

"I can't forgive you." She slowly pushed his hand down and moved away, unable to bear his touch a moment longer.

Wisely, he remained where he was, as if sensing that reaching for her again would be the worst mistake he could make. "Not now," he asked solemnly, "or not ever?"

Unable to find the courage to put full voice to how much he'd wounded her, how the darkness of that time nearly destroyed her, she whispered instead, "I think... I think our picnic's over."

RICHARD MARBURY, DUKE OF POMPERLY, WATCHED THE TWO figures walking together up from the beach in twilight's darkening shadows. He noted the way Belinda rested her hand on Thorpe's arm, how his hand reached up to cover hers—only for a moment before dropping back to his side. A gesture of tenderness and affection. One she marked by stiffening ever so slightly, but in her connection to him not shifting away.

Then Pomperly turned away from his carriage window and signaled with a sharp rap of his cane to the roof for his driver to move on.

So the rumors he'd heard about the duchess's youthful liaison with Maxwell Thorpe were true after all. And from the looks of things, the two were picking up right where they'd left off.

"Not if I have anything to say about it," he grumbled.

Belinda was the perfect choice to become Duchess of Pomperly, and nothing was going to get in his way of making her his. Certainly not some upstart baron's son turned army officer who didn't have the good sense to realize when he was overstepping. *Very much* overstepping, in fact, to think that he could win himself a duchess.

Oh, she might find him pleasant enough as an old friend. Or

attractive enough for an assignation or two, to take care of whatever physical needs hadn't been satisfied since Winchester died. But certainly nothing beyond that.

A *brigadier's* wife? He snorted. Even Belinda wasn't reformer enough for that.

No, she was meant to be a duchess. *His* duchess. Well-cultured, already familiar with the demands of the rank and how to navigate the highest levels of Society, possessing a nice fortune of her own and so would never need to touch his—she was perfect. Doubly so, considering that she was barren and that he already had heirs from his previous duchess. There would be no children to interfere in their marriage.

No mere army officer was going to steal her away.

He'd just have to make certain that Thorpe was put in his proper place... all the way to Africa.

CHAPTER 4

*W*hen Max reached inside the carriage stopped in front of the barracks to help Belinda to the ground, she hesitated to slip her hand into his. Only a heartbeat's uncertainty, but in that moment, he knew she remembered their kiss from two days ago, and her regret ripped through him.

Then she put her gloved hand into his and descended gracefully to the cobblestones.

She'd arrived for her visit to the barracks, and not a moment too soon. He'd spent all of yesterday with her at the hospital, meeting the pensioners and watching as she read books to them, helped mend their clothing—even helped one dress himself, a man whose leg and foot had been badly damaged in an explosion. If anyone from the *ton* had seen a duchess do such a thing, they surely would have suffered apoplexy on the spot. But Belinda behaved as if she were privileged to help.

She'd made her point. The pensioners needed her, and they needed one another.

He only hoped that today she'd realize how much the army needed well-trained cadets.

"You look lovely," he told her as he bowed over her hand, then placed it on his arm to lead her through the gate. He was acutely aware of every curious stare cast their way from the soldiers gathered in the yard.

"Please stop saying that," she admonished with an exasperated sigh. "Your charms won't work on me."

He clenched his jaw. "I'm not saying it to—"

"And you cannot seduce me to your side either."

That brought him up short. He halted, stopping her next to him. "Pardon?"

She fussed with her gloves, not daring to spare him a glance. "Your kiss."

"*My* kiss?" As if she'd had nothing to do with it. As if he routinely staged elaborate picnics on beaches only to have his wicked way with unsuspecting ladies. "That kiss was *not* a seduction." Not by a goodly ways, although for the life of him, he couldn't have said why he'd done it. Except that he couldn't resist. "And you were a willing participant."

"That doesn't mean that you should have done it."

Oh, he was pretty certain that was *exactly* what it meant, and she knew it, too, which was proven by her careful dodge. But he didn't want to risk a slap in front of the men and silently led her forward, toward the enlisted men's mess hall.

"I spent a great deal of time yesterday thinking about it," she continued. He was confident she had. He'd thought of little else himself, especially when they'd been together at the hospital. Close, but never alone so they couldn't repeat the encounter. "It cannot happen again."

"Absolutely not."

She began to nod, as if satisfied with his answer—only to freeze as his comment sank through her.

Her bewildered gaze darted to him. She'd obviously been

expecting a different answer, and her mind surely whirled at a million miles a minute to figure out his reply. If he had agreed with her or was refusing.

Finally, unable to bear the uncertainty any longer, she scowled and demanded, "And what, exactly, do you mean by that?"

He had no intention of answering. Especially when he didn't know himself. Instead, he dodged, "I don't have to charm you to win your support, and I certainly wouldn't attempt to seduce you." Although he'd lost count of the number of times over the years he'd imagined doing just that. He added bluntly, "You're an intelligent woman who trusts in logic and reason, and I'd be a fool to try to use your heart against you. We both know how ineffective that would be."

She hesitated with what he was certain was a cutting reply poised on the tip of her tongue. Then she softened as that unusual compliment sank in. "Then why did you kiss me?"

He purposefully avoided her question. "If that kiss was wrong, it wasn't for the reason you think."

"I *think* we already have enough problems between us," she answered, getting in the last word as they reached the dining hall door. "We don't need to add more, not ones like that."

"Absolutely not."

Her shoulders slumped in exasperation. "Maxwell—"

"Brigadier!"

The shout went up as soon as they entered. As more men took up the call, it echoed through the building and out across the barracks grounds that stretched along Church Street, just a stone's throw across the park from the Pavilion. Infantrymen scrambled up from the benches lining the long tables to snap to attention, then were relieved when Max signaled for them to fall at ease. A comforting sense of familiarity rose inside him as he led her through the hall, a place he knew well, surrounded by men whom he'd trust with his life.

"Brigadier in the barracks!"

She tensed at his side, and her eyes widened as she glanced around the room. He fought back a twitch of his lips at her discomfiture, this woman who was usually so confident that she charged through the world without hesitation.

Briefly placing his hand over hers as it rested on his sleeve, he leaned down to quietly explain, "If it helps, you should know that they're all more concerned about my presence here than yours."

"Oh?"

"I can order them to serve guard duty. You can only order them to serve tea."

The tension drained out of her, and a faint smile of irritation tugged at her lips. "Enjoying yourself, are you?"

"Of course." He patted her hand with mock condescension. "For once, I outrank a duchess."

When she opened her mouth to give him the set-down he deserved, he interrupted, "You've entered a different world, Belinda." He gestured behind them at the dozen or so men who had returned to their seats at the table but were still craning their necks to stare curiously at them. "The army is a world unto itself, with its own laws and traditions, its own expectations and loyalties." They reached the end of the mess hall, and he took her hand to help her sit on the wooden bench at the head of the long table. Standing behind her, he took her slender shoulders in his hands and leaned over to murmur into her ear, "Today, consider me your guide to that world."

He removed his hat and tossed it to one of the nearby men, with unspoken orders to hang it from one of the pegs on the wall. The soldier stared at him in surprise. Officers rarely entered this mess hall and certainly few of high rank.

Then the soldier grinned as he hung the hat, apparently deciding that all the stories he'd heard about Max were true. That he'd rather spend his time with infantrymen than officers.

"Why do I need a guide?" she challenged. "I've spent a good amount of time around soldiers, you forget."

"Around officers." Instead of joining her at the table, he crossed to the little cast-iron stove in the corner, where a pot of coffee sat heating. He lifted the lid and peered inside. "You've probably never had a conversation with an enlisted soldier."

"Many of the pensioners were enlisted men."

"Retired, not actively serving." He returned the lid and turned away, cursing himself for not thinking ahead to have a tray of tea ready for her. But then, hadn't he wanted to show her the way the average soldier lived? Expensive china and tea had never graced the doorway of this dining hall.

"No difference."

"A *world* of difference." He signaled for the men to gather near. Good soldiers all, they joined them at the front of the room without a single grumble.

"Your Grace," Max introduced with as much formality as if they were meeting in a Society drawing room, "these are the men of the Royal Fusiliers."

"The 7th Regiment of Foot, sir," one of the older soldiers interjected.

"Of course." With a deferential nod, he smiled at the man's pride over his regiment. The grizzled sergeant had reason for being proud. Every man in His Majesty's army knew the heroism of the 7th Regiment of Foot and how much they'd sacrificed over the years. "Men, this is Her Grace, Duchess of Winchester."

He held her gaze as the men stared at her in surprise. Most of them had never seen a duchess in person before, let alone been introduced to one, and were uncertain of the proper way to greet her. They shifted nervously, until the sergeant pulled at his fore-lock and nodded. "Your Grace."

The others followed suit, and Belinda gave them a bright smile, as if she were being introduced to peers of the realm instead of coarse soldiers.

"I'm very pleased to meet you, gentlemen." Her soft voice lilted through the dining hall and drew relaxed smiles from the men. Already she was winning them over, exactly as Max knew she would. "The 7th Regiment of Foot... My! That sounds like a very fine regiment."

The men didn't know if they were supposed to make replies to that, and an awkward silence followed until Max cleared his throat and said, "One of His Majesty's bravest. They fought in America and the West Indies before taking on Napoleon on the Peninsula at Talavera and Bussaco."

"Also at Albuera," one of the older soldiers added proudly. "'Twas me first fight."

"A bloody one, from what I've heard." Max's eyes never moved from Belinda.

"Aye," the sergeant agreed somberly. "Gave it to 'em right good, we did!"

"And the sieges, don't forget," another soldier piped up. Although he was too young to have fought on the Peninsula, he openly showed his pride at being part of the storied regiment. "All three of 'em."

Then the men all jumped into the conversation. "Salamanca, too—"

"And Vitoria—"

"Then we stuck it to Boney by chasing him right o'er the Pyrenees and back to France!"

"Stuck it to 'em good."

"Right there on their own soil!"

"Toulouse."

At that, the men all turned their gazes to the sergeant who had quietly spoken that last. Including Max.

The sergeant lowered his eyes to the floor, but not before a haunted expression darkened his face. He added solemnly, "Never forget Toulouse, boys."

A grim silence fell over the room, broken only by the faint popping of coals in the stove and the muted noise of horses and wagons moving in the barracks yard outside.

Belinda glanced from man to man, attempting to understand what she'd missed, before her puzzled gaze landed on Max. "What happened at Toulouse?"

"Hell," he answered quietly.

"*All* hell," the sergeant corrected.

Her lips parted slightly as she pulled in a stunned breath. She gracefully rose to her feet and stepped toward the sergeant.

"You were there, weren't you?" Not a question.

With a curt nod, he looked away. "Yes, ma'am."

Silently, Belinda held out her hand. The sergeant hesitated, then took it in his. She leaned close, bringing her mouth to his ear.

Max had no idea what she whispered to the man, but the sergeant's eyes glistened, and he nodded again. When she released his hand and stepped back, the old soldier blinked rapidly and turned completely away to hide the raw emotions on his face.

Instead of returning to her seat, Belinda went through the group of men, holding out her hand in greeting to each of them, asking their names, where each called home, and how long they had been part of the Royal Fusiliers. Each man beamed when she spoke to him, captivated by her interest in them and by her kindness.

"You've been with the Fusiliers for a long time," Max interjected when she laughed at a joke that one of the oldest of the soldiers told her.

"Aye, sir." The man straightened. Even though Max was here unofficially and doing his best to put the men at ease, none of them forgot his rank. "Over twenty years since I enlisted."

Which would have been right at the start of the wars with the French. Seizing on this opportunity, Max asked, "What was your first engagement?"

His eyes took on a faraway look. "Copenhagen. Been in the army less than three months 'fore they shipped us off to Denmark."

"How old were you?" Belinda asked.

"Just turned one and twenty, ma'am."

Max fixed his eyes on Belinda to gauge her reaction. "Were you prepared for it?"

He snorted in disgust. "The trainin' they gave us was little more than instructions on which end o' the rifle to point at the enemy an' t' keep our heads down when the artillery goes to boomin' off. And marchin'." He scowled in distaste. "Hours o' marchin'."

Belinda asked innocently, "What's wrong with marching? Order and discipline among the ranks are surely important in a battle."

"Aye, ma'am." His nod turned into a frustrated shake of his head. "Until th' first shots are fired. Then it's a scramble on the field, wi' no one knowin' what to do, where to charge, or when to fall back."

"But isn't that what the officers are there for? To give direction to the men?"

He spat on the floorboards. "Officers who themselves ain't had more than a few weeks of trainin' at best? An' trainin' not at all like what they'll encounter i' th' fray, when bullets come a-whizzin' at 'em."

She folded her hands demurely in front of her. "I see."

Max was certain she did. After all, this was why he'd brought her here, so she could understand how little training most soldiers were given before being rushed into battle, along with field officers who were just as inexperienced.

She confirmed her understanding of his scheme when she answered dryly, "I suppose not all officers can be as clever as Brigadier Thorpe." Then she slid a sideways glance at him. "Occasionally, he makes quite good decisions under the pressure of battle."

He fought to hide the amused twitch of his lips at her sly innuendo. She always had been one of the sharpest women he'd ever met.

"So soldiers need more training," she announced. "Do you all agree?"

A round of ayes and emphatic nods went up from the men, and Max gave a silent sigh of relief. If Belinda was ever going to be swayed to support the academy, it would be the soldiers themselves who convinced her.

"What are your career plans, then?" she asked with a sincere smile.

The abrupt change in conversation didn't surprise the men, but a warning prickled at the back of his neck. What was she up to?

One by one, the men all shared their plans with her, and to a man, they all wanted to serve out their army careers as part of the Fusiliers. Not one wanted to be pensioned before he'd given his all to crown and country. The pride Max felt in them warmed his chest and reminded him that he'd not been wrong to pick the military as his life's path. Not when he could serve with men like these.

"And when you're no longer able, what then?" Another question that seemed innocent to the men but which sliced into Max, because he knew where that quick mind of hers was headed. "Once you're too old to charge into battle, or God forbid, should you be wounded? What would you do then, if you couldn't be a soldier any longer?"

One of the younger men shrugged. He was so young, in fact, that freckles still dotted his nose. "Go home to our families, ma'am. Start over there with them."

She pressed, "So you all have families to depend upon?"

Most nodded, except for three men who remained still. One of them was the old sergeant who had fought at Toulouse.

"And your family, Sergeant?"

"Got none, ma'am," he answered quietly, as if a bit embarrassed to admit it. "The regiment is my family, till the day I'm pensioned."

"What a great loss that day will bring to the Fusiliers," she said sincerely. Then she turned toward Max. "Did you know, Brigadier, that in order to be a pensioner at one of the royal hospitals, a man cannot have any family?"

"Yes, Your Grace," he answered with chagrin. "I did know that."

"Hospitals that might otherwise keep a dedicated soldier who has given the best years of his life to crown and country from a life of starvation and suffering on the streets?"

He clenched his jaw. "Yes, ma'am."

Satisfied that she'd made her point, she smiled warmly at the men. "Do not worry. You'll all be given the respect and rewards you deserve, both now and when you retire." Then she added with such conviction that it pulsed through him like an electric tingle, "I give you my word."

Max quietly dismissed the men and took her arm to escort her out. Instead of cutting directly across the yard to the barracks gate and her waiting carriage, he guided her the long way around, along the brick wall that separated the barracks from the inn and houses fronting Marlborough Place.

When they were well out of earshot of the soldiers, she commented dryly, "I think I made my point about the hospital."

She had. And yet… "And I mine about the academy."

"Then it seems that we're right back where we started."

Not back where they'd started, but more firmly entrenched than before. Due in no small part because of their past. Even now, the tension flowed around them as palpably as the salty sea air and only increased with each step they took leading them away from the main part of the yard and past the service buildings framing the perimeter.

"The War Office wants the academy," he reminded her as gently as possible. "I think it's time you accepted that and turned your kindnesses toward helping the pensioners relocate."

"Why can't you see any other perspective but your own?" Aggravation colored her voice.

"I am trying to see your point. But you're an outsider. You have no idea what the army needs to protect its men and—"

"Do not dare to try to put me in my place by telling me that I don't know what army life is like. The War Office will be breaking their promise to those men." He could feel her breath grow short as her frustration mounted, and not with the War Office but with *him*. "I know what it means to place your trust in someone, only to have it destroyed."

He halted as the words slammed into him, grabbing her elbow and pulling her to a stop. "You are letting the past cloud your judgment."

"Cloud my judgment?" With a bitter laugh of disbelief, she tried to yank her arm away, but he held tight, refusing to let her go. All of her pulsed with anger as she accused, "You used me!" She drew her hands into fists. "I loved you, and you used me just to advance your career."

Fury flared inside him. *Enough.*

He pulled her into an open storage room and kicked the door closed behind them. In the dim light cast by a small window high up in the wall, his gaze bore down into hers as he stepped her back against the stone wall. No surrender, no quarter—

This fight was ten years in coming, and he'd be damned if he'd retreat now.

"I didn't use you," he bit out. Every ounce of his will fought for restraint against the anger and pain he'd kept locked inside him all these years. "And I sure as hell didn't break my promise to you."

"You told me you loved me, that you wanted to marry me—"

"I did want that." *Christ!* He'd wanted that more than he'd wanted anything in his life, save for wanting the best possible life for *her.*

She pushed at his shoulders to make him step back, but he refused to budge. "You let me believe it just so my father would arrange for a better post for you. One that gave you a better chance at promotion. When you didn't need me anymore, you abandoned me."

"I *never* abandoned you." Her accusations ripped fresh wounds into him.

"You refused to return to England when I needed you, and it nearly destroyed me." Even in the dim light, pain shone in her eyes. "Why, Maxwell?" Ten years of confusion choked her as she forced out, "For God's sake—*why?*"

That single word was the one question he'd *never* wanted to answer, preferring to take the truth to his grave. But he should have known that Belinda would make him walk through the fires of hell.

"I made a choice." The *right* choice. He was as certain of that now as he'd been ten years ago. "I did what was best for you."

"For *me*?" Disdain darkened her face. "The best thing for me would have been for you to return to England and marry me."

The very *worst* thing. He bit back a curse that she refused to let this go. "You would have resented me."

"*Never.* I loved you. I wanted to marry you and—"

"For God's sake, Belinda! Don't you understand?" Furious that she refused to let this go, he grabbed her shoulders and humiliatingly confessed, "I wasn't good enough for you!"

She stared at him, shocked speechless.

"I wasn't good enough for you," he repeated, the guilt over hurting her so brutal that he shuddered with it. "I couldn't give you the help you needed, but I *could* give you a better life. A life without me."

He released her shoulders with a jerk and stepped away so that he couldn't see any more of her pain. It would absolutely undo him.

"I loved you enough to let you hate me for it. *That's* why I asked you to forget me." The powerlessness he'd felt then rushed back over him now with full force. A cruel reminder of the man he'd once been, of how far he'd come since then. Without her. He forced out around the tightening knot in his throat, "And it *killed* me, Belinda. I had no money, no rank of consequence, mounting debts—" Now that he'd made his confession, the words poured out of him in a wave, carrying with them all the guilt and anguish he'd kept inside him since the night he wrote that letter beneath the monsoon's rains. "You deserved better than being married to some junior officer stationed halfway around the world, with no prospects back in England and no other way to provide a living."

"You're a brigadier." She touched a shaking hand to his arm. "We would have married and—"

He yanked his shoulder away, out of her reach, and wheeled on her. "I was *nothing* then!"

When a tear slipped down her cheek at his outburst, he raked his fingers through his hair to resist the urge to reach for her, to brush it away and stop the trembling of her lips with his own.

He sucked in a ragged breath to gain back his control. "It took years to be promoted—years in which you would have been forced to live in near poverty on whatever few pounds I was able to send home from my pay. You deserved so much more, and Winchester gave it to you." Even now the thought of her in that man's arms sparked fury and anger inside him. "I knew you'd hate me for what I did, and I was willing to pay that price. For you."

"You had no right—*no* right—to make that decision for me!"

"I had every right," he replied quietly, closing the distance between them. "Because I loved you."

"Because you thought I wouldn't be—"

"Because I loved you." Another step.

She fiercely shook her head. "No! How could you have done—"

"Because I loved you," he repeated firmly. That was the answer to all her protests. The *only* answer.

One more step, and she was in his arms, shaking violently and sobbing openly in both anger and anguish. Raw pain seeped from her, and he held her close, taking on her pain for himself.

"I loved you, Belinda," he murmured into her hair, "with every ounce of my being."

She shoved at him to push herself free of his embrace, but he tightened his arms around her. He was *not* letting her go. Not this time.

"I couldn't help you." He squeezed his eyes closed against the cost to his pride that this admission forced him to pay. He'd never felt less like a man than the moment ten years ago when he realized the truth of that. "In order to help you, I *had* to let you go."

"But we loved each other!" A sob gripped her. "We could have... We could have..."

When words failed her, a great shudder pierced her. She finally understood the same truth that he'd realized all those years ago. That they could have done nothing.

She buried her face in his chest and cried, harder than he'd ever seen a woman cry in his life. Every sob was an agonizing slice into his heart.

Not letting her go, he lowered them both slowly onto a large grain sack resting on the floor and held her in his arms as she cried out all the torment fate had thrust upon them. She clung to him, and he'd never seen her more fragile than at that moment, when she cried as if she might break. He hadn't been there to see the pain he'd caused her when she received his letter, but he was living it now. A brutal torment.

"Don't cry, love," he whispered, his lips at her temple. "No more tears, please." God, he couldn't bear it!

But he might as well have been begging the tide not to rise or the sun not to set. And truly, the only way forward was through the hellfire of the past. So he let her cry and provided whatever comfort he could. The only words were soft whispers to soothe her, the only movement the consoling caress of his hand against her back.

When her cries lessened into soft sobs, then finally subsided into nothing more than little gasps for air, he shifted her in his arms to rest her cheek against his shoulder and stroke her back. Eventually, her breath came gentle and even, but he didn't release her. Neither did she shift away, remaining vulnerable in his arms.

Yet the difference in her now was palpable. Pain still lingered inside her; he could feel it with every delicate beat of her heart against his chest, pulsing inside him until he couldn't tell where her heartbeat ended and his began. But it was no longer the harsh anguish she'd held inside her all these years or the confusion over why he'd abandoned her. Now there was at least understanding, if not yet acceptance.

He placed a soft kiss to her hair.

Then he whispered what had tormented him since that night in India. "I regret every day that I couldn't be the man you needed, but I have never once regretted giving you the life you deserved." He sucked in a deep breath to steel himself. "Was he a good husband to you?"

"Yes," she breathed out, so softly that it was barely audible. But his heart heard, and the emotions that crashed over him were a mix of love and fierce protectiveness. Two emotions that he suspected she would always stir inside him. "He was kind and generous. He never spoke a word in anger, never threatened... denied me nothing. We were as happy as could be expected."

The swift stab of jealousy tore through him, and he couldn't find the power to speak. To tell her how glad he was for her. How thrilled he was that she'd lived the wonderful life he'd always wanted for her.

"But I never loved him," she finished. As if compelled, she added, "Not the way I loved you."

That soft confession revealed fully to him all he'd lost by letting her go, and instant mourning for that life nearly brought him to his knees. But he needed to ask the question whose answer he feared most—"Do you hate me?"

Her heartbeat's hesitation nearly broke him.

Then she gave a soft shake of her head against his shoulder. "How can I hate you when you loved me so much?"

His eyes stung, and he squeezed them shut. Her voice lacked conviction, but she'd said the words, and he'd desperately needed to hear them. Hope stirred inside his hollow chest that he'd be able to eventually persuade her to forgive him. No matter how long it took.

"Maxwell." His name was a plea for compassion, an entreaty to give her guidance as to what to believe about him.

He cupped her face in his palm and rasped out, "I never stopped loving you, Belinda, even after you forgot about me. You need to know that."

Her hands twisted his uniform in her fists, and her heart pounded against his chest as she pressed into him. "I never forgot you, you damnable fool," she chastised in a gentle whisper. "Not one day."

Both seeking absolution and giving solace, he touched his lips to hers.

She inhaled sharply at the tender contact but didn't pull back. Instead, she softly returned the kiss, her trembling lips moving tentatively beneath his.

In that kiss he tasted the forgiveness he sought. More, that kiss held a second chance at the future they'd been denied, with Belinda back in his arms. Where she'd always belonged.

"GIVE ME A SECOND CHANCE," HE WHISPERED ENTREATINGLY against her lips.

A second chance? Belinda pulled away and stared at him. His quiet declaration simply stunned her.

Taking her surprised reaction as an invitation, he reached up to trace his thumb over her chin and back along her jaw. That small touch of affection sped through her, blazing a trail of warmth and need in its wake.

"Seeing you again and holding you in my arms makes me realize how much I still want a life with you. The one we'd planned." His deep murmur seeped into her, filling her with the happiness she remembered. "Say that you'll forgive me and give me that chance."

She pressed her fist to her chest to physically calm her racing heart. A second chance with Maxwell... All of her yearned to have just that—the life with him that they'd been denied. She was still drawn to him as strongly as ever. Perhaps even more now that she knew the truth about why he'd broken off with her, now that she knew how much he'd loved her. At that moment, with Maxwell holding her in his arms, she could almost believe the past ten years and all the grief had never happened. As if anything could be possible again.

And yet...

"If you're saying all this only to gain my support for the academy, it won't work," she warned, putting voice to her worst fears that all this was only a lie. That the second chance he wanted was simply another opportunity to break her heart.

"Then how about to gain your love?"

Did he really mean... *love*? She was too stunned to answer as he brought his lips to hers again and kissed away her surprise.

Despite her reservations, she sighed as his mouth moved gently against hers. At first, the kiss was tender and hesitant, then growing more bold with each passing heartbeat in which she didn't stop him from claiming more. How could she, when this was exactly what she'd always wanted, what she'd longed for years to experience just once more? His lips on hers, the masculine taste of his kiss, his strong arms slipping around her to draw her against him...

She surrendered with a whisper. "Maxwell."

All those kisses he'd given her in the past had been nothing like this. For heaven's sake, she could *taste* the difference in him. The maturity that the years had brought to him, the tempering of experience, even an underlying patience that certainly hadn't been there before—it all worked together to sweep her away, until there was only the strength of him beneath her fingertips as she splayed her hands over his shoulders, only his presence filling her senses until she shivered.

When she melted against him, boneless in his arms, a groan sounded from the back of his throat, and his tongue plunged between her lips to capture all of her kiss. She reveled in his need for her and enjoyed her own answering passion. A passion that now had her stroking her tongue over the length of his and encouraging him to claim even more.

"Belinda," he rasped out. Awe laced through his voice, as if he couldn't quite believe that she was real.

"Yes," she whispered. *I'm real. I'm here with you. The way I always wanted to be.*

He kissed down her neck to her collarbone. He tongued the pulse pounding wildly in the little hollow at the base of her throat before trailing his mouth lower to the scooped neckline of her dress.

Belinda wrapped her arms around his shoulders and clung to him, rolling back her head with sheer delight.

"Dear God, how good you feel." He nuzzled his face against her shoulder. "I'd forgotten how soft you are, how tempting... how much I missed you."

As if to prove his words, his hands caressed up her body to her breasts to strum his thumbs against her hardening nipples through the dress. He'd touched her like this before when they'd been courting, but his hands hadn't been as expert then. His attentions had never been on her as intently as they were now to gauge every reaction he drew from her, no matter how small.

Belinda shamelessly arched herself against him, wishing her clothes weren't between them. Wishing her body was bare to his eyes, his hands, his mouth… wishing he was working to quench the burning ache throbbing between her thighs now instead of so devilishly stoking it with each touch and kiss. She was a widow and knew what intimate pleasures a man could bring to a woman. But only Maxwell could make her heart ache just as fiercely with love as he made her body burn with desire.

"I—I missed you, too," she forced out the admission between increasingly harder breaths that were quickly becoming pants.

Lifting her onto his lap, he buried his face against her cleavage with chuckle. "Only *missed*, hmm?"

He licked into the valley between her breasts in a brazen allusion to what he would do if he could strip her dress off her right there in the supply room. If he could lie her back on the flour bags and feast on her as if she were one of the exotic dishes he'd presented to her at the picnic. She couldn't fight off a soft moan as that deliciously wicked image filled her mind. For one desperate moment, she wanted him to do exactly that.

Then he audaciously tugged down her neckline, and she gasped. The tight stays and chemise beneath made it impossible for him to set free her entire breast, but her nipple was visible to his hungry eyes, then to his greedy lips as he captured it in his mouth and suckled her.

"Perhaps—" She forced out the admission chokingly between alternating gasps of surprise and whimpers of need as he tortured her with sucks, licks, and soft bites. "Perhaps it was… a bit more… than simply missing."

He smiled against her flesh, and the devilish expression curled liquid flame through her, so hot that her thighs clenched. She watched without a trace of shame as his mouth worshipped at her breast, as he rolled her nipple between his teeth and then placed a delicate kiss to the sensitive point.

"Good," he purred as his mouth captured hers in a languid yet sultry kiss that held the promise of all the wanton things he wanted to do to her. "Because I sure as hell longed for you." His words were an enticing torment. "So many sleepless nights when you were all I could think about, when I wanted nothing more in the world than to spend just one night making love to you."

She closed her eyes against the pleasure he gave her and against the soft confession poised on the tip of her tongue that she'd wanted the same.

"Give me a second chance." He nipped at her neck in an erotic cajoling that pulled straight through her, down to the ache building between her thighs. "Let me prove to you the man I've become."

"Yes," she whispered breathlessly.

A deep sigh swept through him as his shoulders sagged and his forehead rested against hers. He placed another tender kiss to her lips. Then he pulled away, climbing quickly to his feet.

She fluttered her eyes open, confused. A surge of cold loss passed through her with a shudder. He was... *leaving?* After giving her the most thrilling kisses of her life?

As if reading her mind, he leaned over to touch his lips to hers. Then he murmured in a husky voice that was more promise than explanation, "If we don't leave now, I'll have no choice but to make love to you right here."

His audacity sparked a low heat inside her, and she nearly begged him to do just that.

"You'll not have to worry about dinner with Pomperly then if anyone should happen along and find us." His lips quirked into a lazy grin. "The scandal of it would drum me right out of the army and keep you from ever being invited to a royal affair again."

A bubble of laughter spilled from her, and she didn't fight his help in rising to her feet, straightening her dress, and leading her from the supply room. Or how he wrapped her arm around his to escort her back toward the gate, walking so closely to her that he could whisper in her ear simply by lowering his head... whispers of love and desire that stirred such happiness and longing through her that her insides melted.

Everything had changed between them.

Again.

CHAPTER 5

$\mathcal{M}$ ax watched Belinda over the rim of his wineglass. His attention tonight focused solely on her, despite being in the company of sixty other guests at His Majesty's small dinner in the Pavilion's grand banqueting hall.

He couldn't tear his eyes away from her. Dressed in a gown of dark blue silk that shimmered beneath the lamplight of the three-tiered crystal chandeliers, she was simply radiant. Her skin was luminescent against the sapphires she wore around her neck and at her ears, made to appear even more satin-soft by the curls of her auburn hair piled high onto her head. Every inch of her was perfection, and he couldn't help but wonder if she'd taken such care with her appearance tonight because of him. Because this was the first time he'd seen her in all her formal splendor.

But knowing Belinda, it wasn't to show herself off or titillate with how breathtaking she was. No. It was an imperious warning of exactly what he was getting himself into with such a powerful duchess.

Yet she had no idea how proud he was of the woman she'd become. Or how captivated he was by her.

She belonged at his side. Tonight proved that. A connection stretched between them like a ribbon tying them together. One that had always been there, even during the years when half the world—and her marriage—had been between them.

She felt it, too, based upon the way she'd leaned close to him during the reception in the saloon before dinner, when she'd not removed her hand from his arm even as they'd chatted with the other guests. The little gesture was just possessive enough to spin heated arrogance through him to think that every other man in the room wanted to be in his boots tonight when he escorted her home. Alone. Even now, seated by precedence at opposite ends of the massive table, she took surreptitious glances in his direction.

Another glance... He rakishly raised a brow as his lips curled in private innuendo.

Caught, she quickly turned away, but not before a flustered blush pinked her cheeks.

Seated beside her, Pomperly narrowed his eyes in irritation. But Max only gave the man a slow, confident smile, and the duke haughtily lifted his nose into the air.

Her rank as a duchess had put Belinda right beside Pomperly, despite her scheme to be free of him. Against Belinda's best attempts to keep conversation balanced between guests on her left and right sides, Pomperly was always turned toward her in his effort to monopolize her attention. But he never managed to keep it long before her gaze strayed once more down the table.

Surprisingly, Max felt not one jot of jealousy toward Pomperly. Belinda was on his arm tonight, and his world pulsed electric because of it.

The last course finished. Everyone stood, the women to go through to the saloon and the gentlemen to rise in courtesy to the women.

Seizing the moment, Max circled the table to come up behind

her and stopped her with a touch to her elbow. Then he leaned down to bring his mouth close to her ear so that he wouldn't be overheard.

With an amused roll of her eyes, she interrupted before he could speak, "If you're going to say that I'm lovely, then—"

"Not lovely."

That surprised her. She glanced at him, wide-eyed, over her shoulder.

"Tonight, you're simply breathtaking," he murmured. She'd always appreciated bluntness, so... "I'm out of my mind with desire for you."

She caught her breath. That soft inhalation pulsed through her and into him, warming him through with a longing he hadn't felt in ten years.

"I want nothing more tonight than to get you alone to prove it," he admitted quietly.

For a moment, she didn't move, letting that possibility whirl inside her mind. Then she admonished gently in a breathless whisper, "Maxwell, the pensioners..."

"Let them find their own women," he teased, purposefully diverting her from the objection she was about to raise, the problem that now stood between them like a wall. "I want you all to myself, Belinda." Hospitals and academies be damned. After spending the evening in her presence, seeing the sparkle in her eyes and hearing the soft lilt of her laughter, his patience hung by a thread. It was all he could do not to toss her over his shoulder at this very moment, to march her straight down to the beach and make love to her. "And I intend to have you."

He released her elbow and stepped back before he lingered too long and gained unwanted attention from the other guests.

Not daring to look at her again, now that he'd made a frontal charge and significantly raised the stakes of the attraction between them, he snatched up a cigar and bottle of port from trays carried into the room by half a dozen footmen. But he knew she was staring, because he could feel the heat of her bewildered gaze on him the entire time she slowly left the room to join the ladies.

"So it's Brigadier Thorpe, is it?"

He didn't recognize the voice at his side as he turned back toward the table. But he should have known—

The Duke of Pomperly, who had clearly sought him out on purpose during these few moments when the men were all changing seats and settling in for conversation over port and cigars.

"Yes, Your Grace." Max smiled coolly as he set the bottle of port on the table, claiming a new chair halfway down the table but still toward the bottom of the hierarchy. "I don't think we've yet had the pleasure of being introduced."

"Surprising, since we have such a dear friend in common." He ignored the opening for proper introductions and plucked at an invisible piece of lint on his kerseymere coat sleeve. "Her Grace seems quite enamored of you."

Dear God, he hoped so! "We've known each other for years."

If Pomperly caught the territorial presumption in that casual reply, he didn't show it. "General Mortimer assures me that you're very well respected within the ranks. That he knows no one else currently serving His Majesty who is as fine a soldier as you."

Max reached for the brazier the footman placed in front of him to light his cigar. "General Mortimer is too generous."

"He also feels that you would be the perfect man for the new post in Africa." Pomperly tugged at his jacket sleeves, his old-fashioned ruffled cuffs getting in the way. "Whoever gets that position will be a very fortunate man. His career opportunities will be endless."

A warning pricked at his gut. "A very fortunate man, indeed."

And a man who wasn't him. His future was right here, in Brighton.

Pomperly's attention returned to the invisible lint on his sleeve. "You should know that I have connections within the War Office and, of course, as you've seen tonight, a close relationship with His Majesty."

Max's gaze flicked across the room to King George, who most likely wasn't even aware that Pomperly was in attendance.

"I'm also an old friend of the duchess." Pomperly's nose tilted into the air with an arrogant pride. "A very *dear* friend, you understand."

Max tensed at the innuendo that Belinda's acquaintance with the duke was an intimate one, unprepared for the hot jealousy that flashed through him. And for his pity for the duke that immediately followed, because Pomperly was a fool to think that Belinda would ever give herself to a man like him.

"I could help you acquire the Africa post."

Ah, there it was! The reason Pomperly had sought him out.

"I would be happy to put in a good word for you."

Yes, Max was quite certain of it. After all, it would be damned hard for him to interfere in the duke's pursuit of Belinda if he was in Africa.

"I appreciate your generosity, but I'm committed to the Brighton academy." He puffed at the cigar, sending a cloud of smoke into the air. Then he pointed it at Pomperly and smiled. "But I'll be certain to let Her Grace know of your offer... when I escort her home tonight."

Snatching up the bottle of port, Max walked away, ending the conversation before Pomperly said something that made him pummel the man senseless and get himself court-martialed.

Blowing out a hard sigh, he sank into an empty chair near

General Mortimer and poured himself a glass. He nearly laughed to see his shaking hand, which was trembling with equal desire to both punch Pomperly and to caress Belinda.

Then he leaned back in the chair, letting his pounding heart slowly return to its normal beat. At *that* he did chuckle to himself. Because nothing about his heart would ever be normal again.

If he successfully established the academy, he would be promoted, and everything he'd ever wanted would be his. A successful career in the army, a post in England...

But not Belinda. The one thing he wanted most of all.

He thought he'd put the past behind him and found a way to move on without her. But that was before he'd seen her again. Before he'd kissed her and remembered all the reasons why he'd once fallen in love with her. And why a part of him had never stopped.

Yet old scars often gave way to new wounds, and if he couldn't find a compromise for the hospital and academy—and soon—he feared he would lose her all over again.

Led by the king, the gentlemen launched into animated stories about horses and hounds, as was to be expected in after-dinner conversation, along with the more bawdy stories that were certain to follow once the port was half gone. In Africa or India or England, whether of rank or not—none of that made any difference whenever a group of men gathered after dinner. The stories were all the same, the boasts just as unbelievable, the jokes just as coarse. Only the fineness of their clothes and the quality of their drink signified any difference.

Including King George, who was proving himself to be the loudest and bawdiest of all. Max had never been in such close proximity to His Majesty before tonight. Despite being a baron's son, he'd certainly never moved in the kinds of circles that gave access to royalty, and he wasn't prepared for the way the king insisted that the men behave as if this were no different from any other after-dinner gathering in any other gentleman's house.

The forced sense of casualness should have unnerved him, along with the way Pomperly continued to send him narrowed glares when the duke wasn't doing his best to ingratiate himself with the king. But all he could think about was Belinda and how beautiful she looked tonight. How flustered she'd become when he said he wanted her. How much he longed to hold her in his arms and caress her, to taste her sweetness and hear the soft mewlings of pleasure that would fall from her lips—

He rose to his feet. "Would you excuse me for a moment, Your Majesty?"

No one cared that he'd breached protocol by addressing the sovereign before the king had spoken to him. Least of all King George, who waved a drunken hand in his direction to signal that he didn't care what Max did.

"Unable to tolerate all the fine food and drink, eh, Thorpe?" General Mortimer called out. "Thought His Majesty's officers were made of stronger stuff than that!"

He laughed good-naturedly, not falling for the bait. "I'd like to catch a bit of air to clear my head before we return to the ladies." He paused just long enough for effect before adding, "As Her Grace's escort, it's best to have all my wits about me."

The men laughed at that, having been on the receiving end of Belinda's razor-sharp wit themselves. Except for Pomperly, whose mouth tightened into a hard line.

Even as Max sauntered from the room, his mind whirled to figure out a way to clear Belinda from his head long enough to get through the evening without embarrassing—

He stopped. And slowly smiled.

Belinda waited in the hallway, as if they'd planned a rendezvous.

"Tired already of all those pleasures you men insist on keeping secret from us ladies?" Despite her teasing, an unspoken challenge laced through her words.

He stalked toward her, shamelessly raking his gaze over her. His gut twisted, the urge to possess her so strong that he throbbed with it. "Those aren't the pleasures I'm craving tonight."

As he stepped in front of her, so close that he could feel her body warming his, she replied in a throaty murmur, "What pleasures would those be... exactly?"

"The kind that will leave you breathless and begging." Not caring if a passing footman might see, he lifted his hand to shamelessly caress the side of her breast.

The heated tone to his voice was undeniable, even to his own ears. But then, all of him was on fire as he dared to strum his thumb over her nipple through the silk of her dress and draw it into a hard point.

She forced out between pants, "I don't beg... for anything."

Grinning at her obstinate pride, he slid his hand down her body to clasp hers and promised wickedly, "You will."

Then he strode away, pulling her quickly behind him as he led her deeper into the palace. His willing captive.

When they reached the end of the long gallery, he shot a quick glance behind them to make certain no one would see where they'd gone. Snatching up the candle from the wall sconce, he led her inside the dark waiting room near the king's apartments, then closed and locked the door.

He backed her against the door and kissed her. A whimper fell from her lips, and a glorious sensation of triumph poured through him. She wanted him as much as he did her, both physically and emotionally, her heart eagerly waiting for him to reclaim it.

He let the fierce possessiveness he felt for her invade his kiss, certain from the way she trembled that she could taste it in him.

Good. Because nothing and no one—not a post in Africa, not a hospital or academy, not even another damned duke—was going to take her away from him again.

"I PLAN ON GIVING YOU ALL KINDS OF PLEASURES TONIGHT, MY love," Max purred. "But we'll start with this." Then he licked his tongue around the outer curl of her ear and sent a shiver of raw need coiling through her to land in a heated ache between her legs.

A soft moan fell from her lips. She could barely believe this was happening, that he was here with her, kissing her. That he wasn't simply a dream from which she would awaken into tears, exactly as she'd done countless times before. But he *was* real, and so were the liquid flames of need heating through her.

He'd changed. He wasn't the same man she'd fallen in love with all those years ago—he was *better.* The connection between them was stronger than ever, so was the desire to physically reveal the emotional bond that had never vanished. She loved him, always had. If possible, she loved him even more than before, now that she'd seen firsthand his dedication to his men, now that she'd experienced first-hand his strength and resilience.

He'd asked for a second chance, and as the old feelings engulfed her anew, she offered up a silent prayer that he'd take this opportunity to love her… tonight and always. Which was why she didn't stop him when his hands shoved up behind her to unfasten the tiny pearl buttons holding her bodice snugly in place.

The silk sagged over her breasts, then fell away completely as he swept his hands over her shoulders and pushed the soft material down her arms, baring her to the flickering shadows of candlelight.

A low growl sounded from the back of his throat as his hot gaze raked over her. "You're not wearing stays."

She wasn't wearing *anything* beneath the silk except for stockings. This dress fit too tightly, its specially made bodice reinforced to lift her bosom and hold it in place. She'd chosen this dress tonight precisely because of that, hoping in the secret recesses of her heart that something exactly like this would happen.

But now that it was—

She inhaled a nervous breath and asked softly, "Am I... am I what you'd imagined?"

"No," he admitted. That single word seared through her, nearly undoing her before he added, "You're more beautiful than I'd ever dreamed."

Happiness burst through her. The way she'd always imagined this moment was nothing compared to the heated reality of it, with his smoldering gaze lingering over her flesh as if he'd never seen a woman before. Her nipples drew up taut as he drank in the sight of her, and arching her back as a wave of female power surged through her, she shamelessly let him look his fill.

Then she granted him the permission he sought. "Give me the pleasure of your touch, Maxwell."

"Like this?" He lightly traced his thumb over her nipple. Barely a touch at all, but electricity jolted through her. As he continued to circle her in a reverent, featherlight caress, a damp heat grew between her thighs.

She bit back a pleading whimper, wanting more. He obliged and claimed her breasts in both hands, her fullness nearly spilling over as he massaged them against his palms.

She gasped as he lowered his head to take one between his lips and suck. Oh, simply exquisite! She brought her hands to the back of his head and dug her fingers into his soft curls to press his mouth harder against her.

He laughed at her eagerness, and the deep sound rumbled into her. Her breath came so labored now that her breasts rose and fell fiercely against his mouth, and he suckled at her again, this time drawing her deep with each hard suck that left his cheeks hollow from the ferocity of it. She felt each great pull shoot through her to the merciless throbbing at her core, and a low moan tore from her.

"You like that," he murmured against her breast. The tip of his tongue teased at her nipple before he nipped playfully at her.

Oh, she did! But now that he was hers, now that her love for him could be set free, she wanted so much more and panted out in a wicked challenge, "What... other pleasures... do you crave?"

In answer, he grabbed her hands and pinned her arms over her head as his mouth captured hers, surprising her with his swiftness and catching her openmouthed. His tongue plunged between her lips to ravish the kiss in great, deep sweeps of possession.

"This," he rasped hotly against her mouth as he pressed his hips forward into hers. The hard bulge jutting into her lower belly was unmistakable, and she shivered at the tantalizing contact and all the pleasures it implied. "I crave this, with you."

He bent his knees slightly, low enough that when he pressed into her as he rose up, the hard ridge of his erection slid enticingly into the valley between her thighs. The skilled motion caught the top of her crevice and the little nub buried within, grazing across it just hard enough to send an electric tingle spinning through her.

She wasn't an innocent. She knew what his hard body was capable of doing to hers, and she yearned for it. She tightened her arms around his neck, holding her breath in anticipation of another, harder stroke. Her sex clenched tightly even as it longed to be invaded.

But the next stroke didn't come, and her eyes fluttered open in confusion.

As she stared up at him, she realized why he'd hesitated. This moment had to be a meeting of souls and hearts, a meeting of true lovers… a meeting halfway. And it was her turn to express how much she wanted this. How much she wanted *him*, now and for the rest of her life.

She reached a shaking hand down to tug up her skirt, feeling no shame in what she was asking. She grasped his hand and placed it on her inner thigh, mere inches from the hot ache he'd flamed inside her.

"I want your touch." She slowly slid his hand up her leg until it reached her intimate folds, then she guided him in long, slow strokes as she rubbed his palm against her.

Oh, sheer heaven! She couldn't keep from quivering against his fingers in wanton invitation. Only a fleeting embarrassment swept through her that her wetness slicked his hand, so great was her need for him.

"I've longed for this since the first time I laid eyes on you. I wanted your hands on me, exploring, pleasing… My love." She leaned up to place a kiss of permission against his throat. "Touch me."

With a groan, he stroked his hand against her, stealing her breath away and leaving her sagging against the door. All of her yearned for an even greater pleasure, for the release her body begged from his, and she stepped her legs farther apart to claim it.

His finger slipped inside her, and she shivered at the delicious sensation. But his intimate strokes only grew the ache, not quenched it. With a cry of frustration, she thrust her hips forward to meet each stroke of his hand.

But even that wasn't enough. Desperate for release, she wrapped her leg around his, spreading herself even wider. When a second finger filled her, she rolled back her head as the pleasure gripped her. All the tiny muscles inside her clenched down hard around him, greedily drawing him deeper to satiate the unbearable hunger—

With a single flick of his thumb, she broke with a gasping shudder and buried her face in his shoulder to stifle her cry. But he held her close with his arm around her waist as he continued to stroke into her to prolong her climax and give her as much pleasure as possible.

Bliss overtook her, and she fell bonelessly into his arms.

"I craved the pleasure of *you*, Belinda," he murmured against her temple as he slowly peeled off her dress and left her in only her stockings. "Every ounce of your love. Every moment with you."

Then he lifted her into his arms and carried her to a chaise longue. She luxuriated in the feel of the velvet beneath her as she leaned against the sloping back, but not nearly as much as she relished his stare as he stood at her feet and gazed hungrily down at her, removing his cravat and loosening the buttons on his waistcoat. Then he dropped to his knees and rapaciously crawled up the length of velvet cushion toward her, every tigerlike move boldly proclaiming what he intended.

With a sigh of surrender, she closed her eyes and spread her legs. A heartbeat later, his mouth claimed her.

The kiss stole her breath away. Her intimate flesh was already sensitized from his fingers, and this new pleasure nearly undid her. She could scarcely bear the way his lips and tongue plundered her—no, he was *worshipping* her, and it was the most erotic, most exquisite sensation she'd ever experienced.

"I craved you." His hot breath tickled against her. "The pure deliciousness of your heart. The sweetness of the sparkling girl I fell in love with."

Then he placed a single kiss so reverently against her that she couldn't stop a soft sob from escaping her lips.

Yet regret swelled inside her. She wasn't that innocent girl any longer. Fate had given that innocence to another man, and she would never be able to share that special intimacy with Maxwell now.

Except...

Her heart pounded furiously as the idea struck. She couldn't give him her innocence, but she could give herself to him in a way she'd never given herself to any man before.

She pushed at his shoulder to shift him away as she slipped out from beneath him.

A confused expression clouded his face, but he let her go, only for that look to change to one of predacious hunger when she lowered herself to her knees at the edge of the low-rising chaise and draped herself across the velvet cushion on her belly.

"And I craved *this* with you," she breathed out as she turned her head to look at him. With her hips perched at the edge of the cushion, her bottom rose into the air in decadent enticement, and she spread her knees, offering herself to be taken.

"Please, Maxwell," she begged. "I've waited so long for you, for this moment... please. Let me give myself to you, just like this."

All of him shook fiercely with desire and emotion as he slid himself over behind her. "Are you certain?"

The sweetness of his hesitation nearly broke her. She nodded and rested her head on her folded arms. "But I've never before..."

Her breathless words were so soft that she wasn't sure he'd heard, until he leaned up to place a tender kiss between her shoulder blades. As his large hand caressed a slow and possessive circle over her bare back, she knew that he understood what she was offering. That he was experiencing this special moment as magically as she.

She closed her eyes in anticipation as she felt him rise up on his knees behind her and reach between them to unfasten the fall of his breeches. A tremor shivered through her when he slowly slid his erection between her thighs and against her folds. He grew slippery from her wetness. Each smooth glide across the length of her cleft made her quiver with need, each push forward brought his tip to tease at the aching nub buried within.

A whimper of need strangled in her throat. She writhed against the edge of the chaise, less to ease the fire inside her than to tempt him into giving her the release she craved... his body inside hers, making love to her. "Maxwell, please!"

This time when he slid forward, he changed the angle of his hips and pushed inside her. Her body expanded around his, and she moaned with pleasure as he moved deeper, sinking into her until his pelvis pressed against her buttocks, until he was sheathed completely in her tight warmth. She inhaled a ragged breath, wanting to engrave upon her mind the exquisite sensation of having him inside her, filling her completely. When he clasped her hips and began to stroke—oh, it was simply heaven!

She'd dreamed for years about Max making love to her, but nothing in all those fantasies compared to this. Because this was so much more than physical pleasure. This was a meeting of hearts and souls, an exchange of the strength and resilience that underpinned the affection they shared.

This was pure love. And it undid her.

Her hands gripped tightly onto the cushion as she welcomed his hard thrusts that brought him as deep inside her as possible, filling her body with his and inundating her senses with the raw masculinity of him—the scent of port and tobacco, the rough friction of his breeches rubbing against the backs of her thighs, the hardness of his muscles as he strained into her.

With a plaintive moan, she pushed back to meet each

oncoming thrust with one of her own, until he shoved his hand between her belly and the edge of the chaise to search for the aching, swollen nub buried there. His finger delved down, stroking against it hard and fast, relentlessly—

"Maxwell!" The choking cry tore from her as her hips bucked up against him and her thighs spasmed.

She shattered, a shivering and shaking climax that sent ripples of bliss pouring through her.

"I love you!" She arched into him as she tossed back her head and let her release claim her. "I love you so much!"

He grabbed her hips, holding her tightly to him as he gave a final thrust deep inside her. She gasped at the desperate sensation of vulnerability that pierced her, only to shatter a second time when she heard the low groan of his own release, when she felt him jerk inside her and spill himself. Her greedy body drank him in, quivering around him as he strained to empty every drop of himself inside her—giving her every bit of his heart and soul.

Whispering her name, he collapsed on top of her. His body folded over hers, enveloping her beneath him as his strong arms went around her and gathered her close, his cheek resting against her bare back. As if he never wanted to let go.

Sheer happiness blossomed inside her. There would be more battles between them, more conflict over the hospital and the academy in the days to come. But at that moment, held safe in his arms, she knew he loved her.

CHAPTER 6

*M*ax sat sprawled across the chaise longue and watched Belinda dress, certain he'd never been happier in his life.

She loved him. He could barely fathom it. But she was also giving him the opportunity to prove that he deserved her. In that, he'd never let her down again.

He pushed himself to his feet and leisurely approached her to button up her dress. But he couldn't help slipping his arms around her waist and bringing her back against him. He placed a lingering kiss to her nape and smiled against her flesh when he felt her tremble.

"If you keep that up," she warned as she straightened her bodice and smoothed down her skirt, "we might very well end up right back on the chaise."

He groaned at the temptation. "While I would love nothing more"—he took another kiss before stepping back—"we need to return to the party before we're missed."

She laughed, her eyes gleaming at him in the mirror over the fireplace as she fixed her hair. "Not at one of King George's dinners." She reached up to pin her hair into place. "Before this evening is over, half the guests will be finding their own unused rooms."

"Is that what Pomperly hoped with you?" Oddly enough, he felt not one prick of jealousy.

"Most likely." She twisted a stubborn curl into place and pinned it securely. "But it would have been a very cold day in Brighton before I fell for his entreaties."

"You fell for mine."

She smiled like the cat that got into the cream. "Because yours are irresistible."

In reply, he lifted her hand to his lips and placed a kiss to her palm. Goose bumps sprang up along her arms. Like magic.

"If you keep that up," she repeated, her voice suddenly husky, "we won't need the chaise."

When she cast a meaningful glance at the rug in front of the fireplace, all kinds of deliciously wicked thoughts spun through his mind.

If she kept saying things like that, he might very well have her naked again before she could speak his name. Reluctantly, he released her hand and stepped away.

"The next time I make love to you," he promised, "will be in a soft bed with all the silks, velvets, and down you deserve."

Turning back toward the mirror as her cheeks pinked, she tried to hide the effect that his comment had on her by focusing on the last hairpin. But she couldn't hide her breathlessness as she asked as casually as she could muster in mid-blush, "So there's going to be a next time?"

"That depends." His heart stuttered. He was afraid of her answer. "Do you want there to be?"

Her gaze slid across the room to the chaise. She hesitated before answering, just long enough to lick her lips. "Very much."

His restraint broke. He closed the distance between them with a single step and had her back in his arms, his mouth ravishing hers, before she could finish her soft gasp of surprise. The sound changed into a throaty moan, and he drank it in, reveling in the happiness she sparked inside him. *Never* had he met another woman like her, and he never would again.

When she arched her breasts against his chest, he groaned with frustration. "We can't, love."

She twirled her fingers in his hair. "Oh, I think we can."

He laughed and wrapped his arms around her to pull her into a large hug. He nuzzled her hair. "We didn't take precautions," he reminded her gently, although not regretting making love to her. "We can't take that risk again."

She stiffened in his arms, then slowly pulled back. "You don't know? I thought everyone knew…" She turned away as she explained softly, "I'm barren."

He cupped her face in his hands, gently forcing her to look back at him. "Why do you say that?"

A brave smile tugged at her lips in what she must have thought was the proper expression for grim acceptance. The same way experienced soldiers sometimes smiled before the inevitability of battle. "I must be, to have been married for so long and not gotten with child."

"It takes two to create a child. Perhaps Winchester couldn't father children."

She gave a sad shake of her head. "I didn't get with child tonight." Then, slipping out of his arms to turn back to the mirror and finish the last adjustments to her hair, she forced out teasingly, "So you'll have to find another way to get me to marry you."

When she reached for her discarded gloves, the shaking in her hand was unmistakable. So was the grief over not having children.

"Then how about because we love each other?" he quietly proposed.

She froze, the first glove halfway on her hand. Sudden tension filled the room, and a long, awkward silence passed between them before she busied herself again with tugging her glove the rest of the way on.

"You don't have to say that. Just because we…" She gestured with the gloved hand in the general direction of the chaise longue. "I don't expect marriage."

"Too bad. Because I do."

She startled. The other silk glove slipped through her fingers and piled softly on the floor at her feet.

He picked it up, then took her hand and slowly helped her into it. A satisfied warmth twined through him. Who knew that dressing a woman could be as erotic as *un*dressing her?

"You—" She forced out the words, moon-eyed, "You truly want to marry me?"

"Always have." He lifted her hand and kissed her gloved fingertips. "I was hoping you wanted the same."

"I do, but…" The soft whisper died on her lips.

"The pensioners." He knew her nearly as well as he knew himself.

She nodded, her worry about the men darkening her eyes. He loved her all the more that she would so selflessly think of a group of old men in the middle of his marriage proposal.

"I cannot marry you, Max," she said achingly, as if the words pained her. "If we cannot find a way to save the hospital, then this will always be between us. I'll never be able to look at you without thinking of them, how you were sent to remove them and how I couldn't stop that."

Her words twisted inside him like a knife. The academy was still wedged between them, the tension surrounding it as thick as ever. "I'm not giving you up, Belinda. So we're just going to have to find a way."

With a faint nod, she echoed quietly, "We'll find a way." But doubt furrowed her beautiful brow, and she said the words as if she didn't fully believe them.

Yet, for the first time, she spoke as if they were working together to find compromise rather than as adversaries. She was acknowledging the possibility of a future together. And he liked it. A great deal.

"I've been thinking." She tentatively bit her bottom lip. "The academy needs to be opened too quickly for the War Office to construct new buildings, correct? Which is why you need the hospital."

"Correct."

"So the cadets cannot be moved to another building. But what if the pensioners could?" Her face shone with hope. "What if we found another building that could be turned into a home for them? That way, they could all stay together, right here in Brighton."

He took her hands in his and gave them a sympathetic squeeze as she eagerly waited for his reaction to what she was certain was a grand compromise but which in reality wouldn't work. "The War Office would never agree to the expense of purchasing and maintaining a second property, not when there are other hospitals where the men could be sent."

Her slender shoulders sagged as her hopes were dashed. "Then what do we do?"

"We find a solution." He touched his lips to hers. "Together."

She nodded and stepped into his embrace.

He rested his cheek against her hair and sighed out a silent breath. Thank God she didn't ask how, because he didn't have a bloody clue. But even as he held her encircled in his arms, he knew he would lose her if they didn't.

AS BELINDA HAD PREDICTED, NO ONE PAID ANY ATTENTION WHEN they slipped into the saloon to rejoin the party, least of all His Majesty. He was too busy staring at Lady Roquefort's bosom to care about anything at that point, except how to be rid of Lord Roquefort.

They entered separately, of course, and fifteen minutes apart, for which Belinda was glad. It gave her time to calm her soaring heart and catch her breath before Maxwell could stride into the room and steal it away again.

"Coffee, please." She smiled at the footman as she stepped up to the buffet where tall, silver urns sat surrounded by delicate bone china cups and silver spoons edged with gold. All of it was monogrammed with the king's initials.

"I thought it best to tell you this in private," a deep voice said quietly over her shoulder.

Her smile froze, although her heart stuttered with dread. "Yes, Duke?"

Pomperly gestured with a scowl at the other footman to pour him a cup. "You have my full support with the hospital."

Relief poured through her, and her smile turned genuine. "Thank you, Pomperly."

"Of course, my dear. I know how much that place means to you."

"To the pensioners, you mean." She accepted her coffee from the footman. She would still have to fight an uphill battle to persuade the War Office to keep the men here in Brighton, but at least now she had an ally. "Your support will help convince the rest of the board."

"And I'm hoping that the new post in Africa will help convince Thorpe," he muttered as he sniffed at his own coffee. "I plan to send a letter to Lord Palmerston."

She frowned, not understanding. "The secretary?"

Taking a sip of coffee, he smirked. "He's a close acquaintance. If I tell him how much Thorpe is hoping to be reassigned to the new African command, I'm certain he'll send the brigadier off packing immediately for Egypt and spare your hospital. That's why he's here, after all, pressing so hard for his academy."

"You've misunderstood." She gave a faint laugh, despite the prickle of unease that rose inside her. "Brigadier Thorpe wants to start an academy here because he believes soldiers need better training. He's hoping that this academy might save men's lives."

"Is that what you think?" He clucked his tongue as if she were a naïve child who needed to be placated.

"I know so. The brigadier told me himself."

"Then he's lied to you."

The brusqueness of that slammed into her.

Maxwell picked that moment to walk into the room, looking every inch like the commanding officer he'd become during the years they'd been apart. Tall. Strong. Proud. Instead of glancing her way, he approached the group of fellow officers who had gathered by the French doors.

As doubt began to creep into her bones, all pretense of a smile faded. "No, he was quite earnest with me." *Look my way, Maxwell... Make me believe... Dear God,* look *at me!* "His motivation is to create better officers."

"His motivation is to gain a promotion to major-general." Pomperly set his cup back into his saucer with a jarring clank, as if finding the coffee—and Maxwell—distasteful. "Thorpe couldn't care less about those old men or the cadets. The only man he cares about is himself. Surely you've noticed that. General Mortimer claims he's just as ambitious as when he was younger." He gestured impatiently for the footman to add liqueur to his coffee. "You knew him then. Surely you can see the same in him now."

She lowered the cup from her lips. The coffee tasted like acid on her tongue.

"If he's offered that commanding post in Africa—one that's a jewel in His Majesty's imperial crown—I'm certain he'll accept immediately." He took the freshened cup from the footman. "And forget all about those of us he's left behind in Brighton."

Her stomach tightened into a sickening knot. "You are mistaken." Maxwell had told her that he loved her, that he wanted a second chance with her, that he wanted to marry her…

"Don't be fooled, Belinda. That man will do everything in his power to establish that academy and help himself to a promotion." He lifted the cup to his mouth and mumbled from behind the rim, "Even charm you into believing he's sincere."

Numbness gripped her, except for her heart, which had already started to ache. She clung desperately to what Maxwell had told her, to the tenderness she'd felt when he made love to her, when he asked her to marry him. They *would* be married…

But not until after they found a solution for the pensioners, after he no longer needed her help to establish the academy and secure his promotion.

Her chest burned as she realized what the timing of that meant. And she'd been foolish enough to suggest it.

Yet she forced out, "He would never do as you're suggesting." She *had* to believe that, had to believe that he was a different man now than the one who'd so selfishly used her before. "You're only saying this because you don't like him, because you want to court me yourself."

"I *do* want to court you. But I'm telling you this as a friend who doesn't want to see you be hurt." He gestured around the room with his coffee cup. "But you don't have to believe me. Others will tell you the same. General!" Pomperly called out as General Mortimer circled through the room. "A word, if you please."

The portly general stopped in front of them with a nod to Pomperly and a shallow bow to Belinda. "Your Graces."

"General." Pomperly made the man wait while he took a long sip of coffee, then fussed with his cup as he returned it to its saucer. "I was just commenting about the new African command post, how Brigadier Thorpe would be the perfect man for it."

"Indeed!" Mortimer folded his hands behind his back, which only made his belly jut out farther. "I'd recommend him for it myself, if Thorpe were open to the idea."

Her heart stuttered hopefully. "Then he doesn't want to go to Africa?"

"Heavens, no!" He looked at her as if she'd gone daft. "Deserts and camels, sandstorms and wild beasts… Who in their right mind would want that?"

"Someone who's hoping to be promoted to major-general, I suppose," she prompted gently, fishing for any denial on the general's part that would prove Maxwell's innocence.

Mortimer laughed. "Thorpe has better plans for himself than Africa, I daresay."

She stiffened, her fingers tightening on her cup. "Oh?"

His eyes sparkled with admiration at Maxwell's audacity. "If the creation of the academy goes well, he gets the post he's wanted since the day he purchased his commission." He leaned toward her, as if sharing a grand secret. "London!"

Her gaze darted to Maxwell, whose attention finally wandered away from his group as he glanced around the room, but not yet finding her.

She somehow summoned the strength to ask, "And a promotion to major-general?"

"That goes without saying. He knew he'd be promoted when he made the suggestion to the War Office to open an academy here."

"*He* suggested the academy?" She prayed she'd misunderstood, prayed that this whole conversation was a mistake—

"Directly to the secretary himself."

Dear God... No, that couldn't be. She stared at Maxwell, oblivious to the rest of the room around them, even as his face blurred beneath the hot tears welling in her eyes. Still, she held her head high and somehow managed to replace her well-practiced smile, even as her heart cried out that she was a fool to ever let him back into her trust. But she couldn't react, *had* to keep calm no matter how much she wanted to scream... because she was a duchess, after all. And a duchess would never let the world know that the only man she'd ever loved had once again used that love against her.

"Had an entire proposal worked out, including a six-month timeline for implementation. Said we needed another academy to train officers. Said Brighton was the best place for it and that he knew people on the hospital board he could sway to support his cause." General Mortimer smiled at her, not realizing that he'd just cut out her heart. "He must have meant you, Your Grace."

Somehow, she forced her smile to grow brighter. "He must have." She set aside the coffee before her trembling hands spilled it. Or worse, let it smash against the floor.

"If you'll excuse me." Mortimer sketched a bow that included both of them. "I promised Lady Agnes Sinclair that I'd share with her what's been happening in the Americas." He chuckled with amusement. "The old bird's ready to send the cavalry against the Americans again, just for spite!"

"As good a reason as any, I suppose," Pomperly drawled, lifting his coffee to his lips. Once the general strode away, he added in that same condescending tone as before, "Perhaps now you'll believe me when I say that *I* have your best interests at heart."

Her heart... Nothing was left of it.

"Go away," she whispered, her smile still firmly in place. "I no longer wish for your company."

Pomperly's mouth fell open. "Belinda, how can you—"

"Leave me alone! Tonight and for the rest of my life."

His face turned red, and he gestured at Maxwell with his cup. "You don't mean that you still believe that arrogant bastard's story that he—"

"What I believe is none of your concern." Now that the flood-gates had opened, revealing what she truly thought of Pomperly, she found it impossible to hold back the venom, even knowing that he would turn the board against her, that she would lose all support in saving the pensioners' home... but hadn't she been destined to lose this battle from the beginning? "It never has been, and it *never* will be."

"I could have made you a duchess!" he seethed. In his anger, he grasped the coffee so tightly that his fingertips turned as white as the bone china cup.

"I *am* a duchess."

"A barren widow." He laughed scornfully. "Not even a true dowager."

The vitriol behind that snapped her polite patience. "I would rather be a light-skirt than become your duchess." She arched an imperious brow and added, "Although I strongly suspect that there would not be much difference."

Enraged, he slammed down his cup and splashed coffee onto

the tablecloth. He glared murderously at her and stalked way, without deigning to spare her a word in reply.

She looked up and saw Maxwell staring at her from across the room. The anguish returned in a brutal blow so fierce that she flinched. She glanced away before tears could fall and give her away to the other guests. None of them would care that she'd given herself physically to him tonight. No, they'd cut her for daring to love him.

Love? She nearly laughed at the bitter irony. Oh, so much more! Because tonight, when happiness had flowed in her veins, she'd dared to imagine a future with him.

His brow furrowed as he stared at her. She couldn't look away. Even with all the pain pulsing through her with each heartbeat, knowing once again that he'd plotted and schemed to use her, she couldn't break the spell that this devil held over her. And most likely always would.

But it didn't mean she had to sell her soul.

Summoning her strength, she walked toward the door, to walk out without a word to anyone, without permission from King George—to just *leave*. To walk into the cool night and disappear into the darkness. To drown herself in misery until no more tears would come. Then, when the pain subsided and she could breathe again, she planned on waging war on Maxwell, the likes of which he'd never seen before in his entire military career. If he thought he could so easily use her again for his own advancement, to harm old soldiers—

A hand at her elbow stopped her. "Belinda."

She sucked in a harsh breath through clenched teeth at the sound of Maxwell's voice, even now having the audacity to twine its way so heatedly down her spine and remind her of all the love she'd thought they'd shared, the coming together of hearts and souls... *Ashes.* It was nothing but ashes!

"Are you well?" Concerned thickened his voice, but was that worry for her or for his precious academy? Did he think that she'd been wounded and needed solace, or had he come over to find out if she'd persuaded Pomperly to protest the closing of the hospital? "Did Pomperly upset you?"

"Yes," she answered, not turning to face him. She somehow found the strength to remain calm. "As a matter of fact, he did."

He stiffened imperceptibly, but she could feel it. God help her, she noticed everything about this man, and always had. It devastated her that she was still so connected to him that she couldn't stop it, even now.

"What did he say?"

"He told me the real reason why you're in Brighton." Her numb lips surprised her by being able to form words. "Why you want this academy."

"To save men's lives." The same excuse he'd given her from the beginning.

The same excuse she could no longer bear! "To earn a promotion and new post in London, you mean. After all, that was why you proposed the academy to the War Office in the first place, wasn't it?"

She glanced over her shoulder, needing to see his reaction. Needing to sear closed the fresh wounds he'd given her tonight.

He tightened his jaw, not denying it. With each damning heartbeat's silence that passed, the burning anguish inside her grew more intolerable. All the while, she was keenly aware of the room around her, of the guests who might be watching and waiting for her to show any sign of vulnerability that they could use against her.

"Such an easy plan for your success... convince the board to support the academy, and you get to return to London as England's glorious hero. All you have to do is cast out a few dozen old men from their home." Then she forced out, each word a knife to her heart—"And pretend you love me."

His fingers tightened on her arm. "*That* is not true."

"Stop lying!" She'd been such a fool to believe his words of affection. But no longer. "I know why you're here—why you're with me tonight—why you... why you..." Oh God, she couldn't even say it! *Why you seduced me.* "Because once again you wanted to advance your career at the cost of my heart."

"What I wanted, Belinda—what I have always wanted—is *you.*"

"No. You want an academy so you can be promoted and assigned to London, and you want it so badly that *you* approached the War Office with the idea for it." Only summoning all her strength kept her from clenching her hands into fists. "General Mortimer explained everything."

"*Not* everything." He stiffly glanced at the other guests to gauge whether he and Belinda were drawing attention. But anyone who happened to glance their way would see nothing out of place. Just two old friends and dinner companions looking as if they were discussing how long they wanted to remain at the party tonight after the king retired. "This is neither the time nor place for this discussion." He gestured toward the open French doors. "Walk with me in the garden, and we'll talk."

"Never." She would *never* let herself be alone with him again.

"Give me the chance to explain. Because I do love you, Belinda. I always have."

"No." She blinked rapidly, needing all of her will to keep back her tears. "*Not* always."

His head snapped back, that harsh reminder striking him like a slap.

"When did you realize that you were losing the fight over the academy, Maxwell, and that you had to increase your attack in order to win against me? That you needed to do more than throw a picnic?"

"Is that what you think tonight was?" Subtly, so that no one else would see, he pulled lightly at her glove to remind her of how he'd stripped her bare. "That I seduced you in order to win you over?"

She pulled her arm away so he couldn't touch her. "I learn well from my experiences, and you used me once before. Why should I think you're no longer that selfish cad, when you're simply repeating all the motions?" Despite the heat of her anger, her blood turned to ice. "Congratulations, Maxwell, you've proven yourself to be a bastard." Her voice cracked as she added, "Again."

Unable to stand the torture of this evening a moment more, she walked on through the door and out of the palace.

CHAPTER 7

"Oh no, you don't!" With the fear of losing her already pounding away inside him, Max caught up with Belinda just as she reached the line of carriages waiting in front of the palace. "You are *not* leaving."

She hurried to her carriage. "I'll claim illness. His Majesty will understand."

"I don't give a damn about His Majesty." That drew a wide-eyed reaction from the tiger who opened the door for her that bore the Winchester insignia. The same door that Max wanted to drive his fist through. With an angry grimace, he waved the man away and took her arm to help her into the carriage himself. "I care about *you*, Belinda."

"You can stop with the empty flattery." She yanked her arm away and stepped up into the compartment unassisted. "There's no point in it now."

"More than you realize." Without invitation, he swung inside and shut the door, calling out to the driver, "Go!"

The carriage jerked to a start as it moved away from the palace, fast enough to keep her from jumping out to flee.

Although, based on her furious expression in the light of the carriage lamps, not fast enough to keep her from shoving him out.

"You are wrong." He leaned across the compartment toward her, elbows on knees and hands clasped to keep from reaching for her. "About everything."

"Then deny it," she challenged. "Deny that you approached the War Office with the idea of turning the hospital into an academy."

"I can't," he snapped out, matching her rising anger. "Because I did go to Palmerston with the proposal."

"Because you wanted a promotion."

"Because I grew tired of watching good men die! Of hearing the cries of boys barely old enough to grow beards calling out for their mothers and sweethearts as they lay dying in the mud, coughing up blood with each gasping breath, missing arms and legs, faces blown off—" He let loose a curse he never should have uttered in front of a woman. "All of them terrified and in pain, frightened even more by the cries of others who were dying around them, the screams of horses, the artillery still firing in the distance." He looked down at his hands as they shook. In his mind, he could still see the face of every man whose hand he'd held while they died. "And you can do nothing but pray they die quickly, to put you out of the misery of their pain."

Even in the dim light, he saw her face pale. Yet her eyes remained just as disbelieving. "But you also did it for yourself, so you could be promoted. Which was why you picked *this* hospital, wasn't it? Because you told them that you had connections on the board that would make it easier to garner support."

"I do. Colonel Woodhouse, for one. We served together in Nassau. And the other men on the board who served in the military, who have connections to the War Office." His eyes fixed hard on hers. "But I did *not* mean you."

She gave a bitter laugh. "You knew I was still involved with the hospital. You had to know that I would be here."

"I didn't know for certain." Then he admitted, "But I'd hoped."

"So you could seduce me if your plans went awry?" She tore off her gloves and slapped them onto the bench beside her. "You *used* me, Maxwell. For the second time, you let me believe that you loved me only to advance your career."

That accusation was brutal, but not nearly as shattering as watching the tear slip down her cheek. His breath caught like fire in his chest at the sight of her pain.

"I came here so I could see with my own eyes that you've had a good life," he said quietly, in agony that he couldn't reach for her without making everything worse. "That the choice I made to let Collins have you wasn't for nothing."

"Let Collins have me?" she repeated, as if she'd misheard. As if begging to be told that she'd misunderstood.

But he didn't deny it, letting the true meaning behind that soft confession reveal itself.

She stammered in confusion, "But I—I never told you about George… You *couldn't* have known—not until after we—" Wretchedness marred her beautiful face, and she breathed out, "You knew. You knew when you wrote to break off that he'd offered marriage… How?"

Wordlessly, he reached into his breast pocket and removed the old letter. The one he'd carried with him every day for the past ten years, so he could read it whenever he doubted that he'd made the right decision to sacrifice his happiness for hers.

As he held it out to her, his hand shook. He'd sworn to himself to never show this letter to her. But now fate had given them the opportunity to rewrite their future, and *everything* needed to be revealed. If they had any chance at all of finding love again, there could be no more secrets.

She hesitated to take it, as if it were a snake ready to strike.

Then she snatched it from him. Her shaking hands held it up to the light of the carriage lamp. As she read, another tear slipped free. When she finished, she crushed it in her fist and pressed it against her breast. Her slender shoulders rose and fell with each gasping breath she took to steady herself.

"Damn you." Her eyes burned with a fire that stole his breath away. She cried out, raging at him, "Damn you both!"

"We wanted only the best for you, and the best I could do was let you go." He deserved every daggerlike accusation that she leveled at him for keeping this secret, but even now, while hating that he'd ever had to make that choice, he still couldn't regret his decision. "If I had told you about that letter, you would have tried to talk me out of it."

"Yes!" Frustration pulsed from her, and her fingers gripped the edge of the bench beneath her. As if needing to restrain herself from physically striking him. "Because I loved you! Because I needed you to… to…" Her words choked off, in proof that she realized what she was saying. That her need at the time went far beyond the help that he'd been able to give.

"You needed me to let you go so that you could marry Collins," he finished soberly, a great grief swirling inside him at all that fate had stolen from them. "I knew you'd have argued with me to reconsider if you'd known the truth. That you'd hate him for writing to me and would refuse to marry the man. So I had to let you think that I was a selfish bastard who had used you for his own gain, when it was the furthest thing from the truth."

"I deserved to know," she choked out, fighting back sobs. "You should have told me before now."

"And ruin your marriage by turning you against your husband? Or destroying your memory of him? Dear God, Belinda, that letter is bringing you pain even now. Think of the damage it could have done had you known before."

"I *deserved* to know," she repeated, and her pain clawed into his heart.

"For that, I am truly sorry. But I will never be sorry for wanting to make you happy, or for stepping out of the way so that Collins could give you the life you deserved. The one I never could." He reached for her hands then, unable to stop himself. He held tight, refusing to let go even as she attempted to yank her hands from his. "So you can hate me all you want to. God knows I certainly deserve it. But at least now you'll hate me for the truth."

She stopped trying to pull away. Instead, she hung her head as her tears came in a rush, no longer able to stop them.

"The truth is that I never used you. Not ten years ago, not tonight." He reached up to cup her face against his palm. "All I have ever done is love you."

An incoherent whisper of pure anguish escaped her, and his heart shattered.

Moving to sit beside her, he gently tugged her onto his lap and wrapped his arms around her. She shuddered and shook against him as she tried to come to terms with the past ten years and everything that had happened between them. But she didn't shove him away.

"I don't hate you," she whispered between sobs, her face buried against his neck. "Although you deserve it."

Relief swelled inside him, and he squeezed his eyes shut as he placed a kiss at her temple. "I know."

He prayed to God that she'd give him the chance to be chastised for that every remaining day of his life. Because it meant that every day would be spent with her.

"Deny it," he challenged gently, throwing her earlier words back at her. "Deny that you love me. Because that's what it will take to make me leave again." He reached up to caress his knuckles over her cheek. His voice cracked as he rasped out, "Because I sure as hell still love you."

She slowly pulled back. Anguish lingered in her watery gaze, along with a hesitancy to put her full faith in him, and that bothered him, enough that regret panged with each beat of his heart. But there were also the beginnings of forgiveness and understanding, and he clung desperately to those. Because he would never survive losing her a second time.

"Fate has given us another chance, and I'm not going to let it slip by without seizing it." He gently wiped away her last tear with his thumb. "I want a life with you, Belinda. I will do whatever it takes to have that."

Cupping his face between her hands, she brought her lips to his. In that kiss, he could taste her love. And her forgiveness.

She placed the crumpled letter in his hand. That letter had started all the pain and loss, and he never wanted to see it again. He turned to throw it out the window—

Flames lit the darkness. He could just see through the narrow streets that angled down toward the water the rush of people heading toward the fire and the smoke that billowed into the black sky. A sickening realization flashed through him.

"The hospital's on fire." He pounded his fist against the roof of the carriage as he shouted to the driver, "To the Royal Hospital —now!"

Belinda hurried to keep pace with Maxwell's long strides as they raced through the park and down Church Street, having left the carriage behind in the road that was jammed by traffic. They squeezed through the crowd gathering in front of the barracks, joined by the soldiers who filed out of the yard at the commotion to crane their necks to see for themselves what was happening. But the flames from one of the hospital's buildings shot up into the sky farther down the street and lit up this area of Brighton like a lamp.

They stopped in front of the hospital, and Belinda panted to catch her breath. Her chest tightened, both from the white-gray smoke filling the cobblestone street and from the terror that seized her. Her panicked eyes searched the growing crowd for the pensioners, to make certain each man was out of the building and safe. But it was impossible to find them all amid the commotion. Even in the light from the fire, she couldn't make out faces in the crowd, and the shouts that went up all around from the men and the piercing cries from the women only added to the unfolding confusion.

"Buckets!" someone shouted, and another cursed at every able-bodied man in the street to get in line to be part of the bucket brigade. "Buckets!"

Maxwell released her hand to join the effort.

"The pensioners!" Belinda grabbed his arm. "Some of them might still be inside."

He glanced over his shoulder at the building as the flames burned high into the night and blew out a determined breath. "Stay here."

He cupped her face in his hands to place a kiss to her lips, then he was gone, running toward the building. He tore off the sash of his dress uniform and dunked it into the trough to wet it through. Then he wrapped it around his head to cover his nose and mouth and raced into the burning building.

Her heart stopped. Oblivious to the commotion around her, she stared at the doorway where he'd disappeared and helplessly wrung her hands. *Dear God! Please...* She could see nothing through the windows but flickering red-orange flames. The roar of the fire and the shouts of the men were deafening, but her pounding pulse beat so hard that the rush of blood through her ears drowned out all of it. Each breath came labored, terrified... *Please God, save them. Save* him... *Please!*

A movement in the center upstairs window caught her attention. The outline of shoulders and a head silhouetted against the fire, hands grasping at the window casement to throw up the sash—

One of the pensioners was trapped inside.

She let out a fierce cry and pointed at the building, shouting as loudly as she could to get attention. *Anyone's* attention who could help. But amid the confusion of fighting the fire and the crowds now jamming the street no one heard her. No one else seemed to see the old man or hear his terrified cries for help.

Without thinking of her own safety, Belinda ran into the building to save him.

Heat engulfed her immediately and prickled at her skin, and she coughed as she breathed in the acrid smoke. Unable to see more than a few feet ahead, she staggered toward the main stairs in the center of the building. She'd been here so many times that she knew the place by heart. Thank God for that, because she needed to make her way up the stairs and down the hallway to the room where she'd seen the man, and in the smoke that stung her eyes and made each breath feel like an inhalation of fire, she was as good as blind.

Her fingers groped along the staircase banister as she tentatively made her way upstairs. She shook with fear, but determination surged through her veins. She didn't stop to think if what she was doing was foolish or even potentially deadly. Her concentration was on the pensioner and saving his life, the way the pensioners had saved her life all those years ago.

A spasm of coughing seized her lungs as she reached the top of the stairs, forcing her to her knees in an attempt to catch her breath. But she wouldn't stop. *Couldn't* stop. She would not let that man die!

She crawled forward on hands and knees. Her evening gown caught beneath her legs with each crawling stride until she had no choice but to yank it up to her thighs and crawl on. The cinders burned at her hands and her legs, and pain shot through her knees so badly that she cried out, only to be relieved when, a few moments later, the pain grew so intense that her knees turned numb.

"Help me!" the pensioner cried out, still clinging to the window. His voice trembled with terror and was little more than a breathy rasp, his throat raw from inhaling smoke and shouting. "Please—someone help me!"

"I'm here," she called out, then fell into another fit of coughing. Still making her way forward one determined inch at a time, she lifted her hand toward him, silently begging him to come to her, to let her lead him out of the building—

Until she saw the cane and the twisted leg and foot it supported. Her heart sank as tears of terror and grief blurred her vision.

She could barely move herself through the building. How would she ever be able to get him out, too?

But she would *not* leave him. Taking as deep a breath as she could without triggering another coughing fit, she held her breath and pushed herself up to her feet to rush across the room to him. Around them, the flames ate at the wooden beams overhead and at the walls, and the heat that had first prickled at her skin now burned. The building groaned and creaked as the fire devoured it.

She grabbed his arm and put it over her shoulder, then leaned him against her side. Slipping her arm around his waist, she held tightly to him as she began to walk toward the doorway, one agonizingly slow step after another. By the time they reached the hall, her lungs burned from holding her breath, and she fell to her knees to gasp at the air closer to the floor. The man stumbled and fell into her, but thankfully he didn't crash to the floor.

"Almost...there..." she assured him, but the distance between where they were now and the door leading out into the cool night seemed as far away as London.

Taking another deep breath, she held it as she rose to her feet and dragged the man along with her. So heavy! She staggered forward with such effort that her muscles screamed for mercy.

They reached the top of the stairs just as his damaged foot gave out, tumbling them both forward onto the floor. Exhausted and terrified, she cried out as tears streamed down her face. The helplessness overwhelmed her, and for the first time since she'd run into the building, she lost all hope of getting the man out alive.

"Belinda!" A shout broke through the roar of the fire.

"Maxwell," she choked out, unable to speak any louder. On her hands and knees, she reached a hand toward the dark form charging toward them through the black smoke.

"Here!" He shouted over his shoulder as he knelt beside her. The flames were closing in upon them, the thick layer of smoke lowering rapidly and threatening to poison what little good air hovered just above the floor. "Over here!"

His arms went around her, and she clung to him as he lifted her. With a cry, she reached back toward the old man, who lay on the floor, sobbing and coughing. But another dark form emerged from the fiery shadows. Oliver Graham grabbed up the pensioner and followed quickly after them as Maxwell ran down the stairs with her in his arms, then outside into the night.

The rush of coolness and the fresh air shocked her, and a

shudder sped through her so intensely that a soft scream left her lips. The heat that had danced across her skin and burned at her lungs quenched instantly, leaving in its wake a coldness that was just as painful. Each gasping breath of cool night air that filled her lungs shivered into her, and she spasmed as she lost her breath, choking on the fresh air like a fish out of water.

She clung desperately to Maxwell as she struggled to catch back her breath, even as he carried her away from the building and eased her down onto the dew-dampened ground.

"I told you to stay put," he snapped out, but his anger was lost beneath the trembling of his hands as they smoothed over her face, then over her body... down one arm and up the other, then down her legs, checking for burns and wounds. "What the hell did you think you were doing? You could have been killed."

He pulled her to him, rocking her in his arms. He buried his face in her hair and crushed her against him so tightly that she was afraid she'd lose her breath again.

"Never again," he threatened, his voice rough with emotion. "Don't *ever* do anything like that again, do you hear me?"

Despite the fierce pounding of her heart at how close she'd come to being seriously hurt, or worse, she gave a soft laugh as she rubbed her cheek against his shoulder. Always the commanding officer, even now.

"I lost you once, Belinda. I *never* want to lose you again."

In that embrace, she felt all the love he carried for her, and she knew then that they could survive anything that fate threw at them. The fire had reminded her of what she'd known all along... that she needed Maxwell as much as she needed air to breathe.

She held tightly to him, her arms around his shoulders and her cheek pressed tightly against his. She watched over his shoulder as the building gave a loud groan, and the roof fell in, sending a shower of sparks and flames shooting into the black sky.

Yet the men who fought the fire didn't give up. She watched as the old pensioners organized the soldiers from the barracks into long lines of bucket brigades and showed them how to use shovels, pitchforks, and pickaxes to toss dirt onto the fire to keep the flames from spreading. Another group of soldiers had followed the lead of the more able-bodied pensioners and were beating at the flames with wet burlap sacks. They were working together, with the younger soldiers taking orders and learning from the pensioners.

"Maxwell," she breathed out as her heart began to pound hard and fast again, but this time with hope.

"What's wrong?" Concern thickened his voice as he turned her on his lap to cradle her in his arms. "Do you need a doctor?"

"I'm fine—better than fine. I think..." A tentative smile tugged at her lips, and she reached up to place her hand against his cheek. "I think I've found a way to save the hospital."

He grimaced. "There might not be a hospital left after this fire."

"Oh, there will be! And your academy, too." She threw her arms around his neck and hugged him with glee. "It will be perfect!"

Then she kissed him with all the love she held for him in her heart, all of her hopes and dreams for a future finally having its chance to be made real. Together.

Absolutely perfect.

CHAPTER 8

"Gentlemen, thank you for waiting." Max escorted Belinda into the enlisted men's dining hall at the barracks.

In the sennight since the fire, the hospital's administrative offices had been moved to the barracks, so that the offices could be turned into temporary quarters for the pensioners. A move that Max now found fitting, given the changes that were about to occur.

The members of the hospital board climbed to their feet at Belinda's presence, but instead of sitting, she waved them all back into their places. "My apologies for our tardiness." She turned the force of her smile on Max, whose heart jumped. He prayed he never got used to this feeling. "We were waiting on a message from London with news that you might all find surprising."

That was an understatement. He was certain all the men present would be floored by the decision Palmerston had sent posthaste from the War Office, one Max had brought back himself, returning just in time for the meeting. So recently, in fact, that he still wore his dusty riding breeches and redingote, and his hair was mussed from the wind. Stopping only to change out horses, he'd made the trip in a handful of hours.

"What's going on, Thorpe?" Colonel Woodhouse called out, ignoring the duchess. He was the first to sink into his chair in front of Belinda, not bothering to hide his disdain for her.

Max bit back his anger at the man's disrespect. No matter. By tomorrow, the colonel would be on his way out of Brighton and out of their lives… to a new post in Africa. As General Mortimer's aide-de-camp.

He glanced at Belinda, who fought back a happy beaming. Cleaning up after the fire and assessing the damage had kept her busy for the past sennight while he'd been away in London, submitting a new proposal regarding the academy. One that had her gliding through the world as if on air.

"Plans for the academy have changed," he announced.

"I'll say they have," Pomperly interjected. Around the long table, the men shook their heads at the damage the fire had done. "The place is burned to the ground."

"Not burned to the ground, Your Grace," Belinda corrected. "Just one building, one that the War Office has given us permission to rebuild as a new dormitory for the cadets."

"You've had a change of heart, I see." Pomperly's gaze slid knowingly to Max. As if he could see through his jacket to his breast pocket and the special marriage license resting where the letter had once been. "Whatever has changed your mind about the academy?"

"The fire," she answered. Joy lightened her voice. "More exactly, seeing how the pensioners and the cadets worked together to fight it. I realized that is what everyone needs—to be together."

Warmth grew inside Max's chest at the private meaning

behind her words, even as confused frowns greeted her from around the table.

"During the fire, the soldiers were taking orders from the pensioners," she continued, trying to explain the same rationale that he'd explained to the War Office, "and the pensioners were sharing their knowledge and experience with the soldiers. Both sides were calling upon their strengths to work together to effectively fight the fire. Because of them, only one building was damaged, and the main hospital was saved. If they can do that to fight a fire, then surely they can work together to train better soldiers."

The board members exchanged uncertain glances, then looked at Max for further explanation.

"Therefore, instead of closing the hospital and relocating the pensioners," he announced, "the buildings will be shared. The pensioners and cadets will live together, so that the cadets can learn from the wealth of experience held by the pensioners, and the pensioners—"

"Will feel needed," Belinda interjected, "and know that they haven't been forgotten by His Majesty's army."

Whispers went up from around the table as the men leaned together to share their thoughts.

"There will be separate training and sleeping areas, of course," Max clarified, "but they'll share the same common areas and take all their meals together."

"Not in separate facilities for enlisted men and officers either," Belinda added. That had been one of her stipulations for the War Office. "But all together, in one dining hall."

At that breach of tradition, the whispers turned into low grumblings.

"The officers will have enough time in encampments and forts to live separately from their men," Max put in. "When they're in training, they should learn everything they can about the men they'll be commanding, right down to how they think. What better way to do that than sharing meals and time together between duty shifts?"

That put an end to the grumblings. The men hesitated to express their thoughts about the changes, each waiting for another to speak first.

"It's for the best, for both the cadets and the pensioners," Belinda asserted. "Be assured that I would not support it if it wasn't."

The men nodded at that, knowing her reputation as a stalwart patroness of the hospital. Their resistance was softening.

"You should also know," Max announced, "that I've volunteered to remain here in Brighton to lead the establishment of this new joint facility." He didn't dare look at Belinda as he shared the news that he hadn't had time to tell her. "And to lead it into the future in my new post as its governor."

He heard her catch her breath. Her surprise crackled through the air between them like electricity.

"And I'll be serving as the liaison between the board and the governor," she added, her voice trembling from the news that he was staying right here in Brighton. With her. "To ensure that the pensioners will be treated as the heroes they are."

Max nodded. "Shall we put the new proposition to a vote, then? All those in favor of supporting a joint venture with the academy as part of the existing hospital say aye."

A round of agreement went up from the men, including Pomperly, who grudgingly voted in favor of the proposition. Then the duke stood, sketched a small bow to Belinda, and retreated from the room. Beaten.

The others stayed only long enough to congratulate Max on his new position and to wish Belinda good luck on hers.

"Governor?" Belinda repeated when they were finally alone.

"There wasn't time to tell you before the meeting. It came after I proposed our compromise to the secretary. I had nothing to do with it." He took her hand and raised it to his lips, placing an apologetic kiss to her fingertips. He wanted *no* misunderstanding between them about this. "Are you upset?"

"I'm thrilled for you." With love shining in her eyes, she laced her fingers through his. "We did it. We found a way to save both the academy and the hospital. It's over now."

"Not over." Max slipped his arms around her waist and drew her against him. "There's another compromise we need to make."

She stiffened warily. "Which is?"

"Since we'll both be working closely together to run this joint venture, I suggest another joint venture. Marriage." He caressed his thumb over her bottom lip when she stared at him, wide-eyed and openmouthed. "Seems to me the perfect way to make our jobs easier."

Her eyes sparkled as she returned his teasing. "Undoubtedly. It would save a lot of time waiting around for paperwork and messages if we could just pass them back and forth to each other across the breakfast table."

"Or just deliver them in person." He nuzzled his mouth against her ear. "In bed."

She laughed and hugged him tightly.

"Marry me, Belinda," he murmured, all teasing now gone. "Just as soon as we can."

"Yes." She threw her arms around his neck. "Oh yes!"

He grabbed her and twirled her in a circle, and she laughed with happiness. When he lowered her to the ground, he followed after with a kiss, one into which he tried to pour his heart and soul, all his love for her... all their hope for their new future.

"You should know, however," he warned when he finally

shifted away, "that there is one thing about which I will never compromise."

When she imperiously arched a brow in quick challenge, he thrilled to think how wonderful his life was going to be with this fiery woman. "Oh?"

"How much I love you."

Then he lowered his head and kissed her again.

AUTHOR'S NOTE

Although the Royal Hospital Brighton and its conversion into an academy is a fictionalized event for this novel—and so is the fire that ultimately joins its two missions—it is based on real places and events.

The hospital itself is modeled on the Royal Hospital Greenwich, which served as a home for pensioners, beginning in 1692—taking its name from the original sense of hospital as a place for helping those in need, although it did have an infirmary on its grounds that helped the wounded and ill. Located in buildings designed by Christopher Wren, the hospital received oversight from a board of governors until 1873, when it changed from being a pensioners' home to the Royal Naval College. It trained men and women until it closed in 1998.

The fire is also based on real events at another royal hospital. On New Year's Day, 1872, the Royal Sussex County Hospital caught fire. It was saved when volunteer firemen and a detachment of the 19th Hussars worked together to save the building. The hospital has been expanded and renovated many times over the years, taking it from a 19th century hospital to a modern facility with cutting-edge technology and services. Its mission continues today.

HELLO, EVERYONE!

As I write this, fall is slipping into winter, and I'm looking forward to afternoons huddled beneath a blanket on the sofa with a big mug of hot chocolate and lots of books to lose myself in. That's one joy of being a writer—now I can say that all those hours spent with my nosed pressed in romance books qualify as "research."

And speaking of romance...I hoped you enjoyed spending time with Belinda and Max. There's just something wonderful about a man who's dedicated to both his country and to his true love, isn't there? And I soooooo very much enjoyed writing this story. The ending came as a complete surprise to me while I was writing the story, and I thought, "Of course! They work together!" And voila! A happily ever after ending for both our couple and the pensioners.

I also wanted let you know that I have an exciting new series debuting in February! The Lords of the Armory series, based on

Marvel comic book heroes, follows the heart-thumping adventures of a group of former soldiers who have dedicated themselves to stopping a criminal organization named Scepter, who is bent on overthrowing the monarchy and destroying all that these men have pledged their lives to defend. Once more they find themselves taking up arms and fighting side by side, like brothers...with a little help from some very special women. A glimpse of book one in the series, **_AN INCONVENIENT DUKE_**, follows below. I hope you love it!

Thank you for reading and enjoying my books! If you want to stay in touch and keep up with my latest releases, best contests, exclusive content, and more (including all those pictures of the roses from my garden), be sure to sign up for my **newsletter.** You can also follow me on **Bookbub** where you'll receive news of all my releases and on my **social media sites.**

♥ Happy reading!
   Anna

Enjoy this special glimpse of chapter one of book one in the new Lords of the Armory series by Anna Harrington, **_AN INCONVENIENT DUKE_**. Marcus Braddock, Duke of Hampton and former general, is back from war and mourning the death of his beloved sister, Elise. Marcus believes his sister's death wasn't an accident and he's determined to learn the truth, starting with Danielle, the beautiful daughter of a baron and his sister's best friend. Danielle is keeping deadly secrets of her own. She has dedicated her life to a charity that helps abused women—the same charity Elise was working for the night she died. When Danielle's work puts her life in danger, Marcus comes to her rescue. But Danielle may not be the one in need of rescuing...

AN INCONVENIENT DUKE EXCERPT

May 1816
Charlton Place, London

arcus Braddock stepped out onto the upper terrace of his town house and scanned the party spreading through the torch-lit gardens below.

He grimaced. His home had been invaded.

All of London seemed to be crowded into Charlton Place tonight, with the reception rooms filled to overflowing. The crush of bodies in the ballroom had forced several couples outside to dance on the lawn, and the terraces below were filled with well-dressed dandies flirting with ladies adorned in silks and jewels. Card games played out in the library, men smoked in the music room, the ladies retired to the morning room—the entire house had been turned upside down, the gardens trampled, the horses made uneasy in the mews...

And it wasn't yet midnight. God help him.

His sister Claudia had insisted on throwing this party for him, apparently whether he wanted one or not. Not only to mark his birthday tomorrow but also to celebrate his new position as Duke of Hampton, the title given to him for helping Wellington defeat Napoleon. The party would help ease his way back into society, she'd asserted, and give him an opportunity to meet the men he would now be working with in the Lords.

But Marcus hadn't given a damn about society before he'd gone off to war, and he cared even less now.

No. The reason he'd agreed to throw open wide the doors of Charlton Place was a woman.

The Honorable Danielle Williams, daughter of Baron Mondale and his late sister Elise's dearest friend. The woman who had written to inform him that Elise was dead.

The same woman he now knew had lied to him.

His eyes narrowed as they moved deliberately across the crowd. Miss Williams had been avoiding him since his return, refusing to let him call on her and begging off from any social event that might bring them into contact. But she hadn't been able to refuse the invitation for tonight's party, not when he'd also invited her great-aunt, who certainly wouldn't have missed what the society gossips were predicting would be the biggest social event of the season. She couldn't accept and then simply beg off either. To not attend this party would have been a snub to both him and his sister Claudia, as well as to Elise's memory. While Danielle might happily continue to avoid him, she would never intentionally wound Claudia.

She was here somewhere, he knew it. Now he simply had to find her.

He frowned. Easier said than done, because Claudia had apparently invited all of society, most of whom he'd never met and had no idea who they even were. Yet they'd eagerly attended, if only for a glimpse of the newly minted duke's town house. And a glimpse of *him*. Strangers greeted him as if they were old friends, when his true friends—the men he'd served with in the fight against Napoleon—were nowhere to be seen. *Those* men he trusted with his life.

These people made him feel surrounded by the enemy.

The party decorations certainly didn't help put him at ease. Claudia had insisted that the theme be ancient Roman and then set about turning the whole house into Pompeii. Wooden torches lit the garden, lighting the way for the army of toga-clad footmen carrying trays of wine from a replica of a Roman temple in the center of the garden. The whole thing gave him the unsettling feeling that he'd been transported to Italy, unsure of his surroundings and his place in them.

Being unsure was never an option for a general in the heat of battle, and Marcus refused to let it control him now that he was on home soil. Yet he couldn't stop it from haunting him, ever since he'd discovered the letter among Elise's belongings that made him doubt everything he knew about his sister and how she'd died.

He planned to put an end to that doubt tonight, just as soon as he talked to Danielle.

"There he is—the birthday boy!"

Marcus bit back a curse as his two best friends, Brandon Pearce and Merritt Ripley, approached him through the shadows. He'd thought the terrace would be the best place to search for Danielle without being seen.

Apparently not.

"You mean the duke of honor," corrected Merritt, a lawyer turned army captain who had served with him in the Guards.

Marcus frowned. While he was always glad to see them, right then, he didn't need their distractions. Nor was he in the mood for their joking.

A former brigadier who now held the title of Earl West, Pearce looped his arm over Merritt's shoulder as both men studied him. "I don't think he's happy to see us."

"Impossible." Merritt gave a sweep of his arm to indicate the festivities around them. The glass of cognac in his hand had most likely been liberated from Marcus's private liquor cabinet in his study. "Surely he wants his two brothers-in-arms nearby to witness every single moment of his big night."

Marcus grumbled, "Every single moment of my humiliation, you mean."

"Details, details," Merritt dismissed, deadpan. But he couldn't hide the gleam of amusement in his eyes.

"What we really want to know about your birthday party is this." Pearce touched his glass to Marcus's chest and leaned toward him, his face deadly serious. "When do the pony rides begin?"

Marcus's gaze narrowed as he glanced between the two men. "Remind me again why I saved your miserable arses at Toulouse."

Pearce placed his hand on Marcus's shoulder in a show of genuine affection. "Because you're a good man and a brilliant general," he said sincerely. "And one of the finest men we could ever call a friend."

Merritt lifted his glass in a heartfelt toast. "Happy birthday, General."

Thirty-five. *Bloody hell.*

"Hear, hear." Pearce seconded the toast. "To the Coldstream Guards!"

A knot tightened in Marcus's gut at the mention of his former regiment that had been so critical to the victory at Waterloo yet also nearly destroyed in the brutal hand-to-hand combat that day. But he managed to echo, "To the Guards."

Not wanting them to see any stray emotion on his face, he

turned away. Leaning across the stone balustrade on his forearms, he muttered, "I wish I could still be with them."

While he would never wish to return to the wars, he missed being with his men, especially their friendship and dependability. He missed the respect given to him and the respect he gave each of them in return, no matter if they were an officer or a private. Most of all, he longed for the sense of purpose that the fight against Napoleon had given him. He'd known every morning when he woke up what he was meant to do that day, what higher ideals he served. He hadn't had that since he returned to London, and its absence ate at him.

It bothered him so badly, in fact, that he'd taken to spending time alone at an abandoned armory just north of the City. He'd purchased the old building with the intention of turning it into a warehouse, only to discover that he needed a place to himself more than he needed the additional income. More and more lately, he'd found himself going there at all hours to escape from society and the ghosts that haunted him. Even in his own home.

That was the punishment for surviving when others he'd loved hadn't. The curse of remembrance.

"No, General." Pearce matched his melancholy tone as his friends stepped up to the balustrade, flanking him on each side. "You've left the wars behind and moved on to better things." He frowned as he stared across the crowded garden. "This party notwithstanding."

Merritt pulled a cigar from his breast pocket and lit it on a nearby lamp. "You're exactly where you belong. With your family." He puffed at the cheroot, then watched the smoke curl from its tip into the darkness overhead. "They need you now more than the Guards do."

Marcus knew that. Which was why he'd taken it upon himself to go through Elise's belongings when Claudia couldn't bring herself do it, to pack up what he thought her daughter, Penelope, might want when she was older and to distribute the rest to the poor. That was how he'd discovered a letter among Elise's things from someone named John Porter, arranging a midnight meeting for which she'd left the house and never returned.

He'd not had a moment of peace since.

He rubbed at the knot of tension in his nape. His friends didn't need to know any of that. They were already burdened enough as it was by settling into their own new lives now that they'd left the army.

"Besides, you're a duke now." Merritt flicked the ash from his cigar. "There must be some good way to put the title to use." He looked down at the party and clarified, "One that doesn't involve society balls."

"Or togas," Pearce muttered.

Marcus blew out a patient breath at their good-natured teasing. "The Roman theme was Claudia's idea."

"Liar," both men said at once. Then they looked at each other and grinned.

Merritt slapped him on the back. "Next thing you know, you'll be trying to convince us that the pink ribbons in you horse's tail were put there by Penelope."

Marcus kept his silence. There was no good reply to that.

He turned his attention back to the party below, his gaze passing over the crowded garden. He spied the delicate turn of a head in the crowd—

Danielle. There she was, standing by the fountain in the glow of one of the torches.

For a moment, he thought he was mistaken, that the woman who'd caught his attention couldn't possibly be her. Not with her auburn hair swept up high on her head in a pile of feathery curls, shimmering with copper highlights in the lamplight and revealing a long and graceful neck. Not in that dress of emerald satin with its capped sleeves of ivory lace over creamy shoulders.

Impossible. This woman, with her full curves and mature grace, simply couldn't be the same excitable girl he remembered, who'd seemed always to move through the world with a bouncing skip. Who had bothered him to distraction with all her questions about the military and soldiers.

She laughed at something her aunt said, and her face brightened into a familiar smile. Only then did he let himself believe that she wasn't merely an apparition.

Sweet Lucifer. Apparently, nothing in England was as he remembered.

He put his hands on both men's shoulders. "If you'll excuse me, there's someone in the garden I need to speak with. Enjoy yourselves tonight." Then, knowing both men nearly as well as he knew himself, he warned, "But not too much."

As he moved away, Merritt called out with a knowing grin. "What's *her* name?"

"Trouble," he muttered and strode down into the garden before she could slip back into the crowd and disappear.

To continue reading Marcus and Danielle's story, **click here.**

ABOUT THE AUTHOR

I fell in love with historical romances and all things Regency—and especially all those dashing Regency heroes—while living in England, where I spent most of my time studying the Romantic poets, reading Jane Austen, and getting lost all over the English countryside. I love the period's rich history and find that all those rules of etiquette and propriety can be worked to the heroine's advantage...if she's daring enough to seize her dreams.

I am an avid traveler and have enjoyed visiting schools and volunteering with children's organizations in Peru, Ecuador, Thailand, and Mexico, and I have amassed thousands of photos I unleash on unsuspecting friends who dare to ask about my travels.

I love to be outdoors! I've been hiking in Alaska, the Andes, and the Alps, and I love whitewater rafting (when I don't fall in!). I earned my pilot's license at Chicago Midway (To all the controllers in Chicago Center—I greatly apologize for every problem I caused for you and Southwest Airlines), and it is my dream to one-day fly in a hot-air balloon over Africa.

I adore all things chocolate, ice cream of any flavor, and Kona coffee by the gallon. A *Doctor Who* fanatic (everyone says my house *is* bigger on the inside), I am a terrible cook who hopes to one day use my oven for something other than shoe storage. When I'm not writing, I like to spend my time trying not to kill the innocent rose bushes in my garden.

https://www.annaharringtonbooks.com/

Manufactured by Amazon.ca
Bolton, ON

20478272R10081

FOR ERINN

HIP-HOP IS AMERICA'S BUTOH.

–Akira Kasai

Dear Craig,

I'm a ghost now.

I don't exist anymore.

Not even like how I used to, you know?

At least, in a minute I won't.

This is the last one, okay C.?

This is like, Marconi or whatever—I don't even know if you're hearing me.

Are you hearing me?

Shane and his dad are looking for me—they've got those Lee-Enfield bolt-actions—but I've got the thing right here in my hands. I don't know how you pictured it, but it kinda looks like this retro sci-fi bug or some shit. Like it doesn't look like it could be a real thing, but it is a real thing, and there's this button, and all I have to do is push it.

The 7-0-9, man—it's so beautiful.

I was curious what it would really look like, you know? Like, would it look like the tourism commercials or would it look like something else—like the tourism commercials but also kinda run down and white trash, you know—because that's the way I imagine you, baby, and anyway, I guess the latter is closer to the truth but what does that even mean?

And I feel really bad for Nina and Carter, but shit happens, doesn't it?

Anyway, I'm glad to have known you, and I'm glad you picked me out of the bunch to be the one you fell in love with, you know? It's, like, cool or whatever.

*It was super fun and fucked up and it was like really beautiful—
so thanks.*

Who knows, you know?

Nothing's for certain I can tell you that much.

*Maybe things will work out or maybe they won't but either way,
it's okay, okay?*

*All I really know is that it started while I was in Upper Canada
and you were in the Euro zone—and all the shit that was going
on at the time, but other than that, nothing is true, okay?*

Love you, baby.
Brit

They came for us in the night.

We didn't know at first, but they were there.

The three of us dreaming in bed with the sounds of the traffic and the all-night convenience store right there on the corner, and the dive bars down the way, and the drunks.

They came for us first in our dreams—barely noticeable— a shadow within a shadow in the corner of a dreamed room, the trunk of a car.

Later, we thought we could hear them. First, behind the walls of our apartment; just outside the window, hanging from the eavestrough or in the branches of the trees out front—then finally, we thought we could see them: news footage, music videos, porn sites—they were right there, flitting around the edges, in disguise.

At last, we could feel them in our bones and in the beating of our blood.

And I still don't know where it all started.

But it had something to do with the Painting Game.

The Painting Game, Shane's dad, the Radio Room, and the war.

They're tied together somehow—and then everything came to an end.

And that had to do with me.

I came a long way to find what my life meant, you know?

From the bars and the back alleys of The Metropolis to the tenements of T Dot to the cliffs and the hills of the 7-0-9— sometimes I thought I'd never make it.

But I found what I was supposed to do.

It was like the seed of a flower inside me.

And the seed of that flower was a flame stretching up into the heavens that would never die.

That's what I am.

And this is how it happened.

One day the satellite plunged into Lake Sludge.

Shane, Nina, and Brit watching the shaky video footage on the news.

A black cylinder, glinting darkly in the light, dropping out of blue sky.

An enormous splash. Debris flying up. Shock waves in the water.

It replayed over and over again, the angle of the satellite in mid-fall suggesting some terrible consequence.

They're in the car now, but will never be safe. The three of them knowing they just have to keep moving. And Carter, poor little Carter, with his PTSD.

The man at the toll beside the ferry terminal watching as they pass.

It actually made them feel good to see a person behind the glass.

The black smoke from the ferry's chimney hangs in the air above them.

They blow by a hitcher on the gravel shoulder of the highway.

Just another refugee.

Her cardboard sign saying HOME.

Nina's like, it's 1991. But it's not your 1991, it's ours.

And it's not even 1991, it's 2024.

It's like sci-fi or whatever.

We're ahead of you fucking dumb shits, but also, we ain't.

We're, like, an alternate universe or whatever.

We're like hardcore over here—we ain't your world.

But we are your world.

I don't even know what it is we is, but we are, so like, deal, I guess.

This here is your world.

Don't care what you say:

This is your world.

They call him Shaky, Milk, Dead Fox, Skeet Love.

He'll rap only in front of the mirror at home, a straight-up genius, thinks Nina, legit.

Skeet Love, Shane says, That's like, Rock, yo. Like where my dad is. That's a fucking Rock term and that's me, so fuck you.

Know what that shit means?

Naw, fewl, of course you don't, you're dumb as shit. But I'm not.

I'm not, and here's why:

It means I'm like dirt, yo.

Like, shit.

Like, shit on my whole life, dawg.

And there ain't nothing that makes you smarter than being shit.

Skeet.

Like, what's Nina say about it?

Like, a derogatory term for urban, white, working-class.

Someone who's up to no good.

A total outsider, like every damn day of my life.

That's me.

(Except, not.)

So whatever, and anyway, like I said, Fuck you.

Nina and Brit checking his flow.

His hands, the cut of his shoulders.

At first, Brit was only around occasionally, now she's here all hours.

When she met them, Brit was on top of the moon.

Like, over the world.

Seriously giddy.

That's sometimes the way she talks when she's excited—she mixes shit up.

Shit is always getting mixed up—totally—like your world and this world.

It's messy, G—like where does one start and the other one end?

Or do they even?

Nina and Brit and hours and hours on Karmaloop, Lookbook.

Ecko, Obey, HUF, Billionaire Boys Club.

White Doves, Yellow Airplanes.

Nina's got the best clothes, Shane the best drugs.

The two girls changing outfits while Shane paces and smokes, flexing his trophied lats in the bedside wall mirror—this world, and that, man, like legit.

Shane's like, Know how many crunches I can do, motherfucker? Well neither do I cause I lose count after a thousand. Chin ups? Whatever. This body is tight, yo, like tight as shit, like a virgin—for real.

He's old school, thinks Brit, sells pills for five bucks a pop when everyone else is into powder.

They go to a club, the dance floor crazy, Brit and Nina making out for the crowd while Shane leans at the bar sipping a cooler.

He hates beer, has a gluten intolerance.

Nina once said, Shit, you're so skinny, baby, it's hot. I wish I was sick. I wish I had cancer.

She pictures herself, like him, with her ribs showing through. She could kill anything with ribs like that. She could destroy the universe if she were that thin, her knee bones knocking together painfully in bed.

She sees herself emaciated, grinning.

She winks and the skyline is flattened.

Waves her hand and all the buildings utterly devastated.

Blackened bodies, ash on the wind.

Drop another twenty pounds and you're the shit, she thinks, she smiles.

In the club, she screams over the music:

Ever wanna just, like, destroy the fucking world?

Brit smiles back at her. The vamp fangs she bought online glow in the blacklight.

When Shane first saw them, he was like, Keep that mouth away from my dick.

But not really. Really, he was totally down.

Brit's fangs—they're good for a week and then fall off—two white little talons, like bullets.

Brit's a poet—the fucking legislator of the wound is what she told Shane and Nina when they first met.

Nina and Brit coming off the dance floor covered in sweat.

Shane thinking how everyone in the club, every eye in every head, is watching them.

They rent bikes from a Thai kid outside and peel through the streets, neon blinding them.

Left, right, left, left and right.

If there's anyone following them, they ain't anymore.

Not yet, Nina thinks, wanting to vomit. They come to a park and throw the bikes to the ground.

Sprawled on the grass. Trying to see stars through the smog above their heads.

You guys are my family, Brit says, her eyes huge in the dark. I feel like I'm home.

Nina punches her shoulder, retches and pukes.

Sour Puss and grenadine, a puddle of blood.

Brit says, Take the *in* out, and you've got a grenade.

Nobody laughs.

Nina's spinning.

On the train home, Nina with her head on Shane's lap, KO'd.

Shane watching the other passengers.

Dude in a suit with his eyes all over Nina's body.

Another looks at them over the top of his newspaper.

The soundtrack in Shane's head screams bad cop drama.

They get off two stops early, Shane carrying Nina, and Brit trailing behind.

Later, Brit watches the two others sleep on the mattress. She meant what she said. The sun is up, Monday morning traffic on the street. A fan by the bed blows strands of Nina's hair into the air.

She pops another of Shane's pills. Red Butterfly. When they wake up that afternoon, they find her on the fire escape cross-legged. Her eyes as shiny as a polished gun barrel.

Soon, Leo will get out of prison, and when he does, he'll come looking for Nina.

She belonged to him, but now she belongs to Shane.

She puts her nose behind Shane's ear and says, You own me, baby, you own me.

She snuggles closer to him in bed.

He rolls over to face her, his fingers in her hair, and she's thinking how lovely it is to have his fingers in her hair.

The thing he does when his fingers are in her hair is that first he smooths it all down—almost like he's petting a dog or a cat, and then his hand comes down over the curve of the back of her head, and with her hair in his hand, he sort of clenches his hand very gently and tenderly into a fist, and then releases her hair and smooths the back of her neck.

Then he'll tuck some loose strand of hair behind her ear, and he'll kinda cup the spot where her jaw and neck connect—kinda right where her earlobe is.

Then he'll caress her earlobe between his thumb and fore-finger, and run his hand down her neck until his warm palm meets her collarbone—and then he'll do the same thing again, and again.

You wouldn't think someone like him could be that way—so sweet—but he is.

And when he's like this with her, she worries he isn't brutal enough for the world or something, but maybe he is brutal enough—and anyway, maybe it's not something she needs to worry about.

A phone call will come and it'll go like this:

Skeet Love?

Yo.

This is Dr. Dre. You a fuckin' genius.

No shit? Dope.

Here's a million dollars.

Sweet.

ODB came back from the dead for this shit. I played him yo demo.

But first Shane will make a demo.

But before that, Shane will win a million rap battles.

And there's Nina stage left, watching him embarrass the fuck out of each and every comer.

Like step in the ring, motherfucker.

Like Mohammed Ali.

Shane will make it, and Nina will wear a white faux-fur bolero jacket, a black mini with thigh-high black boots, and her eyes will burn from the camera flashes.

But really, Nina knows, a phone call will come like this:

Shane?

Yo.

This is Leo. Imma fuckin' shoot you dead.

Click-click, Nina and Brit in front of the mirror with Brit's iPhone.

Red-carpet styles. Album cover. TMZ you mothafokkaH-hZzzzZzZZ.

When will he get out, Brit wants to know.

I dunno. Six months, a year.

You scared?

Nope. Whatever.

Is Shane?

Shane is scared of nothing.

How would Brit know anything? They're a month in and already competing for him. She hates this most of all. Why fight?

You're my sister, she says, suddenly. Know that?

Yeah, I know.

Like you said in the park.

You were fucked up.

You were too.

Brit has brought her suitcases to their apartment. She sleeps on a cot in their bedroom, or sometimes between them. Her real family doesn't know where she is, and she guesses that's prolly why the Shit Journal started.

At first it was cause she was backed up—a list of what day and what time of day she took a dump. And then something else began to happen.

It went like this:

MARCH 27, 10:04PM

MARCH 30, 7:00AM

APRIL 6, 3:04AM. ONE FUCKING WEEK!!!!!!

Then it went, amongst letters written to her favourite writer, like this:

SWEAT SWEAT SWEAT DRIPS ON THE BIIIIIIIIIIITCH

BLOOD FROM THE CUNT
YOU'RE THE ONE YOU'RE THE ONE YER YER YER THE
ONE AND ONLY ONLY THERE'S TWO.
I AM A DEATH'S HEAD MOTH. I AM A DEATH'S HEAD.
I AM A HEAD. I AM A DEATH.

But as far as Brit can tell, writing shit down don't change
a thing—trips to the can are like after-school detention—you
sit and sit and nothing happens.

If Leo finds us, Shane'll take care of it.

He's not tough, Brit says.

She takes a pair of fishnets out of a pile of clothes on the
floor.

He's a sweetheart, but he'll take care of it.

How'd you meet?

He was Leo's friend. But Shane only hung out with him
for the coke.

You like this?

Hot. You should wear that tonight.

Think so?

He's got a thing for maids. It's cause his parents had one.

No shit?

Yep. They live on the Island.

He's rich? Wait—what?

His parents are. They get him outta trouble if he finds it.

Sweet.

I know, right? His dad has a yacht. Shane showed me a
picture.

Like, I'm soooo glad I met you guys.

Me too.

For his part, Shane isn't worried about Leo.

Shane is worried about the traffic cameras above the streetlights at the intersection beside their building.

He worries about passing satellites, security drones, bulk data, Google, the webcam on his laptop, shortwave radio frequencies.

Shortwave, yo—shit's a Ouija board, dawg, for real—like it's a plain fact ghosts move through the AM bandwidth, you know what I mean? Like they pass right through everything. Right through me and you and the fucking multiverse— for real.

He's not worried about Leo—Shane worries about the stenciled, spray-painted image of a spider, fangs dripping, on the wall outside their apartment building.

First time he saw it, him and Brit were coming back from the TexaBucks with a plastic bag full of chocolate, soda, and chips.

There, beneath the spider, some homeless dude sat in a puddle of urine.

Shane made fists in his pockets.

It creeped him out.

What more proof do you need that someone's got their eyes on you?

They're everywhere. Watch the news.

Shane went straight to the shoebox in which he keeps his pistol.

Cracked it open and looked clean through the cylinder where the bullets go. Watched himself in the bathroom mirror.

There was no doubt.

They'd found him again.

Shane needs nothing other than Nina, Brit, a blunt, pills, and his iPhone.

And his pistol.

And cash.

And who takes cash anymore?

Thugs like me cause otherwise they track you, G, no joke.

He watches the street from the fire escape.

Brings the gun up and takes a bead on a black guy walking his dog.

Now a white mother with her two babies coming out of the gas station.

Someone stopped at the corner in their car, talking on a cellphone.

He's sure he sees that sucker look up at him.

Ever since he was a little kid he's had to deal with this shit.

One town to the next.

A bus, a train, but never by plane.

Too many cameras and way too traceable.

You go within ten miles of an airport and they've got you in a database somewhere down south with a team of analysts and a tracking device up your ass.

Shane goes out to where the car is parked behind the apartment building and kicks the fender. Thing hasn't moved in months.

No insurance, and he let his license expire last year.

The car was Leo's up until he went away.

Fucking straight up pimp-mobile gone to shit.

Those rims alone cost a fortune.

Tinted windows, leather seats: Leo's old-school five-point-oh Mustang bought in honour, he used to say, of Vanilla Ice.

Leo's old, know what I'm saying? Like for real old. Like ancient. Like practically pre-computer old. Like seriously retro. His first tattoo wasn't Thug Life, it was The Lost Poets if that tells you anything about what shit he listens to.

He's like all political and shit. He's Black Power but he's a white guy who grew up on a farm in the sticks, and was born in, like, 1968.

Leo on the coming revolution: Listen my brother, he'd say, except it was more like, Lissann mah Bruth-ah, shit is gonna git *REAL*.

When Tariq(e) made their appearance that first time during the riots, Leo got their motto tattooed on his forearm.

ONE WORLD.

Like some ancient-history hippy shit, but it worked, and it's no joke—everyone, even half Lebanese Muslim trannies—united under a motherfucking dollar sign—and guess what?—it's dope, yo, like TRUTH.

Nothing pays like looking like an outsider.

But, unlike Leo, Shane is a non-believer. Ain't no change coming. People are dumb as shit, and there's about a million Agents controlling the world—just look at the CEO, yo—you think that motherfucker will loosen his grip? Naw, homey, not likely.

And right here in the parking lot, an old, peeling poster of Tariq(e) in a white gown, a sawed-off shotgun in one hand, cash in the other.

Politics, G—ideas and words—shit's like a virus.

All in one year: LAX, the Strip, the Quake, and the Wild-fires.

Shane remembers—HAZMAT teams all over the news.

Jesus freaks saying it was punishment for Tariq(e).

And since then, like, perpetual crisis: retinal scans, drones, shootings, mass incarcerations, bombs going off—you name it—and the top-end surveillance and craziness beats all those things, like legit—the top-end shit is invisible and everywhere, like radio waves, oxygen, fucking microbes that get into your shit and the CEO and Tariq(e) and the Resistance already know all, and prolly, like, holding hands around a circle of virgin blood most nights.

Shane's got one word for you: Hashtag fucking PIZZA-GATE, G—for real.

Shane calls his father and leaves a message on his voice-mail—old fuckers appreciate that shit. Wonders if the same network operates in the 7-0-9, and thinks to himself, Of course it does. Shit's all connected.

Snowden was a PIMP.

The call means they'll know he's broke. They'll know he's onto them, but whatever. The apartment is bugged anyway. Has been for weeks.

He tried to redeem his mutual funds but the bank got a clamp on his money like tight.

Shane pulls up his hood. Shane is *8 Mile*. He's Milk.

Now he carries his gat everywhere.

How to get money?

MDMA is such bullshit. Your drugs are called, like, Parachute or something. These are called Bombs, you know what I mean? Like Dirty Bombs, bitch.

How to get them stacks?

He picks the girls up from the park where they're all like totally blitzed on pills. Can't even stay hard, later at the apartment, when the girls take turns playing intern.

Nina and Brit have the same thought: Something is wrong with Skeet Love.

Dear Craig,

I'm writing to tell you something you don't wanna hear and that is you've written something beautiful.

You're like I am—you kinda hate yourself and maybe you have good reason. You've done a lot of shitty things in your time. Sometimes you're a horrible, selfish person who thinks you've never been as loved as well as you deserve.

It might be true, I can't really say, but if nothing else, at least you've done this—you brought joy to my life. You really did.

Right now we're only at the very beginning of our relationship. Things will go on from here if it's okay with you. Right now, we've got more time to talk about things and about how we're both doing and what will happen to us.

But I wanted to write you. I needed to tell you that your words touched me. You've done something wonderful for us, and you'll prolly still feel, no matter what, that no one gets you. I don't get you. Not yet, and maybe never. But I feel you, CFP. I feel you, and whatever happens now, whatever you decide happens, it'll be cool, man. You remind me of my dad, like maybe when he wasn't so old and broken from work. But I'd prolly still fuck you. I mean, I for sure would, but that's not something we ever really have to worry about because you're way over there in that world, and I'm right here with Shane and Nina, so whatevs.

Anyway, thanks, and congrats on everything you have. Like the books and your fam or whatever. They love you, and so do I, Craig. I love you and want to see you do well. I'll write again soon.

Yours,
Brit

Nina's like, Fuck, it feels so MINT.

Bitch is a feen for it:

Brit's mouth on her bud while Shane raw-dogs her.

If you've never had it done to you, Nina thinks, you should.

Oh God, it's so good, like legit, like money, yo.

Nina's a good mom. A boy who lives with Grandma; another somewhere else.

One from Leo, and the other from her first boyfriend, Nick, who's now, like, the manager of a Best Buy or something in some shit town up north.

She's never laid a hand on those boys. She was good with them.

It kills her that it's been so long since she's seen them, but it got too hard. Like brutal. Like murder, man.

She's a good mom.

Her oldest, Carter, starts school in September—or the Training Program.

Last picture she saw, he already had the brush-cut.

But, yeah, it's straight-up mint, she'd like you to know.

Can't keep your eyes off that shit.

But now Shane's gone weird on them.

His weapon don't work.

Only sometimes it don't.

And anyway, Grandma got cash. Pop died from a work-place accident. Head clean off from the blade of a forklift.

She got a nice house and it's better for everyone.

And this is the best summer of her life.

Even better than the one she met Leo and dropped school like something hot.

You can't judge, you don't know.

There's something beautiful about life. Even here, now, in this apartment. The afternoon sun beaming in. Even right there, cars like shiny jewels in the parking lot of the TexaBucks. Man, it's the best. This here's the shit. The gold, the blood, the real dangerous stuff. The paper, the pills, the pistol, her pussy.

It's the shit, I'm telling you.

This life's the most beautiful shit in the world.

Look—all three of us got shiners.

On the train or in the street, people see us, and stare like seriously.

The three of us, G—we're like everything.

We're a trinity.

We are the world.

We are the children.

Mine's old and like yellow and there's a gash under my eye from Nina's ring.

The girls are purple for Brit and like a kinda fucking sea green and blue for Nina.

This our shit, okay? It's what we do, and some nights at the apartment the three of us join hands in a circle, and like, we close our eyes, and all we do is like breathe together, know what I mean?

It's like a ritual but it totally ain't satanic or whatever— The Painting Game—it's a holy thing on the side of all that's good and light.

It's love, haters.

We don't eat feces on toothpicks or some shit like that.

Or like fuck goats or whatever.

It's like legit, human activity.

We hurt each other, we hit each other, and it's love, okay?

And we wear it right here on our faces, right?

It's our bodies, that's what it is.

And Nina made it and she's like so generous she shared it with me and Brit and now we're together in a way that no one else could ever be.

And sorry-not-sorry, motherfucker should never talk this way—like what—this bitch ain't queer—but my shit is deep, know what I mean?

Bitch has got eight eyes, eight legs.

Sees everything. Knows all.

When he saw that graffiti outside their building, Shane was like, Oh shit.

Then, two days later, there was that black sedan, totally Agent, like for real CIA or FBI or ATF—fucking HOMELAND, parked on the corner. Dude inside trying to be all like non-chalant.

David Koresh: Now there was a gangsta.

And now the CEO's legions in the government are onto Shane.

Why?

Don't know.

The CEO like seriously—a face made out of boiled meat—pushing buttons and making calls from the Mansion with a team of fucking Pinkertons running the show.

You feel those eyes on you every time you go out that door.

It's fucking trippy, G.

That same homeless dude—like, what is this, a fucking drop-in?—shuffles around, picking butts off the sidewalk.

He's got something to do with it.

Some nasty United Nations bitch-ass punk, except they got rid of the UN like last year, remember? And the Occupy bitches were like, Make the building into low-income housing!

Shane goes over to him.

Yo like what the fuck do you want?

Shane puts his hand on the butt of his gun, but thinks better of drawing it. It's like just what they want. Next thing you know, they got your prints on record, Mom and Dad kidnapped, the girls sold into slavery.

Dude's like, What?

Find somewhere else to hang, Shane says.

Then he sees that black sedan again right there in the parking lot of the apartment building.

Puts his head down and speed-walks around the corner like turbo-styles, he's gone.

He first saw that image, the stencilled spider, while reading about the Illuminati. Shit's fucked, dawg. A thousand silvery threads connected to a thousand marionettes. Think the CEO is a thing? Think Tariq(e)'s for real? They ain't, they ain't, (and BTW, thinks Shane, fuck your gender-neutral personal pronoun or whatever) but this is real: Shane pulls the hammer of his pistol back.

The House of the New Swamp. That's what they're called.

Here's Shane on their website. Trying to figure out what in fuck they're all about. It's just about the most incoherent thing he's read since high school, when the teacher assigned an excerpt of James Joyce.

Yeah, yeah, whatever, the Twin Towers coming down—inside job, no shit—but it's the first he's heard of the New Swamp, and the first he's seen of their emblem: the very same stencil on the wall in the doorway.

Straight up Doomsday shit.

How a cataclysm will bring about the rebirth of some kind of alien behemoth they believe hibernates under Atlantis.

Like Ktulu or some shit.

Bitches be trippin.

And here's some sad artist rendition of that sucker: some kinda hairy squid monster with fangs and eight eyes.

Like seriously?

But poor Shane, he's really kind of an innocent, you know—his heart is caught in a web looking at that shit.

The Euro Zone might be safe.

Bitches got enough wind and solar to keep going for years.

When everything ends, and these fucking alien-collaborating-New Swamp-Jesus Freak-Illuminati-homeless-secret network motherfuckers pull off their coup.

Meanwhile, Shane's bank account says, You ain't goin' nowhere, bitch.

Meanwhile, Dad and Nina and Brit with ball-gags in some cult sex dungeon for a gang of rapist Baltic millionaires.

Meanwhile, an intergalactic UFO raises Jesus and Elvis and Tupac straight up out of the ground, and some Somalian Muslim Vegan terrorists nuke Washington.

Meanwhile, Leo getting out of prison, and that bitch is pissed.

And Shane's like, Dad, can you like put money in my account pretty please?

Be cool, Shakey, he thinks.

He orders a double Big Mac with fries and a Coke.

Fuck celiac.

Bitch is like starved.

Bitch needs a plan.

It was last year that Brit noticed the problem.

She was absolutely paralysed with fear.

Ever see one of those girls, who like starts going bald?

Not like cancer or anything, but like their hair starts falling out? At twenty?

Can you imagine?

It's like genetic? I think it is?

Well—this was last summer—she got out of the shower. She'd been looking down at her vajayjay? Thinking about a baby? How she wanted one someday? And then, she'd looked down further at the drain.

Like a motherfucking wolf spider with its babies on its back, except not—because it was really a really giant tangle of hair—Eww—and so that's when she went online? And found that olive-oil treatment?

And it saved her life, for reals, she says.

Who'd wanna fuck some cue ball?

Maybe if she were punk, but they're stank.

But really her deepest worry isn't going bald.

She pictures the drain in the bathtub of her papa's four and a half.

She knows someday, someone will prolly murder her.

But that's not her worry either.

Oh what's the word? What's the word she's looking for?

You know what? There are two choices for a girl but it ain't really a choice at all.

You can be fuckable or invisible, and that's it, yo.

Just that drain going down underground.

That's what she sees when she feels that way.

And it's the scariest shit.

Scarier even than being some bat-shit crazy balding crack-head lookalike.

Nina wants you to know something, and it's this: $$$$$$$$$.

Dollah billz.

Shane's been gone for hours when she steps out into the hallway.

She's going to buy beer, but also is kinda looking for him.

Wild Cat, man. Shit makes you crazy but it's cheap as shit.

Shane's not answering her texts.

They need cash.

Bitch's got twenty bucks and five forty in TexaBucks.

She's hoping she'll leave the apartment and when she comes back, Shane's home.

She buys eight cans of beer and has enough left over for a small bag of Doritos.

A man in a black suit is there watching her as she waits for her change.

For sure, her A$$ is slammin.

She's getting skinny.

She's like a buck fifteen now.

She's wearing pajama bottoms and flats but her ass is the event horizon.

It's magic, man, that A$$.

The perfect jiggle.

Back at their building, she has a good look at it in the mirrored doors of the elevator.

Going up.

Before it happens, there's this kind of rush of blood through her heart.

She believes in ESP.

It's like totally true.

She's got a gift.

Years from now, when the happy ending comes, and her and Shane and Brit are remembering this shit together, it'll be this moment in her memory that marks the beginning of their fucked-up adventure together.

It'll be right now, in this hallway outside their apartment, where she'll begin to find her happiness, she knows it, like for reals for sure.

She's walking down the hall from the elevator when she hears the click and then feels, like, a big hard dick in her back, but it's like not a dick, because it's a fucking gun, and holding the gun is Leo.

Sup, he says. I'll have one of those beers.

Dear CFP,

I'd say you're insane but that may be too complimentary. I think you prolly like too much people saying that sort of thing about you. Especially someone like me. I'm only eighteen years old. But I'm smarter than most. Maybe I'm smarter than you. And anyway, despite my admiration, I'd put you in a pretty moderate range, intelligence wise. That's not really your deal. Your deal is heart. Me too. That's why I think about you this way and why I like you.

There's nothing ever that's been invented in the history of the world that's gonna kill people like us. Nothing ever, I promise you.

And I know how badly you'd just like to say Good Bye or whatever—that's something you think about a lot, but that's just not very good for any of us—and you have so much work to do, you know?

My family needs you, and yours does too, okay?

Love
Brit

BK blows.

McD's got flow.

Skeet Love on the mic—

Yo yo.

Shane's stomach like a cannonball of napalm.

Like white phosphorous.

Before they were all murdered, what's in his gut could kill a clutch of demonstrating Palestinians.

Out on the street, the McDeal don't help him with figuring out what he's gonna do, and worse, he's gonna do damage to that toilet back at the crib.

That shit like literally, except not literally, a motherfucking war crime.

But now here's the very same homeless motherfucker in his face, right here on the sidewalk outside McD's.

Don't hurt me, he says. I need to talk to you.

Shane lifts his shirt and flashes his gat.

Don't hurt me.

What do you want?

You're in danger, dude says.

Fuck you, says Shane.

He moves to step by him but the little fucker blocks his path.

Shane, listen to me, you and the girls are in trouble.

This is some lame-ass B-movie shit. Like here comes Roger Moore or whatever.

How do you know my name?

Crackhead just laughs.

Shane's about to bitch-slap this clown, but then he sees like Agent Man, like for sure the same guy who's been watching the apartment since forever, pull up in that black sedan, Mister Ninja Super Agent.

They run.

Down the alleyway past the McD's.

Dead end.

They crouch together behind a dumpster.

Shane remembers suddenly, when he was a kid, uncovering a rats' nest beneath a dumpster just like this one behind a butcher shop one blistering hot summer.

That's just what Crackhead smells like.

Blood, offal.

Bitch smells like a million miles of ass.

A writhing ball of rats, their jaws working blindly.

Shane breathes through his mouth.

They wait.

Shane's heart, bass drum pounding.

But Agent Man don't show.

They're sitting there for like ten minutes, and nothing.

Okay, Shane says. Spill.

So then Crackhead begins in with the whole story: How Shane and the girls have the CIA on their asses because of Shane's old man. How it isn't just coke his dad smuggles, but the hardware components for a dirty bomb, and how the Feds think Shane may have some of those components. Crackhead says Shane had better be like ultra-careful, because it's common knowledge in some circles that the government has been cloning people for years—and not that pleasure-clone plastic-surgery shit that Brit went through, but like espionage, sabotage, whatever *age* you like.

Crackhead says some more things that are too risky even for me to repeat. The last thing your narrator needs right now is trouble with the law.

What about the cult, the New Swamp, Shane says.

But then BAM! BAM! BAM!

Shots fired.

Shane pictures some kid's science-fair volcano times like a billion.

Like the fucking Yellowstone Supervolcano.

Just one more way the world's gonna end.

Shane makes some fucked up sound in his throat.

It's like: GAH—GAH—GAH.

He runs for it, hearing the ricochet of bullets in the alleyway.

Crackhead is gone like he was never there. Total vanishing act.

Amongst others, one lesson stands out for Shane:

If that's what it's like in a gunfight, he won't be popping caps anytime soon.

Inside each beautiful thing is a secret and the secret is even more beautiful than what's carrying that sucker.

See here, a fucking jaguar, G.

Right here a toucan like a cluster of jewels.

This is what Shane's dad does.

Bitch is a millionaire.

A team of poachers out there all over the world sending Shane's dad this Serengeti-jackpot-winning-golden-ticket-four-legged motherfucker, this deep-dark-jungle-triple-seven-straight-up-pimped-out-prize-winning-point-blank-period-winged-creature miracle of evolution.

Anacondas? Shane's dad's done like 50 of them.

Shane's dad with a lab over in the 7-0-9 and a tanker full of formaldehyde and enough rubber tubing to stretch a line from here to the moon or your ass or wherever the fuck he wants.

But inside, see, that's where the beauty is.

Shane wants to know how many keys of coke his old man has shipped this way and the old man don't know—a fuck of a lot, he says.

So that's money right there and ain't no way no how no one knows nothing about it.

Except maybe they do.

Anyway, shit's always like that.

There's this beautiful thing like totally totally beautiful, and inside there's this other thing that makes your face go numb from the glory, yo, like know what I mean?

Leo's like, Shee-it, I ain't had a beer in two years.

Nina's sitting on the couch.

Better take it easy though, he says. I get drunk enough I might rape you with this.

He holds up the glock and smiles at her.

Where is that faggot boyfriend of yours?

Leo's got lots more tattoos. Prolly an asshole wide as the North Atlantic. Jail time and all.

He ain't answering me, Nina says. She's wondering, Where is he, where's Brit? As if in answer, a text from her:

Imma get stoned bbg Wanna join? Smiley Smiley Heart.

You guys are in a heap of shit, Leo says. Know that?

Why?

Shane say anything to you?

Bout what?

Anything.

No.

Maybe the bitch don't even know.

Leo, what do you want?

I want a decent future for Carter, he says.

And then Shane comes in, looking like death.

Fuck my life, Leo says. They find you?

Ordinarily, coming home to this, Shane'd be like, Blam blam blam, here's a fucking hat-trick of bullets for you, bitch, but he's just standing there.

Nina says, Baby, you hurt?

Leo's like, We need to get the fuck out of here. Like. Now.

Tommy was this guy she met when she first came to town?

He does tattoos out of his basement apartment.

Sketchy as fuck, but discount prices.

Piercings too, and dermal shit, which Brit is totally into, but scared.

See their tools, man? Like he could rip out your uterus if he wanted.

Scarier even than the clinic she went to because at least like they put you under?

Brit can't remember if they fucked, but she's pretty sure she blew him once.

Anyway, he texted her, and she met him at the park.

He's like, for sure, a real artist?

He's one of those quiet types. Sort of just smokes a lot of weed.

And Brit is saying how what she is, is like, a poet?

But not a poet like Shane's a poet, but she's like an artist too?

And her life is her art and her art is her life, but also like she just, like, really loves words—like all of them? Every word in the world.

They're sitting under one of those giant lilac trees they have in the park when up pulls this crazy-ass brand-new white Cadillac, and inside the Caddy are Nina, Shane, and some hard-looking dude with those awful white-boy dreads.

Nina yells to her, Get in the fucking car!

Brit sees that Shane is like all fucked up and shit.

Like totally a ghost, you know? Aghast.

Like what the fuck?

And she's up and running over the grass to them.

Meanwhile, Tommy is still sitting under the tree, just kinda weirded out by it.

Poof! Brit gone in a puff of smoke, like Abracadabra style.

And the Caddy peels off, tires screeching into the rush of traffic parkside.

Here they are—one big happy family driving in the car.

Nina in the passenger seat, Shane driving, Leo with his pistol out on the backseat behind Shane, Brit next to him.

Fuck, Shane, you been livin alright, huh, Leo says, watching Brit's legs fidget.

Traffic's fucked.

The 401, man, like a dead snake of light—Leo rolling a blunt with one hand, gun in the other.

I can, like, see what new tattoos motherfucker's got on his hands—spiderwebs yo—like a little one on each of the knuckles.

And a new scar on his face running right through his eyebrow, but maybe that's just like a thing he done with a razor because Leo's like that.

That was always the way with that one—always trying to look harder than he was—which must be something I like—because Shane's like that too—he'd kill me if he knew I told Brit about the yacht and the big house and the money and his dad and shit—but this ride is sweet, and I figure what Leo wants—like I can just tell, man, legit like ESP—he wants the kid, Carter, the little boy what we called the Squish back in the day when I had him—the future, man, just what every dumb-ass dude in the world wants—they want to own it all— shit that ain't even happened yet—the land and the sea and the air you breathe and final curtain and all of it—Leo and Shane maybe too are just like the rest of them—they want to own it all and nothing else, yo, for real.

And I'm scared for Granny and Carter and everyone else.

Sometimes she could be such a bitch.

Nina fucking hated her.

She'd put a bolt on the outside of Nina's bedroom door, and Nina was like, Fuck you, and used the window.

A two-storey drop and a twisted ankle.

She'd worn those bike shorts with the pink neon stripes down the legs because they were easy to take off.

The guy—what was his name again? Hobbies included slashing ambulance tires, bricks through windows.

He waited for her round the corner at the park, and she limped the whole way.

Her first orgasm, she thought she'd pissed on him.

He was—what else?—an MC. Or that's what he called himself.

And her poppy had died in that workplace accident.

Nina's grandma, like, pushing that shrink on her and shit.

Pill bottles rattling.

Enough for ten years.

Mood stabilizers and anti-depressants when all Nina wanted was to get fucked.

For real, Nina hated her.

But Nina loved her, too.

That's what's, like, fucked about life.

There's something you hate and you love it too.

She'd like the world to explode, or just fucking burned black, like whatever.

Don't know why.

But it's also the dopest shit ever.

And that's how the Painting Game works too, like legit— you love the person and you hate them too—and you want the world to see that shit and for the person you love to feel your hatred for them.

And now Nina's clutching Carter, listening to what's happening to her grandmother in the next room, and what's happening is that Leo is raping her.

Except he's not really raping her, he's only threatening to do so, which, as far as Nina's grandmother's concerned, is just about the same thing.

First there were screams but now it's just these weird animal whimpering sounds like the time Shane's pit bull got hit by that taxi.

And Leo acting all hardcore.

She took the boy out of the room just as Leo put the gun in her grandma's mouth, and he'd said, This bitch ain't the bitch, this bitch is a copy.

Shane and Brit right here with Nina.

And nobody lifting a finger to help.

Carter looking up into her face, and Nina looking at Shane.

And then that ESP shit happens again—Nina, Brit, Shane—the three of them in matching electric chairs.

Like, buzz, buzz, buzz—blood and brains out every hole.

Wires connecting their temples so they're fried at the same instant.

Like fucking orgasm, yo, except, you know—death.

How could the world be so beautiful, and so fucking cruel?

Shane's like, Yo, Nina, shit's fucked.

And Nina's up, dragging Carter—Shane and Brit behind her—not into the living room where it sounds like Leo's just about done—but outside to the Caddy where she takes Leo's keys from the sun-blind and then, like—VROOM—the whole crew are gone, baby.

Like, G-O-N-E.

Like a bullet baby, into a night black as gun powder.

Dear C.,

Why do you care? Why do you care? Why can't you just let it all go, that's what I wanna know?

No one who knows you has not been affected by you. Doesn't this mean anything? People want you to succeed and people want you to tell the truth and people would do anything for you and wonder why you haven't succeeded and why you haven't told the truth because you are in a position to do so and you have the skill and the wits to do so and what's really at the heart of it is that you have the heart to do so. So, why haven't you?

Look, maybe it's different for me. I'm outside of you and your world and even from way over here I can see it, and I can see you. I can see the green light of your father's car dash just like I can see the green light from our dash. I can see the light. And I can see how the light, whatever way it shines, whatever it decides to reveal and hide, whatever it is, C, I can see that it changes and remains the same. Just like you and me, baby. Just like how we are.

We. You and me and everyone. It's not the big why, it's the big we.

I love you, C. I love you and miss you and wish somehow you'd come back to me. Because even though we could never meet, and never have, even though that's impossible, the feeling I have is that you've left, and not that I'm waiting for you, but rather that I'm searching for you, and that you're searching for me.

Love
Brit

Shane remembers when Tariq(e) appeared.

After the riots started, Shane's dad had written him at the time: The future just got darker for us.

He meant it literally and otherwise.

Tariq(e) in their white gown with the sawed-off and their necklace of pearls—shooting that thing off into the sky from the top of a burned-out cop car.

The way they spoke was straight-up Fred Hampton, and what happened to him?

Commies, queers, feminazis, darkies, artists, writers, the scum of the universe.

They'd come out of their shantytowns right across the country to vote—but it didn't mean shit.

The CEO's campaign had won campaign of the century as voted by the PR Industry/ Department of Information.

That alone should have reassured his old man, but it didn't.

Shane's dad moved to the Rock, like pronto.

As far away from things as possible.

Then there was outrage when Tariq(e) and his gang protested the flattening of the Strip.

Shit's like, a motherfucking parking lot over there.

Here's Shane watching the airstrikes in an HD livestream— smoke and debris and limbs flying.

The streets at first, wild with celebration—then the pinko-commie-NWO counter-attack: sit down strikes in solidarity that shut down the eastern seaboard.

As far as Shane's concerned, they're just flipside of the same coin—all theatre for the real conspiracy that's going on right in front of everyone's faces.

But know what?

That's the way every fucking pimp and bitch in the world is.

Nobody sees shit. Or at least, don't let themselves.

Shane remembers last year when his dad had sent him a fucked-up skin job.

The pelt of a Pine Marten or some shit, Shane don't know. There's like, twelve of them in the world, but the bitches won't hump.

The old man had ruined it somehow—its face was caved in and an eye was missing.

Shane tacked it to the wall of the living room for a laugh.

Forgot about it until they'd grabbed everything they could from the apartment just three days ago, and Shane saw it again still hanging in the same spot.

It gave him the motherfucking creeps.

It also gave him the creeps that the old man had said to Shane once it arrived:

NEVER LET THIS SKIN JOB OUT OF YOUR SIGHT.

So now it's in a suitcase with the rest of his shit.

As a dealer, a gangster, one hard-ass thug, they'd have like twenty visits at that apartment from Shane's clients every damn day.

And not one of them ever said a thing about that skin job on the wall.

I mean, fuck sakes—shit's GRISLY, G.

But that's the way people are, know what I mean?

They'll see something like that and just shut the fuck up, right?

Even though they know something's gone wrong cause your dealer's got some dead fucked-up rodent tacked to his wall.

That's why Leo is bullshit.

All that political shit.

Tariq(e) or whatever, like—know what I mean?

Like people are so used to pretending they don't see shit, that even when they do they don't, you know? Feds don't need, like, mind-control drugs and shit, cause bitches do it to themselves like for real.

And now they're driving to who the fuck knows.

Shane with his eyes on every security drone that whizzes by Leo's Caddy.

Leo must have de-bugged the car or else they'd already be dead.

Fucking nano shit, you know, prolly everywhere around them.

Like an invisible cloud that's programmed for one thing, and that one thing is to keep you in your motherfucking place.

Surveillance, yo.

The fucking Panopticon, like legit.

That invisible cloud, like, the fucking soul, the spectre, of power.

He's sounding like Leo right now, and Leo be trippin, but whatever.

Diff is Shane wants to sign up, yo, and Leo wants to check out.

And anyway, bitch showed his true colours with what he's doing to Nina's grandma right now.

Like, does a clone have rights?

Does anyone?

Yo, like fucking trippy, dawg.

Like maybe we're all clones anyway so who cares?

Fucking Dick, know what I mean?

He had shit figured out like a hundred years ago.

Shane checks the safety on his pistol.
Brit and Nina and the boy crying as they drive.
Like, legit, thinks Shane, we're ready to die.

Craig,

I wonder where this is going, and I really wonder what it all means. You're searching for something, and while me and Shane and Nina are running from something, maybe searching and running are like flipside of the same coin kinda deal, you know?

My dad gave me your first book. People think people like us don't read shit. That we're dumb, don't they? Like because dad was a mechanic he was dumb. But we both know that's not true don't we, Craig? Just look at you, and look at your people. The people who maybe read your first book or your second would otherwise think you're like dirt, don't you think? I know that's probably something that energizes you. That like anger or whatever you wanna call it.

Sometimes I close my eyes, and I can see you. You're working your job and you're serving these people at the fancy resto. And most likely these people are treating you like garbage. I guess that's a common enough thing. Dad always talked about that sort of thing, you know? Like, people hating on you, I guess. Because of your job.

There's this dive you like to go to when you get off work at night, and you like to go there alone, but you always run into someone you know, but this one time you were sitting at the bar alone and some baby-boomer guy asked you what you did for a living and you told him you're a waiter and the first thing he said was, You must have higher aspirations than that, and you were just drunk enough to threaten breaking your beer bottle over his head. You don't do that very often because you're not much of a tough guy are you?

But something you love is that these people who can spend the mad bucks to eat at where you work prolly don't read shit, and they def don't know about your work—but then sometimes, someone will recognize you or something. Like maybe they like indy shit. And you'll get this swell of pride up until the point this random person will start talking about you as though you were some kind of weird trinket they found at the antique shop or the like curiosity store or like that boutique-fashion-outlet, one-of-a-kind, special-order number. And then you go back to your anger again.

Listen to me, okay? I want you to know that you're good. And we're good too over here where we are. We really are good, too, despite your misgivings. Okay? At least. I am. I'm like you. And I'm scared. I'm more like you maybe than anyone you've ever met.

Brit

The best thing that could ever happen to you is finding, like, a suitcase of cash in the trunk of a car you just stole.

Ever notice how the universe provides?

Except not for everyone—maybe it's just God's people—like, yo, who do you pray to, dawg?

Shane prays to green, except it's not green because this is the North and our money is bullshit.

Brown, red, green, purple, blue and then, like, a bunch of lame-ass coins.

Like our money is Gay Pride or some shit?

Like rainbows and jingle-bells?

But anyway, this here suitcase is filled to the top with like everlasting bundles of twenties, so at least those motherfuckers are green.

Like evergreen—the Northern forest, G—money—shit'll never die, know what I mean?

They'd pulled into the parking lot of a TexaBucks and popped the trunk just to see, right, like Leo might have a fucking body back there—who knows?—and then like, BAM, when he opened the case he heard the girls' pussies start dripping simultaneously, you know?

Legit—the big-ass Falls are, like, right there up the highway, but it's also right here.

Like Love Canal, know what I mean? Love Canal and the Hooker Company—you can't make this shit up.

Like, serious puddles on the asphalt from the girls.

And then Nina and Brit are dancing around super excited—trucker dudes and fat moms and dads and old people all staring at them—Shane's like, Yo, like fucking chill.

But no Agents, and no drones—just welfare cases and fucking dumb-ass motherfuckers hawking TexaBucks crack-addict coffee shit and working on their English conversational and missing Sri Lanka or wherever, yo, like I'm serious.

The girls are like—Let's stay at the MEGAHILTON!

And Shane's like—Naw, naw, naw. We need to be spooks. Like total ghosts.

So they ended up at a cheap motel, where, on the bed, Nina counted out the money and the kid watched cartoons and Shane and Brit both paced and paced and paced the floor til the sun came up.

There's one hundred grand give or take, but like Shane says, No planes. But how long before Leo's Caddy is on the radar of the pigs?

There's something going on that Shane'll never mention, but Nina's worried as fuck about.

And that's that Shane's dad is bat-shit crazy.

Not just cause he moved to the Island, which is like, fucked up, no—

Here's a picture of Shane's dad with a Royal Wedding Commemorative Plate.

That should say it all.

That princess bitch who died, you know? Fairy tales that get like totally fucked up.

But Nina thought she was hot anyway. Like that 80s hair-style. Like cool, you know—like retro. Like bowl cut, you know? Munching some royal pussy—MINT. But Nina'd be like, Yo, Di, you gotta shave that shit, yo, know what I mean? Like fucking pube Amazon. Like 1983 or whatever.

And the way Shane talks about that princess bitch, it's like all mysterious like. Shane thinks she was murdered because her bloodline went back to like the Egyptians or whatever, and those guys were like half-lizard people or some shit like that.

But yeah, Shane's dad is seriously fucked, man.

Here's another one of Shane's dad with his prized Royal Daulton Queen Mother Statuette.

Shane's like—Yo, don't make fun. It's cause he believes in the royal family, right? He's from Cornwall, you know. That monarchy shit—he loves it.

Also, Nina's like one quarter Arab, so she's pretty sure Shane's dad is like, Shane, your girlfriend's a terrorist. Even though her family back in Beirut had to bail cause of the war, right? Like 1983, motherfucker.

And Nina's kid sister down south was in a protest organized by Tariq(e), so there's that too.

Like, trouble, you know?

Like, what would Sissy call it? Familial tensions or whatever.
Intergenerational conflict.
But really, Nina has no idea how fucked Shane's dad is.

Shane's at the table in the motel room when it occurs to him. Making ham and cheese sandwiches for everyone, the loaf of white bread at his elbow. Heard of those scientists, G? Like, time travel?

Shit's fucked—like, the multiverse, yo.

He remembers one time back at the crib, the Orton Park bus pulling up down there on the corner—he pulled a bag of bread from a cupboard and saw that something had eaten a hole from one end straight through to the other. Like a mouse or whatever—or a giant-ass cockroach.

Verse—his poetry, yo—will that shit survive a nuclear holocaust? Like forever?

So like how can this infinite thing be expanding, he'd like to know—that's how fucked the universe is.

But anyway, that tunnel eaten through the bread was how those scientists talked about space-time, right? Like you could meet another you in some alternate reality or whatever except maybe it'd be you from the past or the future or maybe you were dead in that one, who knows?

So yeah—it's like this—bread, mayo, cheese, ham, bread—it's simple as shit but not because there's this universe and then the one right next door, right—and that mouse motherfucker back in T Dot was, or like is, or like will be, a fucking CHRONONAUT if you know what I mean. Cute little mouse space suit except it's more like time suit or whatever. Like that's a Lockheed/Disney co-pro blockbuster yo for sure—with TexaBucks fucking fill ups and coffee and ammo thrown in or some shit for good measure—like travel, G—that's dope, and that's what I'm thinking about right now watching the girls sleep and the kid, Carter, is like glued to the TV screen and, based on the way he crams that sandwich into his mouth, like starved—just like his mother.

Brit thinks about how sad it must be to live in a trailer park.

Your mom a hot MILF banging the guy who bullied you in high school.

There was one thing, one possession, she knew she couldn't leave behind when they split the apartment, and it wasn't the Shit Journal, it wasn't her Hitachi, her fun wand, her pipe—it was the print-out copy of the script from *8 Mile*—dogeared, crumpled, a patina of stains on the pages whose provenance she couldn't guess (Tommy, Shane, Nina, Dad, Craig?)—here she is, now, in the bathroom of the motel room, clutching it to her breast, only seven of her fake nails still intact—seven red berets, seven gunshot wounds—and the missing ones—a pinkie, a thumb, an index finger—were those her, Shane, and Nina?

In the next room, the boy with cartoons on bust—BLAM BLAM BLAM goes a gun on the television.

Eminem went west to escape, and they are going east.

The 7-0-9 is a shithole. Like everywhere else.

I'm nothing: not even lame enough to be a real poet like Shane. Like I'm nothing compared to Shane.

A wet red hole is what I am.

She brings her painted mouth down to the cover page and kisses it.

A red wet hole and when I die they'll take my body and bronze my pussy.

I'm through—like done. Like legit, man. Like this—we're going into the very dark heart—the jungle, the past, the deep south on a raft, except not—except a heart made of bullshit—7-0-9, the Rock, the Nova—like the end, fuckers—the end.

Cornwall—where Shane's dad's from.

And the Rock, where they're going.

Here's Nina and Brit checking out the road map of the North North American Zone.

Brit thinking she should see her dad, but maybe not.

She'd be like, Good bye, and he'd be like, I'm going to save you.

And at the edge of the map—nothing.

A white border.

Lines that mean highways and roads and rivers and tributaries which are really all just veins and arteries or whatever. And marked between borders of the provinces, those checkpoints where they, like, scan your eyes with a laser and can read every email and text you ever wrote.

That time Brit got the clap—blood making the toilet water pink—it's there for any motherfucker to read on a screen somewhere, you know?

How to get through? That's what the girls are wondering, and also: beyond the white edge of the map there's those other shitty provinces and then the real end of the road.

Shane's like, Don't worry, you'll love it. Nothing ever happens there. It's, like, chill.

But the girls ain't buying it.

Brit slides her hand under the map and up Nina's thigh as Shane speaks.

It's like pre-modern, yo, Shane says. It's like the Dark Ages, or like pirate days, right?

It's like real. That's why Dad loves it. And it's as close to home as you can get.

It's like the past, Shane says. Like time travel.

He holds up the loaf of bread in its plastic bag as if to prove something.

His eyes so hot just then, the girls not listening.

Nina's sister would say: What you're doing is disrupting hetero-normative relationships.

And Nina would say: That's bullshit.

Nina's sister: a Gender Studies major with a minor in Poli Sci.

Brit sucks two fingers and pushes them in.

Nina's pelvis rising off the mattress.

After the orgasm comes, she sees the shadows in the room darkened in its bright motherfucking aftermath—like, the best.

Tsar Bomba—3800 Hiroshimas.

But that was long ago.

And these days, Shane says, they've got something called the Twinkie that makes the Tsar Bomba look like a baby fart.

Shane says, Listen, Michael Jackson ain't dead.

After the Pepsi commercial they chipped that mother-fucker and pimped his brain.

Likewise, you don't know shit about Hitler.

Hitler died of old age in 1986 in Brazil.

You don't like what I'm saying to you but it's only cause you're ignorant of the facts. Or what later became the facts.

Watch Tariq(e)'s speech from the bomb crater down south, or the CEO's State of the Union.

Everybody's chipped, G.

One word for you—CLONE LAB.

Reptiles, yo. They chip you, they pimp your brain, and if you don't do what you're told, you're dead meat. Like meat on a hook. Like Whitney Houston dead—her and her whole family one-two-three.

Or what's worse is the theatre down in the basement of CLONE LAB where they've got you strapped in and rich people watch dude cut strips off and eat you and they applaud and shit like that.

Some of them can't even eat, like, real food anymore cause they've got an addiction to human flesh and that's it.

Celebrities—show me one who hasn't been gaped by a Green-lighter, and I will show you a clone cause clones don't have sex organs.

You ever seen *Hostel*? That's basically the whole story.

Straight up—if you're righteous you know what I'm say-ing and you watch for the signs and even those closest to you—like the way Nina and Brit are with me and vice versa—even then you gotta watch and listen close because even Eminem was took. There's this photo of him and, like, how'd his hairline change so much so quick?

And then Proof was shot outside that club in Detroit and

Slim Shady is like Elvis Presley and who did Elvis give up to those motherfuckers for his career?

His twin brother that died at birth, G.

Because this cult shit goes deeper than language or even consciousness, so how do you guard against that?

And they chipped MJ and cloned him and then they bleached the clone's skin and if you look at his nose you see it's basically like a robot's nose.

The cult. The House of the New Swamp. The government. Your mayor, your fucking representative.

And like Tariq(e), yo—totally in on it all—holding hands with the CEO all the way to the gates of Hell.

Like it's right in front of your face, and you can't see it.

It's the eyes, yo. It's always something about the eyes is how you know—like before they were elected, the CEO's eyes were, like, more human than they are now. And that's another way they get you is they make you do sex torture with another man and Tupac is the same thing too and like Tupac is my boy but it's too bad because it's a proven fact he was in on it so it's the worst thing but also the best thing to be on the run right now because it means they haven't took us yet and I know for sure they haven't gotten any of us except maybe the boy, who may have been chipped and pimped and cloned and planted there at Nina's grandma's, because one thing about those fucking reptiles, yo, those bitches have got long-term plans for all of us and whatever the Ktulu shit is they're planning has got fuck all to do with me so like I said listen up and hear me because none of us are gonna get tooken on this trip and once we get to the 7-0-9 and the old house and Dad we'll be safe as houses like Dad likes to say, so fuck you and open your damn eyes to the truth.

Leo's Cadillac goes through the guardrail beside the road and rumbles through the underbrush, the sound of the limbs of the trees like claws on the paint and the chrome.

Night—plum-coloured air and Nina can't believe how loud it is, the trunk popping open and the tail lights of the car like the eyes of the devil—like the YouTube vid of that interview with Nicki Minaj that Shane made her watch.

In the vid it's some lame affect—like Photoshop or whatever—but this is real, like so real she sees the glow from those eyes on the faces of her boy and on Shane and Brit's faces as the Caddy plummets over a ridge and then there's this boom and crunch and a weird silence once the car is stopped and she sees its headlights shine again for a moment in the distance and then it's gone.

And there's something about that instant—the white light from the car on the trunks of the trees off down the distance—like a camera flash or an epiphany, that makes Nina, like, scared shitless for some reason.

Like, how the truth fucks up your shit, and you don't wanna see it.

She thinks she'd follow Shane anywhere, do anything for him, but maybe there ain't any cult after them and the world is just basically a giant shithole with people killing each other all the time either slowly, like starvation style, or with drone strikes or sarin gas or whatever and there's no plan or web to it other than just killing to grow your bank roll.

But there's also now this soft hissing sound, and Brit's like, It's the tires spinning in the air, and Nina realizes how quiet it is until a transport truck comes hurtling out of the night around the near corner, the four of them gripped briefly in the shock and roar of its engine, and Nina thinks, Like, hey, the truth's just like that too, you know? Sudden as fuck.

Like, whatever—like Shane saying to them back at the motel—This shit ain't safe no more, and so now, here they are ditching that sucker in the woods, a shiver going through Nina as Carter, eyes big and glossy, takes hold of her hand and likewise. The next day at that truck-stop restaurant in the next town, Carter's hands are small and pink mashing French fries in his mouth and they all feel hunted, the suitcase of cash under the table.

Shane outside at the, like, only payphone left on the face of the earth—calling home—slamming the receiver into its holder until the damn thing snaps off and the end you listen to dangles from its wire and every patron stares at him as he comes back in.

Chill, Shakey, she says.

He's bitten his nails down to nothing.

Under his eyes it's blue and grey like the bottom of an ash-tray or some shit.

Shane drums his fingers on the table top. Slams his open palm down and the cups and saucers rattle in their places.

Take off your panties, he tells her and Brit later.

He paid the motel clerk in cash taken straight out of the suitcase.

But it's clear he don't wanna fuck. He doesn't even watch them kiss. Like Shane's tripped out as fuck.

And the worst thing is he gets right down there on his hands and knees and has, like, a real long look at them—Brit, like, giggling, like, What the fuck, Shane—and he's just like, made of stone, man, like, for real Shane's maybe lost it.

But then later, the boy asleep on the floor, Shane staring at the television with the sound turned low, and Brit's clit in her mouth—Nina's, like, happy, man.

In Brit's dreams there's a claw that reaches out from under her. There's nothing—just blackness all around, and she's sitting on a stool in one of those schoolgirl skirts Shane likes, you know?—the tartan or whatever—her breath echoing like, the reverb is crazy, yo. And then there's this three-fingered claw, like it's the branch of a tree or some shit like reaching out from between her legs, like, she feels her puss open to accommodate its girth, and in the palm of the claw—those long scaly fingers coming up to form a kind of cage—it's her, Shane, and Nina holding each other.

Morning—where are they now?

She doesn't know much but she does know that on the Island they have these giant-ass icebergs—Shane talks about it all the time—chunks of glacial ice that break off and drift all the way down south—like total freedom, right? Like just totally independent? Like until the sun fucks them up and they melt into the ocean?

Anyway, that's them. That's her and Nina and Shane and the boy. Except, like, a family? And then maybe that claw comes up right from the bottom of the sea? And captures them?

And drags them down into where there's no light, and given the choice, she'd rather die from fire than ice and darkness, right?

Corvus—like written in the very sky above their heads.

The car they've got now has a moonroof and Nina's looking up. There's no smog out here in the countryside, just a bunch of trees and rocks and shit and the stars are up there looking down.

Sometimes, the car just ripping along the backroads, you can't tell a satellite from some heavenly body, know what I mean? Like, legit—there's the old light of the universe and the new light of the modern world competing for your attention—and Corvus is the giant raven holding an eye in its beak and the eye is either the eye of the devil or the eye of someone who's always watching you on a bank of monitors in a room underneath a Catholic church, like in Chicago or some shit, and they're about to serve up skewers of baked shit and goblets of urine and virgin blood and whatnot—the carnival of beastiality about to begin, know what I mean?

She doesn't like to think this way because it reminds her of Shane.

Shit's like a virus, yo.

Like herpes, or some shit, and once it's in you, it's in you like—no cure.

And Shane says like, You gotta prove to them you'll do anything for them.

You might have to fuck a donkey or a goat or something.

Like gangbang a bunch of ancient motherfuckers.

Like fucking Egyptians or whatever, you know?

And like their dicks are shaped like pyramids.

And that's how they get you, right?

Shane ain't saying where they're going.

It's a gravel road and the mud puddles are reflecting the night sky, Nina studied them when they stopped to let her out to piss, but otherwise everything's dark as shit.

They got the car from a farmer for far too much.

Shane saying, But you gotta be able to trust a farmer. They're like, of the ground, you know? Like check his finger-nails. You know some old dude with dirt under his nails you can trust him straight up.

Unless he's a grave robber, said Brit. Or a murderer.

But farmer dude wouldn't take cash, insisting on a trade while eyeing the two girls and Shane thought about just shoot-ing him dead right there in the parking lot of the truck stop or whatever, you know?

In the grim grey light that afternoon, Nina noticed a kind of low-frequency panic in the air. The coolers in the gas station nearly empty of water and juice, the shelves, like, totally ransacked. A rat-faced manager so fat she was busting out of her cashier smock darted her eyes around the place non-stop. Her eyes like a couple of black birds, man, seriously. A couple of sparrows. Everywhere at once.

Like pre-major-storm tension in the air, you know?

A man hustling his toddlers into the cab of his pick-up, some teenage girl in the flatbed with a rifle over her shoulder.

Carter waved to her. The girl pushed up the brim of her camouflage ball-cap and just looked at him.

Like the levee's breaking or some shit, that's what Nina thought.

She leaned into Brit and whispered: Like, something's up here. Something's going on.

They drive through the night, Shane saying it's safer but Nina don't believe for a second that whoever's after them don't need like light or whatever to see shit. I mean, they've got drones the size of a thumb tack with night-vision and infrared and fucking x-ray for all she knows—but Shane insisted, and now, the sun barely coming up, Shane pulls off the dirt road they're on and into a little clearing where they get out and stretch.

Her boy does his pee in the bushes, she watches him.

Doesn't matter what Shane says, the cult ain't, like, laying a finger on them.

And now the sun, which is not the sun, but something else—Nina's eyes on the horizon—she's thinking about a nuclear holocaust, new beginnings, and like that ESP shit begins to buzz in her brain again—it's coming up and the bloody red glow is on her face.

Shane, where are we going?

It's cool, he says, I gotta plan.

Brit is scratching in her notebook, sitting on the hood of the car.

The sky slowly becomes blue and gold, Nina thinks of the royal family, Shane's dad.

Feel like letting me in on it?

Men and their plans, like, whatever—all those plans. Leo would always say the same shit, up until he got bit and they put him away.

It's cool, Shane says.

He flicks his cigarette into the ditch, and for the first time in her life, she sees his elaborate posturing. Like that mysterious brooding shit, even now, in the middle of the most serious trouble, like, ever.

She goes over to Brit and puts her arms around her, watches her son stab something near the ground with a stick.

Ever since Brit cáme along, there's been something bothering Shane, and what's bothering Shane is that she has a butterfly tattoo above her right ankle.

He should have seen trouble right away. Something that fucked up and you may as well have like a goat man on there, know what I mean?

It's like this—a butterfly is like the ultimate symbol of Satan, and even back then when she first appeared in their lives—even with his dick deep into Brit with Nina spread eagle on the bed in front of her—Brit just like totally slurping away like that—like, seriously hot or whatever—a dog with fucking peanut butter—Shane would look down at that butterfly on Brit's leg and wonder.

To make things even worse, anyone who's righteous knows that a butterfly is THE symbol for an international child pornography ring.

Like, where did Brit even come from anyway?

Yeah, no shit—transformation—but from what, into what?

Like what *they* want you to become, that's what.

He's in the backseat, pretending to sleep, trying to hear what the girls are talking about as Nina drives the car. The potholes huge in the dirt road. Otherwise, just, like, blackness, G. An abyss outside the car window.

Shane wants to know this: can you trust any fucking bitch or any motherfucker in the world?

Cause check it—only paranoid motherfuckers like me will survive this shit, for real.

But can you escape?

Naw, dawg, naw.

Just run is all you can do.

Just run for the rest of your life.

Dear Craig,

So one morning you woke up at your mom's house, and you had had one of your bad dreams, hadn't you? I remember that morning somehow, like, it's weird, baby, the way you and I are connected, you know? And something happened in the dream that had to do with your old life—the one you had when you started writing about me and Nina and Shane—the life that doesn't exist anymore, or at least only exists in the past, right? But anyway, you were sad, weren't you?

Just another sad forty year old who had finally acquired the legitimate drinking problem you'd only pretended to have before.

In fact, that line I just wrote is a line you'd just written that morning for your next book, wasn't it?

The book you began writing in Berlin almost accidently one night in that little apartment you and your wife had rented— but she wasn't really your wife—that's just what you called her at the time and you guys split up before going through with it anyway.

And it wasn't very late in the day, but you'd already opened the flask of rye and you poured up a drink and stood for a while looking at the drain in the sink—how something about the shape of the drain reminded you of the shape of a flower—like a daffodil or something—but it also reminded you of pretty unimaginative things like an eye or a mouth or some shit like that—and also like a sun painted black, or like a black hole— which is what the drain is, if you know what I mean.

You stood there for a long time. You were thinking about your best friend's dad who had died the year before—you'd go see him in the hospital and play crib with him and you pinned a photo of your daughter on the corkboard next to his bed so he could see it whenever he wanted.

When you were a kid, like a little older than me, your friend's dad nicknamed you Scoobie Doo, remember that? He called you Scoobie Doo, but really he was referring to Shaggy, because you kinda looked like Shaggy when you were that age—all skinny and scruffy—but he didn't call you Shaggy— you were Scooby Doo.

And as you were standing there at the sink, looking at the drain, you remembered one of the last times you saw him—he was getting worse, and couldn't even play crib with anyone anymore—he was looking at you and saying, Life is a struggle, Scoobie. Life is just a struggle.

Given where I am right now, I can't say he was totally wrong, can you?

And then you thought some other bad things about when you were a kid and shit like that, like bad things that happened to you and some other bad things you did to people and I guess you'd pretty much gone to the dark place, hadn't you?

You were full on in the dark place that morning.

But then you went outside onto your mom's balcony that looks out onto the cemetery. And you turned around—you were looking for a light—and over on the neighbour's balcony was the neighbour, Suze—and she was holding her little newborn granddaughter in her arms in the sunshine and Suze is like smiling at you and she says to you just then, Oh, I loves er so much—and you're smiling back at Suze and it's a beautiful day today and you don't say anything back—and you find your lighter and sit down and put a cigarette in your mouth and you're like, Man, I'm dumb because what just happened is so cliché, but it's better than death I guess.

And baby, your friend's dad was right, okay?
But you were right too.

I love you, C.
I'm yours and you're mine, okay?

Love
Brit

At first he thought Brit was just a one-time thing. Then he saw how close her and Nina were. Like, how they looked at each other sometimes. It bugged him. Like women were basically evil. All you had to do was read the Bible for that shit. All that blood and all the spinning of the universe, right? Like, the full moon and the rising tide and their cycles lining up and all that synchronicity shit going on. Now how does a uterus know anything about time?

His dad always told him—Never trust em. Ha ha, like if it bleeds for three days and doesn't die blah blah—and his dad would laugh.

According to Dad, women were either like totally beastly or like angels, but you never knew which at any given moment. And there were evil angels too, so there was that problem, know what I mean?

And you know what else? Butterflies taste things through their feet so, like, what could be more fucked up and satanic than that?

If Brit's name was Lucy, as in Lucifer, then that would be a big-ass clue as to what was going on, but Shane didn't think for a second that Satan would be so obvious and dumb as that.

No writing, no peace—that's his problem—weeks since he'd spit mad ryhmes or checked himself in a mirror.

Guess that's why he's so paranoid and pissed off.

But not really.

Really, he's not an artist.

Really, he's just another rich boy with a mental illness and a drug problem, but whatevs.

He feels for the gat beside him on the car seat. The cool shape of the barrel reminding him of the tubing in his dad's workshop. All those skin jobs, like, frozen in time. Dead bodies, bullet holes, fangs and talons—bullets. Like, straight-up bullets.

What was it he loved so much about that taxidermy shit?

Shane looks at the two women in the front seats.

He hasn't the slightest idea what they talk about.

He thinks of the fucked-up Pine Marten in the trunk of the car.

Wrapped in cheesecloth and tinfoil as his father instructed.

He imagines that Pine Marten and wonders if there's enough light in the trunk for its one black eye to gleam, cause that's how he pictures it.

He glances down at the pistol next to him, sees Nina's sleeping boy in dim light.

One thing he's sure of—he'll do like anything, yo.

Anything to save the world.

Like, whatever it takes.

Nina says, I'm scared, and Brit says, Me too.

I don't even know, like, what's happening or where we're going.

It's bullshit, but maybe not, right?

Like, this isn't good for the kid.

I think he's crazy. Sorry, but I do.

I know. Look—in a way it's good this happened. We couldn't have gone on like we were.

I didn't like the apartment anymore. Except you. You were a good thing about it, but it got, like, weird, right? And anyway, you're, like, my sister?

For sure.

Like what's at the end of this road? Like living with Shane's dad? Forever?

It's security. I guess.

I guess, but it still makes no fucking sense to me.

But there's something true about it, you know, says Brit. Like, there's some kind of truth to what he's saying. I can feel it. And anyway, whatever happened to Shane's mom? Is she like dead or whatever?

It's like when I knew I was first pregnant. There weren't any signs, I just knew. I don't know if anyone's even after us, but it feels right when Shane talks about the system and how it works against you.

I'd like to have a baby someday, but I'm scared.

It's like there's a monster inside you. Like there's this hungry little ball of flesh in your guts.

Nina's like, Look, it's been two weeks since we bailed on the apartment, and this whole time it feels like we've been driving in circles.

We got to the border security between Upper and Lower Canada yesterday, but before that Shane had to go over the car for bugs or whatever and we were all basically scared shitless. Shit's meant to explode when you find it unless you got the right gear. Except Shane wasn't scared, of course, Shane was like, Just be cool, see, be cool.

Like, whatever, man. That shit is getting old, fast.

And so there we were in the fucking line-up of cars at like three o'clock in the afternoon.

Shane had been like, Yo, let's go like super late at night, know what I mean? Less heat.

And I said, What? Why? They got you, they got you—same difference. Doesn't matter what time.

And Brit was like, It's way more suspicious to go late. Whatever they want you for, they'll think you'll try at night, like, ninja-style, I guess.

And so we settled on the daytime, and anyway the fucking cops don't make a peep at us. We just pull up and I say to the officer or Agent or whatever like, Yo, we're taking my boy on a road trip like a vacation or whatever and he just waves us through like it's nothing.

So I guess we're having doubts about this whole thing, but it reminds me of back in the day, know what I'm saying? Like, we're total refugees yo. Like my grammy and poppy were when the rockets started falling and the embargo and the sea lanes were cut off, right? And basically Beirut was, like, a moon crater or whatever, you know? And then there was Palestine.

So now we're through the border and back on the road.

What I want to know is how does a single motherfucker in this world keep going? Like legit, man—you see this soil?—like I'm talking about right now roadside we're just cruising along through rural Lower Canada and my eyes keep drifting over to the ditch and all that wilderness and I keep thinking about the soil, you know? Like, there's a million Indians and Frenchies they murdered out there in that wilderness—you ever wonder how the soil has so much life in it? It's cause of death, yo, like for really real—your eye falls on something, like some beautiful thing—like the hills and the trees or whatever—like some really cool shit—like a meteor shower or like city lights from a distance, you know?—and your heart swells up cause what you're seeing is not some cool shit, but like aftermath, know what I mean?—you're seeing death and you're also seeing like everything—like the earth's bounty or whatever— at the same fucking time.

That's what I think about, driving like this. Like somewhere far off to the west I'll see this town or some shit, but what I'm seeing isn't the town, what I'm seeing is like the bones of the people upon which cities are built, you know? But it's still, like, beautiful, you know? You have this total annihilation that essentially happened yesterday—and then you have like today, and like people walking around—like going to the mall or whatever, like running from the NWO like we are or some shit, like whatever or whatever—doing whatever it is they do—and all this beauty is built on like total fucking murder, right? And like that's us, know what I mean?

And the absolute worst thing is that, like, back at that motel, back there before we bought this car from that farmer dude, I fucking lost that really expensive lipstick I got. That black lipstick that cost like forty bucks or whatever and I'm not kidding when I tell you, I wept more for that little plastic tube than when Carter was first taken away from me—cause, after all, when Services came, I was like: THIS BITCH IS FINALLY FREE FROM THE BURDEN—like know what I mean—like to be totally honest with you that's what I thought—like give me some time to rediscover the miraculous beauty of who I am or whatever, you know?

And so when I look at my kid, I see the beauty and all that possibility, right? But I also see all the fucking murder and misery planted like a fucking seed or a fucking cocoon or whatever—like a motherfucking nest of spider eggs—like, like, it's fucking genetics, man—no joke—right there in that little guy—I mean, Carter, my kid—all the hurt and murder and love and beauty or whatever of the world—that's him right now asleep with his head on Shane's shoulder like, totally asleep and the one light in this world is the light of this car moving through the darkness and the one keeping this light alive is me right now with my foot on the pedal right to the floor and Brit beside me with her eyes big as a fucking couple nuclear explosions staring out that windshield cause we're stoned as shit on Shane's pills and like totally feeling the vibe right now.

Man, remember when that sucker MC, Hot Shit, ran for election in T Dot?

Fucker's election signs were everywhere—and the album he released back before he announced, like, all in Liberal red and white? Like, they call that foreshadowing, motherfucker.

Same time, the CEO is like killing the primaries down south, right? Just like, totally trouncing Bush Junior and the Clinton tradition, who had also put out that lame-ass album—the one with like the Appalachian coal-miner chorus shit with the Euro beats? Remember? Cause the CEO was like third party? And the Bush album was all spoken word—like Biblical shit?

And the people saw right through that shit—like for real, that's why the CEO won—you can put out any kinda album you want saying you identify with shit, but hitting the right notes don't mean a damn thing if they know you're just branding, right?

Like what do a few billionaire families know about working in a coal mine, or God, or some shit like that, when everyone knows based on hard fact they'll just sell you out before the oath on inauguration day is done.

So that's how *The Unifying Theory* came together—that's my album—but it ain't finished yet. You have to experience shit to write, know what I mean?

Like, what options does anyone have anyway, you know? Like, fucking robots bag your groceries and a drone the size of a beer can delivers your mail. Politician, Agent or rapper basically is all you got, G, for real, and there's no way Skeet Love is gonna taste the devil's dick so you can forget that shit like yesterday.

Robots and bombs seriously—what's fucked is that the government wants these things destroyed cause that way they have to buy more, know what I mean? Blood keeps this whole world rolling, but it ain't for the people—ain't no jobs or shit like that coming—ain't no jobs period, bitch—except to be a rapper like seriously—a dog's only job is to bark.

So like, there's no diff between my world and yours like—yours—like know what I mean?—so the best thing for me and my family, like Nina and Brit and Carter, is like straight-up murder or whatever—like the best book of poetry ain't like Eminem or whatever—the best book of poetry in the world is like not written yet, but basically it's like me saying how I'm gonna fucking murder you—like death threats, yo, like the best poetry this bitch ever read or could sometime in the future, like, write—so like fuck you or whatever, did I stutter?

Somewhere in the countryside they park the car. Shane checks the map. The last few days he's gotten skinnier. The thin bones at his wrists protrude. Watching him, Brit is reminded of something mechanical—thin pistons working under a skin of rubber. In the dim dome light, he scans the paper. In some distant town, behind the crest of a hill, beyond the reach of their vision, the sounds of fighting. An explosion they feel more than hear. The tree line backlit by a quick burst of light.

The night above their heads filled with stars and satellites— a glossy ultrasound printout of the womb.

Brit is going to bleed, and soon, Nina will too. That's how they call it—not *their periods* or whatever other euphemism someone came up with. It started months ago, back at the apartment, Nina saying—Fuck, man, this bitch is gonna bleed heavy—her hand on her abdomen, and Brit suddenly felt the very same way.

With the GPS and the radio cut, there's no way of knowing what's happened, Shane saying at the time, If the world's gone to shit, it's still better than being found—it's better than being dead.

They pull back onto the road, the gravel beneath the tires whispering to them.

The ocean, Shane says, it's freedom, know what I mean? And that's where we gotta get.

There's no observable evidence of the chase, but they all feel there is one. In the strange blood dark outside the car, a pulse in the air. A quiver amongst the limbs of the trees that stretch up into the sky. Looking out her window, Brit sees the dark veins, the grave black filaments of branches.

And now Shane takes the car off the back road where they'd been and onto some narrow overgrown gravel path. The branches scratching at the windows and doors. The soft hiss of shrubbery at a fender.

Here in the valley, emerging from the darkness surrounding them—the ramshackle beaten-down frame of a house.

So anyway Brit doesn't like to talk about this shit with anyone. It's because of her dad and like, yeah, he's a mechanic or whatever, but like ever since she was a little girl—I mean like ten years ago, man—her dad made her study some weird shit, and before she dropped out and took off—au revoir or whatever to the corner-store wine and smoking at the Catholic school playground in Grade 6—like back in the day—like I'm sorry?—but, it's, like, chess? Or whatever? Like? Chess? You know?

Back when she was a little girl—her and her friends were cheerleaders in the Santa Claus parade—her Dad saying what the fuck's up with my daughter in a super-short CFM elf dress—and Brit being like, DAD YOU ARE SO GROSS!—but it was true—that whole sexualized-child thing—obviously by now, given her previous employment, Brit knows what the sick fuckers want—but anyway, chess!

That game with the knights and the queen and the king and like black and white and good and evil?

When the CEO came to power, he put all chess players under surveillance, so it's super down low, okay?—And anyway, Brit wants you to know she's never even seen a queen's gambit so fuck off and I never wanna talk about that shit ever again alright?

Chess—like checkers for professors, that's what Dad called it, you know?

Like, he'd say, It's space and time except not random enough?

But nobody knows this shit, and know what?—neither do you, you fucking narc.

Something that she loved about it, and that she loves remembering, is the black half-moons under her dad's nails as he taught her the moves.

For a long time it was just Brit, her dad, and her grand-mother—Nanny! Brit would scream from her crib—and Brit knew the alphabet and her shapes and could count to twenty before she was two—her Nanny would say, We've got a bright one on our hands—so how did that go so wrong Brit would like to know?—and anyway, Dad would only say about Mom that he hoped she was doing better so that was kinda like, Brit's entire family history right there.

The black half-moons—her dad's hands—that smell of the garage, like the gasoline and the grease, like where he works, you know what I mean, would be on his hard hands, and car exhaust and some kind of chemical smell clinging to his beard? Like, Brit can hardly even handle the gas station when they stop to fill up.

And even worse, once in some small town, while Shane was filling the tank, she saw some dude in the side-view—she saw some like skinny dude come out with a Coke cradled in the crook of his arm, and like he was like Shane's age but he had a beard like Dad and was in these blue coveralls smeared in grease and was wiping his hands in a rag? And she almost died? Thinking of her dad! Like, waah!

Like, pauvre-bebe-paurvre-sange-mon-petite-sange-little-ape-girl-I-miss-you-Dad-forever-heart-exploding? Like, you know what I mean by that?

But anyway: the queen—like, the most beautiful and elegant and graceful and just like murderous thing in the world. The slender neck of a swan, right? Like deadly, man, seriously.

What's that sword called? The one where the handle's just like a brocade of jewels or whatever? Like pirates or some shit stab each other with them, or like fairy-tale princely dudes will cut the buckles of your corset with the tip and then your like totally perfect titties are out and he can't control himself and shoves his face right into your cleavage?

Anyway she's like that, the queen is.

A total rapier.

Like, a rapier, that's the word.

And all those other dumb-man pieces. The knight, the bishop, the rook—like just bumbling around the stage all day? Like can you imagine?

Once she showed Shane the little travel board she'd taken from home when she ran away—and he was like, Yo, like I'm the king! And she was like, Shane, he's the dumbest-ass piece in the whole game like—he's just this helpless sack of shit.

And Shane just shut his mouth like a trap.

But of all the pieces, she felt worst for the pawns.

They drop like flies, and if they could only make it to the other side, then they become whatever they want—they were her second fave—but what pawn would wanna be a king?

She wanted them to live and grow, you know?

Like, transformation or whatever?

And her dad would say shit about, like, the best games and the best players and shit like that, right? How they were all crazy and shit?

And his favourite player was this Russian dude named Tal, but Brit always called him Tall or whatever but he was actually Latvian and actually like sickly and frail and not tall at all. And Dad always said the thing about him was that he'd just do the craziest shit on the board—like sacrifices, right?—a rook here, and a knight there, sometimes a queen, and it would always or at least mostly work out for him.

But now, because of computers, they know that his mind was faulty, right?

He was a genius but his logic was flawed.

But the way he was and the way he played, it freaked out

and fucked up the people he played and they'd just succumb to the insanity, right? They'd resign—and Brit liked that—like, they were resigned to the way things turned out or whatever.

The vortex, right—like maybe how we are with Shane right now, but whatever—insanity, right—like a black hole or some shit like that.

And when Tal was dying he up and jumped out the window of the hospital to play some grandmaster dude who had come to town to visit before he croaked or whatever?

But the main thing was that Tal wasn't afraid to take chances.

And that's what her dad said to her.

Take chances.

And that's how she ended up leaving home.

Just like Tal did—up and out the window one night, leaving a note for Daddy saying like, DON'T DO NOT DON'T WORRYYYYYY DADDEEEEEEEEEEEE BISOUX BIS BIS BISOUX BRITNEY, only now maybe she'll die some fucking shitty death, you know?

Like Tal did in some hospital bed but maybe worse.

Like maybe a gang of dudes will take turns fucking her ass with the end of a hammer and then club her to death with it?

And Dad will probably blame himself for the rest of his life?

She knocked around her neighbourhood for a few weeks—like so many parties, so many boys, so many girls.

If there's one image she remembers most she really couldn't remember but she thinks it might be like cigarette burns in the carpet or the tiles in the bathroom of one of the houses she partied at?

But anyway, she followed Tommy the tattoo guy to T Dot or whatever.

For something to be at, Shane would have said in that fake accent he sometimes busts out.

She'd written her dad a postcard saying: I'M ALIVE.

The Lockheed-TexaBucks Tower pointing up into the blue.

Like, almost exactly where that long-ago satellite had plunged from.

Like, that satellite we mentioned, like, way back on page thirteen? That's right, motherfucker, *thirteen*. Coincidence? Think about it.

But anyway she went back home and worked for a while in front of a webcam, and then split that shit once she'd gotten the mods done with the cash she made and the whole time she felt like she was just running running running away from she didn't even know what—and that's life, you know?

But life is also like you're driving a car top speed like they are, and you know there's a cliff up ahead somewhere, and you know you're just gonna go right off that sucker only you don't know when it's gonna happen—only that it will happen. It will totally happen.

But this shit right now is too much, and she's seriously scared maybe for the first time ever. Like ever ever. You know?

And so like, Now what Brit? she asks herself, looking at Shane's sleeping face in the gloom.

Now you're stuck with this world.

Or maybe not.

In the dim woodstove kitchen of this house, wind through the gaps of the boards and still, it must be hours now that they've been listening to the sound of distant drums and booms like bloody war echoing up from the valley nearby where they saw that flash and the rattle of fighting and shouts, and there's that smell in the air like smoke that has nothing to do with the wood that burns and pops so sweetly beside them all. The green smell of the woods around them is tinged with something else like ash or something else even that seriously, man, makes Brit tremble where she lays.

I don't know what it is.

Maybe just this house.

Me and Carter spooning and my God he's so big now.

Like I dunno what—but the men are coming for us.

Hordes of them, know what I'm saying?

I can smell this wet dirt smell and this whole fucking place tilts in the wind and fills with air like a sail or a lung except black like you've smoked for a hundred years.

They smell like that.

And they're like thick, man, like seriously. Thick everywhere, these men. And Shane's gone like a stick on me now and it's almost too much.

They are coming. Like for real they are. And somewhere behind them there's fire burning in the distance.

It's like the mob from Frankenstein or whatever.

Like what kind of monster is that?

Like *what have thou wrought*, know what I mean?

It's like Biblical shit, and it's like creation.

Every parent wonders the same thing.

Like, Carter before he was taken away would sit with his Cheerios in the high-chair and I'd look into his eyes and wonder who and when he'd rape somebody.

Like, not *if*.

She feels Carter's lungs filling with air and emptying again.

Sees in her mind the thin fibrous tissues like roots underground, branches against a night sky.

The stars in their heavens—a network, the dots of Morse code.

Billions of cold eyes.

A constellation of screens through which men in far-off rooms watch their every move, fly drones overhead, plan the weather, the next election.

When the floods began she was just a little girl. Videos showed refugees huddled in rain. Trudging through shit and muck and everything else. Life jackets sent out emblazoned with the logos of Walmart, the Seal of the President of the United States of America.

Perpetual crisis, and if it seemed things were going to let up, someone would just invent something else to worry about. It was a relentless churning inside her. Constant war and worry. Everyone trembling in their tiny rooms in the cities.

After she'd left home, met first Leo, and then Shane, her sister began sending postcards from the Midwest with tourist destinations on one side, and the words I AM AFRAID on the other. Likewise, clippings from newspapers and flyers from supermarkets that all seemed to say the same thing: THE END IS NIGH.

Like,

TAKE-STOCK-OLYPSE FOR THE APOCOLYPSE!!!
THREE HEADED DOG FOUND AT DUMP!!!
CHILDREN BORN WITHOUT BRAINS!!!

That summer: at the party where she fell in love with Shane, they were in Leo's kitchen listening to Biggie Smalls. Shane, shirtless, pointed out the dagger tattoo on his left wrist, complained about the heat, said he loved Arturo Gatti and David Lemieux and Sean O'Sullivan, pounded a can of Wild Cat and, once Leo (as he always did) passed out in his bedroom with the TV on bust, raised an eyebrow at her and said, Sup, Nina? Sayin?

Those raised eyebrows of his—it's his thing.

It happened right there on the kitchen table.

Nina saying to him I'm a freak. I'm nasty. I don't give a shit—knowing it was just what he wanted to hear—while

Carter, face to face with his cartoons on the TV in the living room, hadn't yet even been potty-trained.

Carter had his father's eyes.

Leo's eyes. It was hard to look at them.

All her old fuck buddies—some of them dead; others, she supposed, still out there somewhere—but it was like a different universe than the one she was in now.

Even seeing Leo like she had before they split T Dot, it was like he was someone else. Like, not real, I guess. Like that clone shit Shane talks about—everyone and everything just a copy of someone or something else.

She once got a letter from Sis and in it she wrote that everything was nostalgia. They were moving backward in time.

A demolition thunderclap splits the momentary silence of the house.

The world was mad.

Like, crazy as shit.

You think for one second there aren't like government clones everywhere around us?

Think about it, G—if they done it already for those pleasure clones—like the way Brit is—then you know they've got them everywhere. Like, if some billionaire can afford to get a blowjob from, like, Young Jenna, or like, Mary Pickford II or whatever—from like Emma Goldman or some shit (because in case you don't know, they cater to anyone and there's nothing some proto-fascist motherfucker would like better than to have The Most Dangerous Woman In The World in der Hündchenstellung).

You know the ratio of clones to real people in the world?

My guess? It's 50-50.

Like, hopefully.

In the morning Brit wakes with a gun to her head.

Shane hadn't done that sort of thing in a while.

Maybe it was part of their game, but maybe not.

Sometimes he'd strut around the apartment with the barrel of the pistol in his mouth.

Nina called it his Ernest Hemingway routine.

Then he'd like, lay out rhymes with it in his mouth and her and Nina would laugh and laugh.

It was like *The Sun Also Rises*, told in reverse or some shit.

Or like the Hemingway family tree in rewind or like *The Old Man and the Sea*, know what I mean? Do you though? Because I'm not even sure I know what I mean, but I guess it's just some kinda feeling or whatever, right?

Like death or whatever by your own hand.

Sometimes when they got stoned, Nina would read to her and Shane from those books. Brit often felt those were the best days of her life to have someone read to her like that. He was Nina's favourite writer but Brit always thought it was something Nina didn't really feel and just kinda inherited from the smart one, the sister, down at Penn State or whatever. The one whose words Nina ripped off to lord it over them sometimes.

And Brit was skeptical about that anyway because wasn't Nina's sister some feminist bitch? Like, who wanted to take over the world?

The only food they had in the house back then was an ossified hunk of ginger, and at first, Brit didn't even know what in the hell it was til Nina told her.

Good for your metabolism, she said.

They threw it in a pot of boiling water and Nina read to

them and the whole apartment smelled like ginger. And then they drank the water once it cooled. Brit picking the stringy bits out of her teeth.

Nina's mouth—God she loved it.

Brit watched her mouth as she read.

Like a bow or some shit. A bouquet.

Words, man—how Brit hated and loved them at once.

Like weapons, man.

Until she'd met Shane and Nina, she hadn't really given it much thought.

Shane and Nina used words like the way people used clothes or perfume or make-up or money.

The whole world was beautiful and total poison, and weren't words a big part of it? Like a big big part of it?

But anyway, Brit loved Shane shirtless, like how he was back then.

Shirtless and hairless, a thing they had was the girls would shave every inch of him, just for something to do.

A couple razors, a bar of soap and a hot bath—seems alright to me, Nina would say, and what else is there to do?

Like, I'm not some fucking animal, Shane would say. He had this thing where his nostrils flared all the time. Nina thought his nose was too big at first but then she got used to it.

He'd say, I'm like human. Don't need no pelt. We got clothes don't we? Think we need fur? Not me. I say let's evolve, dawg. Like, seriously.

He looked like a horse, and Brit was kinda in love, I guess, is what she'd say about it.

I'm just playing, Shane says, but his eyes are too hot. She's looking at his index finger on the trigger and wonders.

Things happen, decisions are made and milliseconds don't even really describe the quickness or the eternity, you know?

Like, what's faster? Light or thought? And what's more certain? Gravity or knowing? Don't know, man, couldn't tell you.

Nina and Carter still asleep.

Did she love Shane? Or did she "love" Shane?

Who knows, but she's terrified.

Silence.

Grey light coming through the windows.

The woodstove cold dead.

Through its open mouth, blackened coals and ash.

She rises up, gently pushes the pistol away.

He sticks the gun back in his waistband.

Outside, they're throwing their bags into the trunk. Small black birds dart above their heads.

Total quiet now in the far-off distance where, the night before, explosions made the ground tremble.

On the wind and hanging in the grey air, flakes of ash float heavy, drifting down to the dry grass and in the distance where the hills meet, tendrils of black smoke rise up into the sky.

Nobody says shit except for Carter, who's like, There's a fire over there.

That's right, says Nina. It ain't anywhere close to us.

But it is close, Brit thinks. It's right around the corner.

So listen, this here's an education for you. This here's the Book of Skeet Love, legit—yo, like the moon alright?—like if you believe the moon is just the moon then you're prolly someone who believes in the moon landing, right? You're prolly just that type. Like dumb as shit.

Now listen: the moon ain't real. It ain't a real thing.

Just open your damn eyes.

It's a hologram, G.

There's no like actual hard evidence or scientific proof the thing even exists.

I've done a lot of research on this shit.

It ain't real, I'm telling you.

It's the truth alright?

There's two possibilities—spaceship or hologram. So it might exist okay, fine—but not the way you think it does.

Back in the day, NASA shot fucking rockets at the moon and it boomed like a church bell. Like, it's hollow. But I think the rockets just hit the moon's force-field and that's what made the sound.

This shit's all on tape.

The Internet is like freedom, know what I mean? And because of this I know Kubrick faked the moon landing and he also shot *Star Wars* and I know the moon ain't real.

And the moon needs a force-field because what the moon really is is a fucking reptilian eye looking through some quantum periscope.

That's my theory.

First off, it's too big. The moon is too big for our planet. The moon is fucking bigger than, like, a couple other planets in our solar system, so what's up with that?

Second, we've never been in space.

Third, when you look at it, when the moon's full, it looks just like a snake's eye.

It's like the CEO during the State of the Union address. Motherfucker's right eye is just like the moon. Just watch the vid, G, seriously what's wrong with you?

And now shit's blowing up all over.

Like what's over those hills?

Is this the end that's been foretold?

Yo, smoke, motherfucker. Smoke and ash everywhere.

First time it's a flood, and second it's fire.

Like a fucking supernova, that's what's up.

Book of Revelations, Necronomicon, the Annunaki Chronicles.

My whole damn life I always listened to Dad, and for what?

He'd say shit like, We've got the fire inside of us, or whatever. And like, what does that even mean anyway?

He'd say like, Society needs a good purge—like purification or whatever. Like purification by flame, like what you do with souls or steel or cocaine, know what I mean?

You look around at this world and it's all under someone else's control. And you think your own mind is yours but it's not. You've got like a thousand years' hereditary abuse to deal with. You've got the structure of society. You've got an army of clones watching every move you make and a billionaire class keeping you indebted—like, you can feel the hounds at your heels, know what I mean?

And then, the whole thing ends anyway—a nuke or whatever, a plague—either way it's like death or whatever that gets you and maybe in the afterlife it's the same shit, you know? Like God or whatever just keeping his eye on you like non-stop.

But I don't even believe that shit anyway—the afterlife is for losers.

What's the point in trading one master for another is what I wanna know.

Like, Dad don't believe in God, but he believes in the Royal Family so what's the diff?

Don't believe in God, but believes in the Invisible Hand.

And here we are in this car, G. The girls don't know what I had to trade for it and this bitch is like a vault, know what I mean? Like Vault 7 right? Shit goes in—it don't come out. Except sometimes it does. There's a crack in everything—and that's how the shit gets in.

We pull up to the border crossing, the one into The Drive Through Province right? And we know shit's gotten totally real, because the place is a fucking ghost town. Ain't no one there. Like, not one guard.

And Nina's like, WHAT. THE. FUCK.

And the worst thing about it is that there's this lone combat boot sitting in the middle of the road next to the tollbooth, right? One of those standard-issue jobbies there where the arm or the gate or whatever it's called bars the road off and dude checks your papers and your retina.

One fucking boot, shiny as fuck, like, gleaming in this lame-ass weak-ass east-coast bullshit sun.

Like pure death forever and ever amen is what I'm thinking.

Shane rolls down the window and listens—nothing.

Out here in the wilderness, he's becoming something else.

Hair sprouting on every part of his body.

It's like werewolf styles, but not—but something like that, know what I mean?

It's like the werewolf got no choice about what he is or whatever, he just is what he is, right?

Nina talks about it all the time—like that Gothic shit, but Shane isn't getting his dick pierced for nothing. And like, with Brit and the fangs and all that—like monsters and shit like that—Shane doesn't like it one bit. He's a sci-fi guy, not horror.

He's fantasy—he's made up, but so are they.

He's what could be, and they're like what was—but Brit is def the future too and that's something else he doesn't like. It's like hey, bitch, that's my turf.

At least Nina's just a regular bitch who's hot—Brit's a monster, man, like a Frankenstein.

And Shane's read that shit, at least he pretends he has—once you begin altering a human's body you know how long before shit's not even human anymore? God knows.

Or maybe his dad does.

But anyway there's nothing out here.

And Carter, yo, the kid's fucked. Eyes like a couple moon craters. But like, he's hope, know what I mean? Like, I believe the children are the future.

Like maybe the way I once was but not anymore but maybe still could be.

I'm the future too, and it doesn't look good for any of you bitches.

There's not a day goes by where I don't think how Dad hates me.

What I think about when I think about my Dad are the

parts for a nuke rammed up the ass of a dead Pine Marten. Like total extinction, yo—the future.

And anyway, if you wanna know, a good way to keep tight is to practice your hooks, right? Like, power in both hands, like converted-south-paw-peek-a-boo-Mike Tyson-Oscar De La Hoya styles.

You practice your hooks, your pecs tighten up like nothing else and that's how I do it.

Except I haven't been able to much because of the cult or whatever, and you know—how I'm like a renegade mother-fucker and the world's ending and thank fuck for that so there's no future coming anyhow and anyway there's no way I can lug a heavy bag around with us, can I?

And what's worse is I haven't shaved my balls in three weeks and I'm so itchy it's like I've got crabs or whatever, for real.

But there ain't nothing out here.

There's the light.

There's the hills and the trees beside the road and this mist has come down now, hanging in the air, and weird light making patterns in the mist above us—like from the sun way up there in the heavens or else from the searchlight of a sleek black helicopter—who knows?

The nervous system and the circulatory system—some outside stimulus happens, and a bolt of light streaks through your body. Like, is that how heredity works? Except it's through time and space?

There's that experiment where the scientists split some particle in two, and moved the two halves miles apart, and what you did to one particle in the lab would happen to the other at the same time—it's like a real thing—I looked it up some-where—and is that like family and history? We're just these particles reacting to something that's happening right now a hundred years ago a thousand miles away?

So we're sitting there in the car, right?

All of us, even little Carter, staring at that discarded boot, right? The windshield so grimy you can hardly see through it, because we ran out of cleaner fluid, and we haven't passed a gas station for days and days, and have been using the gas from the tanks Shane filled at the last place, but they're starting to run low.

It's rough living this way—the dash covered in food wrappers and empty pop cans, chip and cookie crumbs, a pair of Nina's underwear on there, kept in place by an empty coffee-cup carry tray thingy, you know?

And dust. There's like, a lot of dust in the air? And it's settling on everything. It's hard to breathe. In the sunlight beam through the windshield, there's like a zillion big-ass motes of dust and dirt in the air.

We're sitting here, and it's like dead calm out there in the world, you know?

I feel Shane shiver next to me—he's got the creeps—and I'm glad when he rolls that window down, man, because I've been smelling his dirty feet for like ten days straight now—we're all losing our minds because nobody's had a good wash in so long, right?

So Shane gets out his pistol and gets out of the car, and it's like his head's doing a 360 soon as he's out in the open air.

He's shirtless, just his jeans and his work boots on, and it's like because he's out in the light of the bright sun I kinda see how much weight he's dropped, you know? His abs are like, otherworldly, right? And the muscles in his forearm as he grips the .38 make me a bit, like, ooh la la, right? He's still a beautiful creature after all.

I don't know if you'll know what I mean when I say that sometimes I just hate myself for being this way—like, boy-crazy or whatever—sometimes it's like I'm not in control of my own body—and other times I think I just pretend to be boy-crazy because that's what they want from me, you know? But it amounts to the same thing whether I'm pretending or not.

Like, deep philosophical shit, I know.

Shane walks slowly over to that boot, right?

His shadow is black as shit on the pavement, and the two bones of his shoulder blades look like totally elegant.

He tips the boot over with his toe and stands there looking down at it for a sec.

And in the dead quiet, we can't hear shit because there's nothing to hear—but then suddenly there is—and it's at first this distant roar. Then a scream. Then it's like a fist pounding its way out our ears, and these two fighter jets screech over our heads like super low to the ground. Their big black shadows engulfing us for, like, an instant. Then gone.

Before the pain recedes, Shane's back in the car, gunning the engine. And I hear someone screaming, and it's me. It's me and Nina and Carter and Shane all screaming as the car plummets over the empty road.

First time it happened, they'd been drinking non-stop for twelve hours, straight.

There's a lot you can do in twelve hours, but what they had done was drink.

And the thing about it was that they both hated to eat—like, they hated food and what it did to their bodies—all that gurgling and churning and shit—like yo, they were these kind of gross machines, man—Nina hated it—so they'd get crazy with booze and the whole not eating thing.

They had a room by the bus station—like it was seriously just the smell of diesel and grease and the sound of air brakes compressing and decompressing every second like forever.

This was long before Brit, and Leo finally got bit, know what I mean? And Nina was like, I'm free as a bird yo, and I'm never going back to the shit life I had before. I'm, like, happy.

And anyway she don't know for sure but she's pretty sure Shane made the call on poor Leo—just to get him out of the picture.

The thing they did was, legit, just beat the streets, man.

They'd wake up in the late afternoon and fuck and then shower and would walk all over the city together for hours, just like any couple would do, and then they'd go home and drink enough to feel the buzz and then fuck again because what else was there?

That was their problem.

They were bored-ass motherfuckers, and secretly Nina suspected they were boring people, too—and that's why what happened happened the way it did.

He always seemed to be talking.

He'd put on his giant-ass headphones and listen to beats and nod his head and scratch in a notepad.

Even back then, he had this skull and devil and occult

thing going on—like sometimes Nina felt bad for him—how hard he worked on his drawings. Like six hours later, all Shane would have is like a skull with a blunt in its mouth, right?

Nina would laugh, and Shane would get his feelings hurt.

He was always drunk or high, and he always needed to be held like a baby.

Sometimes he'd rant.

He talked big talk and went on about every single person who he thought had wronged him in the most fucking inconsequential way.

Nina felt her brain dry up. A dead seed, like for real.

They walked the whole city, rode the trains without paying, Nina found a tattoo guy who worked from a basement, while Shane bashed out rhymes for his album, designed the cover art, and they'd buy vodka coolers and smokes and sit in the park until sundown and buy more coolers or whatever else and go back to that little room by the bus station.

The mouths of the bus garage would open and close, and the busses would come out and peel off or they wouldn't come out at all but some dude in overalls would come out of the mouth and smoke in the parking lot, and Nina would watch it from the window while Shane talked and paced around.

And there was something about those days she thinks of, even now, with Brit—that connection between those days with Shane and Brit being the, like, daughter of a bus mechanic. Some mornings, before this renegade shit, she'd put her face in Brit's hair and would swear she could smell the diesel from the garage.

But anyway, Shane, like, he was a total animal in a cage back then.

First time, there was a flash of light and her cheek bone felt hot.

He cried and groveled, made her an ice pack.

She thought it looked hot when she looked in the mirror—totally smoking.

Like, totally.

She came right out from the mirror and popped him one—a left hook to his temple.

She had watched him practice throwing punches so much, she knew what to do.

What's love—accepting everything? Or not having to accept a thing?

It became a game.

Nina called it Painting.

The Painting Game.

Their colours were blue and brown and purple and red and yellow and black black black.

His face, and hers—like legit canvasses, man.

And let me tell you, it's better than anything Shane ever drew or painted before.

When you see that shit on a city wall it's like you're looking at a corpse. Or even worse, like in some gallery where it's like a funeral home or a wax museum.

Some dumb shit with an aerosol or camel-hair brushes.

Concrete or canvas, like whatever.

Because painting is alive, man, and it's written right here on our faces.

And when they introduced Brit to the game, she took to it like crack.

That's how you find true love—you fuck them up, and then it's their turn.

When she told her sister, Nina received a post-card in response, saying:

FUCKED UP. BUT CONSENTING ADULTS.

They went with it.

Like, full on.

The dead seed sprouted.

Maybe they were actually really exciting people, but she didn't really think so—she thought they were even more boring than before.

She held a knife edge to Shane's face one night—That's us, baby, she said.

I still feel that way, motherfucker, Nina says. Like, the front of this car like the edge of that knife. Like, leading the way, know what I mean? Like, we're avant garde as shit.

The curve of that front bumper cuts through space.

For a time, her knuckles so swollen, she couldn't grip a cup or Shane's cock and made Brit do all the work.

So what happened was I was just like totally sick of looking that way?

I started making good money as a cam-girl and one of the other girls told me that I should reinvest my money in my career and in my future and that's when I booked my appointment for the consultation and they said I had a lot of potential—good cheekbones and lips and nice wide eyes even though I thought I looked ugly—like a total meth-faced bitch—but I had a lot of fanboys.

One of my regulars always signed off, Thanks Cumbucket, and that's how I felt about myself?

And also my pussy was like a piece of raw meat, you know?

I put in a lot of hours on that thing.

I've spent more time working that thing than anything else in my life.

I'd always had that innocent-girl vibe going for me, but I was done with that.

When I hit fifteen I was like, girl, you are done being a delicate flower.

They made me look more like Rita Hayworth, right? Like old-timey and sad and like a vamp, too, but I went around town for weeks and weeks with my head completely wrapped in bandages, you know?

And anyway, my nose is smaller than hers, and that's natural?

But I looked like some kinda burn victim or some shit.

And you have to be careful these days because those studios are everywhere and it's so cheap now they'll give any cab driver from Sri Lanka a license and a scalpel, you know?

And it wasn't just my face and my body they fucked with, it was even my nipples: they have this simple procedure thingy where they turn them from ovals into heart shapes, and it hardly cost anything extra, but now, even though I can't ever breast-feed some little monster of my own, my nipples are in the shape of hearts?

And, like, Shane loves it—and so have others? So whatever or whatever.

I have become the picture of love and the picture of love is monstrous—and I love what I've become, you know?

So beforehand, me and Nola, that was the other girl's name who hooked me up with this idea, went to this place where she'd gotten some mods done—she's ancient, man, like, twenty-seven years old—and we worked together at her place sometimes and it went well so I trusted her.

Nola was kinda like my mom or whatever—that was a thing we liked to do on camera, but it was also the truth, right?

Or we both agreed she was my mom without ever having to talk about it, but it didn't feel weird when we performed together or anything, it was just a thing, know what I mean?

But it was Nola who had the idea for me to invest in my career and in my future because she was like, You don't wanna end up like me where the mods at a certain age make you look weird, right? The clinic gets their lasers into you and that bio-chemical shit into you, you start to look a bit reanimated or some shit.

It's true—you see it so much—dead girls on the screen—they're everywhere.

Dead girls with a magic wand or whatever, working the raw meat for you.

Dead girls populating the invisible cloud above our heads—data, man, you know?

Dead girls in the netherworld.

In the real world too.

In the waiting room they had these screens on the walls with an animation of some, like, fire-bird or whatever flying out of the sun—the name of the company was Phoenix Modification—and Nola held my hand the whole time before I went in for the chop-job like my dad would say.

And when I came back out, swaddled in rags, man, did I ever feel excited about things.

I felt just like Jesus Christ.

Like, it was a new morning, you know?

And my sun was rising.

Dear CFP,

So anyway I wrote you all those letters previous because I am a fan of yours, but also because I felt you needed it. I care for you and for what happens to you and what was happening to you was that you had lost someone, so I thought I should write.

You've made it through okay.

Just like I advised, you haven't died yet.

You're still alive, and so are we. We're still here and so are you.

Maybe you'll die when we reach the big end, and so maybe this is a book you won't finish until you're ninety years old—but then, through our magic, I know this book will be finished and available in the spring of 2017, like, years ago—so maybe you'll be dead by then—maybe everything will finally kill you, all this shit—and by that time, given what happens at the end, how that's already written and the future already defined and clear and bright as a flash of light—the present still just totally opaque and fucked up—I can be there with you.

Like dead or whatever, or maybe not, but either way, we'll see won't we, CFP?

Because you may be killing us, but we're killing you too, huh?

It's just the way the Painting Game goes, right?

It goes this way, but it goes the other way too.

I guess we'll see how everything goes eventually.

<3 Brit

First they saw the immense radio towers in the distance aflame and stark against the dark sky.

Where the rocky hills give way to the valley, and beyond that the sea, radio towers as bright as crosses—hundreds of feet up—lining the highway leading down to what? Man, who the fuck knows?

Booms, echoes, the smell of electrical sparks, diesel, ash, grilled meat: a slight warm wind bringing to them through the open windows of the car the scent of something else—marshland, humidity, the air thick, heavy, and somewhere else between the thunderous roars from afar—birds screech and are silent out there in the near wilderness.

Gotta be napalm, Shane says, or some shit like that because whatever it is sticks to shit.

Look—these towers are made of steel, and they're burning, and here roadside, the greenery burns black.

Shit's fucked, yo, like, the world's ending, G.

Through smoke, big birds fly.

They pull up to a roadside gas station—the blinking blue-and-red neon OPEN sign a miracle in the grey—where the mustachioed elderly scarecrow takes cash from Shane's hand—gasoline, and an eight pack of canned Wild Cat for dad—saying something about an uprising, workers, cults, the government—the man's dentures chattering in his head—through the window Shane sees those radio towers burning straight down the line into the distance, and on a shelf behind the man, the television showing scenes of urban and not so urban revolt—troops in the streets of T Dot—Shane would swear he saw their old apartment building in the background of one shot—blood and smoke, homey, like fire everywhere—and in the once green towns—the police have rounded up the malcontents and beaten them to death with boots and batons and fists and have set fire to everything the jets haven't yet destroyed—the reporter saying most rural areas are secure, gesturing to a trench behind her.

The jets and the armor of the soldiers emblazoned with the emblems of their corporate sponsors, the Stars and Stripes.

Craters in the rich soil of the heartlands.

He stares at the screen for a long while wondering what may be waiting for them on the Island.

Like, did anyone even think of that place as part of the world?

Did Tariqu(e) or the CEO ever hear of it?

A freezer in his dad's workshop filled with bodies waiting for chemicals.

He leans there in a studied pose of extreme nonchalance but doesn't feel like he's pulled it off—the scarecrow giggles at him, crazy as fuck.

At the counter, the old man's hands at rest on a pane of plastic under which lie all those unscratched lotto tickets—Your Dreams Come True—and Shane's like, guess the market for that evaporated some time ago, right? Went up in smoke.

Why do we do the things we do?

Shane steps out the door and looks east where the sounds of a war and the beams of the sun are coming from.

He doesn't like to think too much so he thinks of how he'd gotten into this anime porn shit a long while ago—like big-titted cartoon girls hung like horses—and it totally ruined his sex drive for regular pussy. Aw dawg, these bitches—to say they are cartoons is like an insult to the animators, cause these girls are real, like for real—like they're real looking—nearly as real looking as Brit and Nina are except better because they're also not real—they're like these fucking perversions of reality and what's hotter than that? But they're virtual, yo—like they ain't messy the way Brit is, know what I mean? Like all the mods in the world and you're still a person. Unless you're a clone. Or like, Satan.

And what's not real about them is that they've got these giant cocks they fuck each other with, and they've got these sweet little pussies too and they're, like, down for whatever, know what I'm saying?

Aside from this uprising or whatever, it ruined his life.

Anyway, the scarecrow behind the counter is like that, yo.

You just keep doing the things you've always done, right?

Shane guesses he's been here at this gas station every day for the last fifty years, and ain't no way shit's gonna stop him.

You get a taste of something and you like it at first and you keep doing it, and then it comes to define who in the fuck you are, know what I mean by that?

But there's no, like, true self or whatever.

There's no initial state.

There's no human nature, G, grow the fuck up.

Shane's like, it's fucking Pavlov. It's Skinner. Or maybe he's just feeling cynical given that the world's ending, and he's actually like, Naw, G, it's Chomsky and we're all terribly creative and maybe everything's gonna be alright.

So Shane's back in the car and we just creep along this highway.

Cars abandoned left and right.

A sign outside the town says Welcome and someone has flattened the place.

The car bumps over the train tracks that run beside the town.

Rubble, building foundations like sets of blackened teeth.

Right in the center of town there's this waterfowl park shit—like it's a swamp and in the middle of all this—wooden boardwalks that go right out into the middle of it, right—there's this like still water and this like swampy as fuck area? Like, I don't go in for plants, but these cattails are, like, the shit, know what I mean? They tower above the roof of the car and Nina and Carter look up at them.

It's kinda like the most peaceful place in the world?

Fucking bugs big as your thumb whiz by?

The car rolls right to the edge of the water, and, except for the bodies, you wouldn't know that, a hundred feet away, the town's been drone fucked.

Here in the dim light of dawn, bats are still whirling.

Blindness, right—motherfuckers just know—they feel it, they don't just see.

They know, you know?

The body.

The body knows what it knows in its own blind way.

And then, you know, there's all these dead bodies surrounding them, right?

Charred skulls and ribcages, right—like they're everywhere.

I may or may not lose my mind, but I'm not gonna even try to describe it to you—the scene or losing one's mind—

words may or may not do the experience justice, you know what I mean by that? Words are just shorthand for experience, but unfortunately they are also material, and that's what fucks with you I guess. Material gets in the way of meaning but is also just like total meaning at the same time?

But anyway, needless to say—bodies everywhere—this little town stinking of so much shit.

Like horrible things everywhere, that's what we're seeing.

Burned bodies with gaping mouths holding smaller bodies with smaller gaping mouths.

It's like, real, right—women and children burned where they lay.

Prolly raped. Prolly raped before they were murdered and then burned alive.

So, that's what I'm seeing now.

Once people asked what is God?

And they asked what is truth and beauty?

They asked what is love?

What's real?

What's meaning?

What's anything?

Brit's like, When shit gets real like right now, who cares?

Dear Craig,

We're almost home now, and so are you. You're doing well, okay? I just wanted to tell you that. Maybe you think you're at the absolute bottom now, but things could be worse, couldn't they? At least you're not on the run, and at least the world isn't ending for you way over there where you are, right?

I see you, okay? I see you. And I'm there with you, even on those nights when you're sitting alone in the spare room of your mom's apartment, wondering how it all went wrong—I'm there with you.

Don't drink too much, and don't whore around too much.

Don't give up, okay? Not yet, at least.

And don't believe yourself when you tell yourself what a fucking loser you are, okay?

Don't do that to us, baby—it's not true.

You're bringing us all to the point we need to be at for things to feel right—and you're bringing yourself there too, honey, okay—I promise.

You are making me, but I'm making you too so don't forget that.

And last night, I dreamt about you, but it wasn't really you, it was a really super-hot black girl in leopard-print bra and panties—you were rocking this 70s afro thing and you looked so good, C, you were my dream girl.

And we were walking hand in hand through the Christmas Village thing they had at the base of the TV Tower in Berlin and we skated on the little skating rink next to the Ferris wheel and your daughter was there with us too.

I was so sad, Craig. The three of us were so beautiful together.

And that was the whole dream, baby.

It was just us going around and around and around—the moon coming up and going down—around and around forever.

When they tested the first A-bombs way down south, they didn't really know what would happen, you know? Like, the first detonation was the trickiest—there was a chance the explosion wouldn't actually come to an end—like, anything could have happened. They could have opened a door into another world— like into your world or to my world and then who knows—we may have met somehow, you know?

That's what I like to think about.

I want you to think about that too.

Let's know each other a long time, okay?

I love you, baby.

I miss you.

Bisoux Brit

The four of us get out of the car, leaving the doors open, because, like, who knows, right? The interior lights letting out this sickly little glow into the night.

And we walk out onto one of those boardwalks that lead out into the middle of this swamp where the brown water laps at the planks—we're at the very heart of the place—dead center in the water, and the four of us just kind of stand there looking around, right?

Out of nowhere comes this tiny yellow hummingbird, and we watch that little guy just hover for a few moments in the air before us. And it does this quick zig-zag, and stops again, and seems to watch us.

I think Shane may think it's like some fucking drone or some shit, but before he can do anything, it darts off into the foliage, the leaves of which are dusted with ash.

Sure enough, Shane's like, Those fucking things ain't nocturnal so the fucking Satanist Cultist Agent Motherfuckers better start doing their research.

And I'm like, Shit man, he's right.

That's what's fucked, right?

Your boyfriend is prolly like full-on bat-shit, but then, sometimes he's right about something—or he makes some kinda observation that's correct or accurate, right?

And maybe that's what's happening to all of us right now, like legit.

Shane's like, It's fucking mass hypnosis, yo, like fucking wake up, motherfucker—there's a fucking lizard eye watching us every second of the past, present, and future yo—like it sees through time—and that fucker owns all time—open your damn eyes, you dumb bitch.

A human body can take up to twelve years to go skeletal. And that shit's without a coffin, yo—six feet under the ground in, like, ordinary soil.

Everybody knows this shit, but know what—it's cool as fuck.

Your intestines start to go, and those fucking microbes in there get to work on your body—like you destroy yourself, yo—and you've carried that shit around inside you your whole life.

We make this world just like that—every bitch with the fucking seeds of their own destruction inside them—and just look at this world, motherfucker—can't you see it?

And it's true that they're seeds because those microbes are totally flora, know what I mean? They're plant life, G.

And it's like fucking literal, and also not, yo—that seed of your own destruction thing.

I remember when I was a kid, dawg, when Dad first moved to the Island he flew me there for a couple of weeks or a month or some shit.

He'd gotten into this, like, hunting shit—like because he's British he was rocking this foxhunt thing or whatever—but on the Island they don't really have that kinda shit—it's like deer or some shit—except really it's called caribou, but they're like deer, but like not deer, know what I mean?

So first thing Dad says when I'm off the plane is like, You need your gun license, and I had just turned eighteen and was like, Dope—even though he'd sent me a few pistols of his too dodgy to hold onto or whatever—like my dad's a straight G—but they were safe to have in T Dot for a bit til I sold them and sent him the money back.

And it's not like you can just send some fucking pistol in the mail, G. You have to send it all separately in its various components or whatever, you know? Like, the feds are all over that shit. And the real key is the ignition for the gun, right? Like the real live bits that make the bullets fire—Dad sent me those stuffed in the belly of this dead-ass seagull he'd plucked off some beach over there and had buried the parts right into where its guts used to be. Like, I couldn't find them at first and he kinda flipped when I told him.

So anyway I took the gun test thinking they must give out a license to any retard off the street or the boat or whatever it's so easy—but I failed because of my dyslexia, and had to take it again.

Teachers always said I was dumb, but I know I'm not—they had me in Sped right up to graduation—and I know I'm not dumb because I was like, That's the most ironically named high-school class in the books, right?

And like, kids in school called me Retard because of that shit, so I own that term, right?

You take words and you make them your own—and you take the power they have if you know what I mean by that.

But because of Sped, all kinds of people said I was dumb, right?

Like Leo thought I was and look how that turned out for him. And also look at how I've seen shit coming for years, which is why me and the girls and the kid are still alive and on the run and like Leo is prolly a stone corpse right now under a bridge in Upper Canada or whatever with twelve years to go before the bitch gets skeletal—and like the motherfucking feral animals having a feast.

But, second go round, I nailed the gun test and so here's me and Dad out in the middle of some super shitty bog-land who-the-fuck-knows-where tracking these caribou mother-fuckers with a .303 rifle in my hands—like, sick, man, seriously—the bolt action making my cock hard as wrought iron it's so bad-ass.

Those bullets, G—gold talons—menacing as fuck, and I'm

like an eagle, dawg, a fucking bird of prey, yo—and when Dad sees a mound of caribou shit at the edge of this river we're crossing, his red face is split in half with a smile.

Dad's smile, yo—like someone took a hatchet to his face, it's so big.

A real lady-killer back in the day, so he's told me, and I picture all those dead animals at his lab, right?

Soon enough one big-ass caribou head on a plaque in there looking down at us all and all the dead animals, like, frozen in time or whatever.

And so we're stalking this thing over the barrens for hours, G, seriously. Like, my hair's gone grey it takes so long, and Dad's checking the wind and stuff because these motherfuckers can smell you miles away, and we're creeping along because they can hear you from miles away too.

We come over this rise and there down below in the valley Dad sees him first—this big-ass caribou with a seriously stunning rack, G—it's beautiful.

Fucker's just stood there like a statue or some shit, and the only way you'd know the thing was alive and not just one of Dad's skin-jobs is that its ears twitch a little after we've been watching it for a while.

Dad gestures for me to take my shot. I shoulder the rifle like how he showed me and bring the scope up to my eye. Through the crosshairs I take a good long look at that sucker. Fucker's filthy yo—there's mud and shit and like bits of moss and twigs in his fur and shit. Eyes like a couple of those Magic 8 Balls I had as a kid, you know what I mean?—the ones that told your fortune or whatever.

Dad whispers, Take it, Shane, take it—and like, the caribou hears him or some shit because just then he starts to move and I squeeze the trigger and my shoulder feels like it got hit by a bus from the recoil.

He goes down. Gets up. Staggers a few steps.

Dad says, You fucked up!

And I'm like, Naw, I hit him!

You shot him in the ass!

He's right.

There's a big red blossom there.

Blood pouring out.

I fucked it up large.

Fucker doesn't get far. Over the next rise we find him on his knees in a clutch of lichen-covered rocks.

Dad doesn't hesitate.

The sound of the gunshot seems to hang in the air a long time.

Meat's ruined, Dad says. A bullet to the shit-box—what a waste.

He goes about unfolding a big sheet of canvas.

Saws the thing's head off before it's even done bleeding out.

That's when Dad's like, It's illegal to hunt these things by the way.

Because we've slaughtered them all, he smiles in my face.

We leave the headless body behind.

Birds already in the trees call out and watch and wait until we're gone.

Carter hears it first.

We're kinda camped out on one of the boardwalks in the waterfowl park, trying to sleep.

We've just got our dirty clothes rolled up for bedding, Shane asleep with his pistol in his hand, like, on his chest, and Brit with her mouth wide open like she does when she's out cold, her arm draped over me.

At night it gets quiet—we hear the sound of the bats' wings more than anything else—the booms in the distance from the air strikes or whatever are gone, yo, for now anyway.

Carter's like, Mama, there's ghosts here, and I'm like, Ugh, Carter go back to sleep.

But second or third go round—something in his voice scares me—I can hear it too, right—these voices are singing like some hymn or some shit—and it's like fucking Halloween-styles—like creepy as fuck.

I know he's right—ghosts, man, they're with us all the time—it's like the past or whatever, right?

And they're us too.

It's like back when me and Shane first got together and then when Brit came along—like, there's ghosts everywhere, man, we carry that shit around with us, but also they live right here in the soil and in the water, legit.

All the bodies and all those lives, how could they not still exist, you know? It's like, energy, and that shit cannot be created nor destroyed but only transformed if you know what I mean.

It's like quantum shit, but Shane knows more about that than me—and in fact he'd be like, no Nina, it's fucking thermodynamics—but nothing's impossible is my point, and I happen to believe in that shit—you don't come from a lineage of Lebanese refugees without knowing that the past is real and like a tangible thing, know what I'm saying?

Like, it's a physical thing, it's not made up or some shit.

Scientists measure this shit.

Like, subatomic particles know when they're being watched, so how can you count anything out?

And anyway, my grandmother saw her brother blown apart by bombs, and before that, she saw her mother starve to death because of the embargo or whatever.

So how does that not exist forever, you know?

Like in your blood and your genes and in everything you are—it's like history but it's also the future at the same time, you know?

For a few minutes me and Carter just hold on to each other in the dark, and for a sec I think I see some kinda light glimmering through the tree branches, right—but it's just some trick of my eyes or whatever because there's nothing there—it's smoke or some shit like legit.

I can see the car where we parked it near the edge of the water, and everything seems cool except for this like eerie-as-fuck singing going on and I'm like, Yo, like, maybe I'm losing my mind just like Shane is because nothing seems very real just then for sure.

In the town the only standing structure is a church.

Windows blown out and soot covering the big stones of its face.

There's no light there, you can just make it out, you know?

It's this giant grey shape.

And you can make out the clock in its tower and the clock's hands are totally dead, right?

Like, they ain't moving.

Once I wake Shane and Brit, we creep up and go around the back of the church where one of these big-ass oak trees has bitten the dust, like legit—it's huge—prolly hundreds of years old—or at least it was—now it's just a smoldering husk of wood—and the singing is coming from inside the church and we can all hear how it's, like, the same three words over and over again, know what I mean?

We're just trying to scope out the situation or whatever, you know?

And Shane makes a step with his hands for Brit to look in through one of the windows and for a long time she don't say shit—she's just watching—and then she's like, Maybe it's okay, like, let's check it out? There's kids in there, she says.

And Shane, he's showing us how brave he is, because let's face it, we're all freaked out by this shit—man, the singing is not of this earth, right?—he cocks the pistol and we sneak around to the front double doors.

He creaks the doors open a crack with the barrel of his gun.

Down the long aisle strewn with rubble, there's people gathered.

And they're like singing, man, and it's actually kinda loud the way the notes echo up off the domed ceiling and the walls, right? It's like beautiful—but the people themselves look like shadows—they're covered in soot and shit—and from somewhere pigeons fly up and escape with the music through a giant crack way up there and we can see the sky through it.

And I'm not kidding, man, the birds as they flap their wings are in time with the notes of the hymn.

I watch the white feathers go up.

The feathers are notes taking flight, right?

And the people are singing, and some are just whispering the words:

We Shall Overcome.

And then the fucked-up thing happens—and the fucked-up thing is actually like the most beautiful thing—and that's that me and Carter and Brit and Shane are kind of crawling up the aisle—I look over at Brit and she is like definitely crying—like the tears are making rivers down her cheeks through the dirt—and we hear that the people have stopped singing, and almost like magic the four of us, down on our hands and knees, have brought our eyes up at the same time and there's, like, someone's body on the altar—there's a priest or minister or whatever up there leading them, and the body could be that of a man or a woman or a child or something in-between all of these—and the body is so covered in soot that it could be like any race you'd care to name, right?—and what's for sure, what is for like really really happening like legit all the way is that this warm rain begins to fall through the hole in the roof—and the people start up singing again and are gathered around the body, and then we're all crying except for Shane, who's face looks just like one of the statues that line the place—and like, I'm thinking, Shane is fucked up as shit.

And this dead fucker on the altar was prolly cooked in white phosphorous or napalm or some shit, right?—or something else.

We back out of that place, like silent as shit, man, seriously, like total ninja-style shit—but something's gotten into us, know what I mean?

It's the germ man.

It's the shit that's driven Shane nuts and maybe all of us or whatever, right?

That fucking germ, man—hope, and its evil twin—despair.

Motherfucker's just gotta have that shit.

I can already tell you the worst thing that's ever happened, but the worst thing hasn't even happened yet—but it has to do with betrayal, yo, like, how I've been betrayed, right.

It's always the ones you love the most, right, it's totally cliché or whatever—but it's also true like legit—like for really real it's totally true.

I'm sure that's how Leo thinks about me—poor motherfucker—I don't know how many times he told me he'd, like, kill or die for me like no matter what, dawg, and me too—I said that shit to him, and then, like, what happens?—in goes the knife, right?

A blade sharp and shiny as shit, G.

A dagger, G, that's me. That's life, yo—don't doubt that shit, okay? Cause next thing you know the love of your life laughs while you're bleeding out, motherfucker—and that's just human nature—and it'll also be what happens to me sometime, like just around the corner, dawg.

We drive from this town, into that other east-coast province to the south, and it's a wasteland, man.

It's a trip, man—what can I say?

You're the type who, like, prolly loves, like, heavy description, right?

Like, you prolly think what shit means has to do with how shit is described or some shit—like, the land or whatever—but really the meaning of things is in how a bitch talks or whatever—like the landscape and the world is made from the words I'm using.

So basically, just make that shit up yourself, okay, baby?

There's a world, and it's burned black as shit, okay? And that's what we're seeing right now.

Like, you love your details, don't you?

So okay—I'll give you a little taste of what you want—like, I'm a mommy after all and as we come down that highway, the whole black sky is alive with fire and sparks and shit—there's a storm happening, and the rain is like thunder on the roof and the thunder is like something else I couldn't even attempt to describe—like God basically is what it sounds like.

God, man—we're gonna die, okay, baby?—that's what it sounds like.

It's distant, the thunder, and the distance of that like rumble or whatever is more frightening in a way than the fighter jets fucking dropping bombs and shit, like legit, man—the faintness somehow more ominous than anything else, right?

What you don't know is that it ain't technique, it's attitude, right?

But it's both.

That's what Shane likes to say about it.

It's like approach, right?

Like how you approach shit.

Are you in love with the thing you do or do you wanna know what this thing you love can do?

Do you come at something thinking you already know what it is? Or do you come toward it like a child does? Do you approach something like the way you were taught, or do you do the opposite of what you were taught? That's the key, baby, like literally—because like I already said, there ain't no knowing anything. There's no knowing—and thank fuck for that.

Basically it's this—do you love the thing, or do you love what the thing can become?

Big diff, yo.

Same thing with dudes, man, seriously—do you love the tradition, or do you love the living thing?

And that's how come things are the way they are—someone stops loving what you can become and they love you as they think you are—but ain't really you—they've just done you up in costume, baby. And that's when you stick the knife in. You kill their dumb ass because they wanna keep you what you're not.

And maybe I'm dreaming, yo, but I see that city—the Fax, man—in my head, right—like a bomb went off—like black, man, and like, that's love isn't it?

Like you ain't a kid, so I know you know what I'm saying right now—a wasteland, man, like legit like murder up to here—my hand draws a line across my throat.

Things are in flux—ain't nothing static in the world—Shane and his quantum theory and his cult shit—nothing's known—which is all we can know.

Shane used to get *The New York Times* delivered to our apartment and he'd go through the columnists and the op-ed guys and tell me like a litany of things they'd predicted and got like totally wrong—like legit these guys were dumb fucks—but millions of people bought that shit like legit, baby, every single day.

It's because of my dad, Shane told me, He's had me read this shit since I was a kid and neither of us believe a word of it—but it's habit, right?

But Shane believes in the cult and in quantum mechanics, and maybe he's been right all along—it's really something if someone like Shane was tuned into something the big boys in Manhattan or Washington or wherever couldn't figure out.

The particles, though, man, legit, like so much is in flux it's possible to walk through a wall, to fly.

We creep over the empty highway and I'm picturing the empty streets of what once was the Fax's north end—I lived there once, like a million years ago. I was Brit's age, and me and

Leo were here—he was hustling for his bosses back then, moving around like constantly, like, always.

We lived on Falkland, Cornwallis, Creighton, and Agricola.

We lived on North, Gottingen and West.

For two days we lived in a house on Uniacke Square.

When we lived on Creighton there was this bar on the corner Leo went to. It had one of those neon OPEN signs and it was always on. Sometimes, after it rained, I'd look down from our window on the third floor of the apartment building and see the red and blue in a puddle in the gutter and feel like I was in a detective movie or some shit.

Leo sold coke and meth straight out of his pocket there and then tried to shark people at pool but he was never good enough—motherfucker used a house cue warped as a gimp's dick—but he'd be gone all night and spend every cent he made. That's part of why we split for T Dot, but anyway I loved that corner and one summer a boy got shot there and we had to leave.

The black guys told us—this is the most racist city in the North American Zone.

They were like, Welcome to fucking Baltimore.

The Big War had come to those streets, I'm picturing it right now, but the other one, the Secret War, had been going on for centuries.

Fuckers have been under the boot-heel for, like, ever, yo—and the rain is pouring down on all of it.

The only thing that town had going for it when I lived there was like some accident that killed a million people. An explosion like flattened the city, I guess, and now looking out the windshield at the wreckage around us I'm like they'll be charging admission on this shit in the Fax a hundred years from now, know what I mean? Like, today's trauma is tomorrow's tourism.

But anyway, maybe the Fax is flattened or maybe it's not, but thank fuck we ain't gotta go through that town, but if what's happening everywhere else has happened there, those motherfuckers are fucked, like legit.

Dear Craig,

It's okay, okay?

You were never a big believer in marriage, but you popped the question didn't you? And look where that got you.

You were in your robe in the kitchen with the baby and you called out, Can you come in here for a sec, and your wife came in and you said, the baby in your arms, Will you marry us?

She said yes, but you already thought she had other plans, didn't you?

You thought she thought you were a loser, but she didn't think that she thought something else.

She really loved you.

It's all just dreams, okay, babe?

It's just bad dreams.

It's okay, okay?

We have the Painting Game, but you had another game didn't you?

It was the game you were taught when you lived in Vancouver and it was the game that was called Waving Goodbye To Someone You Love.

So many games, aren't there?

We play so many of them but only a few have names we can remember.

But in that game you used to have with someone, you'd picture them leaving you on some rickety and creaking ship that sailed away—they were on the deck of the ship, and you were on the dock, and the thing was that you would just wave goodbye and watch them recede, and that was like, death, wasn't it? But it was also everything, wasn't it, you know? You were waving good bye to her and her and her and him and him and they and they and yourself and me weren't you, baby?

The person leaving wasn't really leaving and the truth is that you were the one going away, weren't you, baby? You were the one dying.

When you played this game, something you'd whisper to them or to yourself was, It's okay, okay? It's okay.

And maybe that's why you worry so much about this book because you feel like you're saying goodbye but you never can tell how shit is gonna go, can you? Nobody ever really knows shit, do they?

Anyway, I was reaching out tonight to you—the ferry arrives in the morning so we're told—and I knew I'd find you out there— I knew you'd be there if I needed you to be—and sure enough you were.

Keep going, okay baby?

We need you to.

Until the end and then we'll see what happens.

Brit

They took the motherfucker right onto the lawn of the White House, and the first thing they did was shave the motherfucker's head—it was fucked up, yo—it was kinda the most fucked up thing I've ever seen.

We're in the terminal watching replays on the big screens.

TV dawg, everywhere—we'd gone so long without contact, when we saw that shit—like the news channel or whatever—we were shocked, know what I mean?

Brit was like, If TV is still working, then is everything okay in the world?

Tariq(e), G, seriously—they shamed that motherfucker, and make no mistake, shame is like the most potent weapon in the world.

They make you ashamed of what you are, if you're not like them—and on the news we watched it happen.

Like Tariq(e), yo, they started crying, and their clipped hair was falling onto their shoulders and shit, and they were like looking like directly into the camera and crying and shit. And then once they were done with the hair, the dudes in the masks made Tariq(e) like pull up their skirt and we saw Tariq(e)'s dick for a second and Tariq(e) was mouthing the words, It's okay, it's okay—Don't worry it's okay, and then the men just shot them in the head and the video cut back to the anchor and just then we were told that our ship had come in.

The ocean is black, and so is the sky.

There's no one on board but us—it's like a total ghost ship, G—the captain and crew and seemingly just one steward and they've all gone bonkers, know what I mean—like legit insane. Like Day-Pass motherfuckers the whole lot of them.

In the night, we list like mad, the rigging groaning and the motor so loud Carter is scared shitless, yo—a mist patterning the circular windows in the lounge where the steward—this fat dude in a dirty shirt with greasy hair and paws like ball mitts—mixes drinks for us on the house because he says we're probably the last guests they'll ever have—VLT machines blinking silently all around us—everything sways with the tilt of the waves.

We've got sixteen hours on this sucker, maybe longer, and we're wondering what's waiting for us on the Island, G, seriously.

Sixteen hours of watching dude split ice with a pick in the sink behind the bar, making Tom Collinses for the girls and Shirley Temples for Carter and the howling wind beating at the windows and otherwise the place is like a tomb—like a mother-fucking tomb haunted by banshees or some stupid shit like that.

But in the cabin, at least there's a shower that works.

And after everyone gets a wash—like, legit, it had been weeks, yo—we all crash out in the two bunks we got, but I can't sleep and leave the girls and Carter in the room and go out on the deck and watch the waves crash against the hull, thinking of our car, the only one on the ship, down there below-decks in the belly of this thing.

Shit changes so quickly, yo. Like, you're cruising along—you've got your girls and you've got your money, know what I mean? You can't see the future but you think the future is gonna be okay, right? Yeah, you're gonna die someday, but not yet, know what I'm saying? It's point-blank-period-like-totally-legit sweet as fuck.

You're living well.

You feel good about shit.

And then, how does it happen, G?

You go back in time and try to figure the exact moment when shit went seriously awry, right? Like that might help you make shit right again, but it don't, because you just can't place it. And everything that happens in the present—like, fuck you, it ain't the present—shit is the past and the present and it's also the future—the whole time, bitch is trying to read it all—you see these angles in your head, legit—everything is happening—and motherfucker is trying to read it all, and you'd never tell he was because maybe he's just like some guy on the bus—but he's trying to read everything that happened and is happening and could happen or not—and that's what is otherwise known as being jaded or like being smart as fuck, dawg, seriously—or insane—and you're doing the same thing too, G—everyone doing their best to read like what this world is or is supposed to be or what was, know what I'm saying?

How it went wrong—I think sometimes it had to do with seeing that satellite fall outta the sky like months ago, you know? Or when I saw the cult's stencil on our apartment building back in T Dot—like maybe that was the moment. And then I think it started even before that, like when me and Nina came up with the Painting Game and that was it—but really I know it began even long before that, right? Like maybe when I was a kid even or even before I was born shit was fucked up and the good times are just like a total illusion, G, for real.

It's like this—even when I was a little boy, motherfucker had, like, serious anxiety—it's how come I pace so much and shit, and chain-smoke like I do. It's because of my dad, right? And he's the way he is because of his dad, and his dad before him all the way back into history.

But because Dad is rich, I had shrinks and drugs and shit when I was a kid and most people can't have that shit because they're broke-ass motherfuckers, right, and I want to be poor so bad—that'd be like the dopest shit ever seriously—but I'm not.

Leo would always say that shit to me—like, You could make the world a better place, but you'd rather pretend you're a bad-ass. He'd say, You had every opportunity in the world but you'd rather wear a costume.

Leo hated me for that, because bitch grew up poor as shit, and really did have to hustle—with me it was like totally the same as the way Nina used to shop online—just some fucking get-up, know what I mean?

And anyway, I'd be like, Fuck you, dawg, but bitch had a point.

Dear CFP,

Don't worry.

You feel the same way about palmistry and astrology as you do about French continental theory, broken window policing, and contemporary literary fiction—like total quackery.

Late at night, I see you on the couch in your mom's living room while the baby sleeps in the spare bedroom, watching YouTube debates from, like, 1982, and thinking to yourself that Foucault makes Chomsky sound like a pragmatist.

But it's okay, baby—in the morning, you look at the jagged lines across your hand and pick out all the failed relationships that are etched right in there—one, two, three, four, five, six, seven, eight—your daughter beside you in the sunlight in the park with her counting book while ducks gather at the edge of the water, waiting to be fed.

We both had to come a long way, didn't we?

I went from the boulevards of my hometown to the ethnic enclaves of T Dot, then all across the east to the 7-0-9. And you've been everywhere else, haven't you, baby?

It's a long way to go—and I feel like for you and me, things are about to change again, aren't they? Maybe we're getting close to the end of our time together, I don't know and neither do you. But unless a miracle happens, that's just the way it goes, doesn't it?

No matter what, the story ends sometime doesn't it?

Last time round, you liked to say that you'd never fall in love again because of what happened—your heart couldn't take it, and you were too old for all the silliness—all that trauma and all those terrible things you did to the people you loved.

Time doesn't heal shit, does it, baby?

Nina knows that better than anyone, but she don't talk about that shit too much, you know? I know you know.

You were coming outta the store with an eight pack of beer, and there on the sidewalk coming toward you was your old lover from years ago, and when she saw you, you saw how freaked out she got, right? She began, like, nervously adjusting her hair and her glasses and this scarf thing she was wearing.

You were already pretty drunk, weren't you? And just then you decided you weren't just gonna let her walk by you without saying something—so you said something—like, Hello how are you or something like that—and you saw how hurt she still was and how angry she still was and how she hated you and how she def was not, like, indifferent to you at all and that's how I know that time don't heal shit, right? I know that because you know it, too.

And then you went back to what you had been calling your studio—that place where we first fucked, except not really—but it wasn't really a studio at all, it was a place you would go to hide because you were forty-two years old and living with your mother and you were ashamed of yourself. Then you texted the girl you were fucking and told her what happened and then you texted her to say you couldn't wait to fill her mouth with your cock and punish her, didn't you?

And then you stayed there all night looking out the window with your CD player and you cried all night, didn't you? You cried so much snot was dripping out your nose and you couldn't breath—and that's when I knew I loved you—because you were doing that for me, weren't you? You were doing it for a person nobody in your world even knows really exists—but here I am.

And there you are, C.

I don't know for how much longer I can write.

But I'll try, okay?

Goodnight.

Brit

So this is the most fucked up shit in the history of the world, okay?

Like legit, man—this shit's a bigger nightmare than what we've already come through for real—like, worse than Leo and the world burned black and Tariq(e) shot the way they were outside the White House and even all those bodies we saw in that little town with their mouths like stretched open from the pain and horror of it all—this is worse than all that shit.

We drive the car off the ferry in whatever town—it's just some shit town from a postcard or some shit—like really pretty and like a total ghost town—just these quaint little clapboard houses and tarpaper roofs or whatever—like legit, laundry on the line in some of the backyards and as Shane pulls slowly outta the mouth of the ferry it's like just totally surreal, you know what I mean?—given everything we'd just come through. It's like we're in some other world, and for the first time since we got him from my Granny's place, Carter seems sort of happy, or whatever, like seriously happy—he points out the car window at some big ugly seagull roadside, and like, I'm thinking: Maybe it's gonna be alright, right?

But it's not alright—the sun is shining and it's, like, beautiful here.

And we're so dumbfounded Shane pulls the car over to the shoulder and I roll down the window and we all watch this seagull with a, like, TexaBucks wrapper in its mouth. There must be like a piece of burger or some shit in there because dude's really intent on ripping that thing apart. It begins just furiously whipping its head back and forth with the wrapper in its mouth. It's kinda walking around in circles and flapping its wings and ripping the TexaBucks wrapper. And its little feet are stomping around in the grass, and bits of the wrapper are coming loose as it does, and Carter begins to laugh at it.

The wrapper is yellow with red lettering, and it's dirty looking. For a sec, the wind catches it and tears it from the seagull's mouth, and he has to fly over a few feet and lands on it and begins tearing at it again, only this time the gull has his feet firmly planted on the wrapper, and it comes apart in no time. Then some other gulls fly over and land beside the first one, trying to get the prize or whatever but our gull swallows the burger or whatever in one big gulp. His neck bulges a bit as he swallows it, and he's up and into the air and out of sight.

Shane puts the car back in drive, and we keep going.

The rest of the world covered in ash, and here, on the Island, it's like God's country, right? It's like, really real here.

And man, the road, right? It's this little beaten down thing that's just crumbling away, and it winds beside the ocean and the ocean is like calm as a motherfucker—there's these cute little tree-covered islands out there in the water—and the birds, man, dozens and dozens of them are wheeling around high up in the sky.

Shane looks over at me and smiles and tells me he knows from the way they're flying that there's a storm coming—Like a fucking motherfucker of a storm, he says, showing off how, like, rugged he is, or pretends to be, even though he's really a city boy or whatever—the Islander thing he likes to bust out for me sometimes—like that story about the caribou he shot— I've heard that one a million times like legit.

And I guess things aren't the same as they once were here—water-breaks and levees are everywhere because of that sea-level shit, right? Shane saying everything here was once so perfect and pristine, but it looks pretty good to me—there's all these cute little hills and boulders roadside and there's this wind blowing and it smells so clean—I see myself in the side-view mirror and, man, I look good, you know—my eyes are like ringed and baggy, and my lips are all cracked and fucked up— the wind blows my hair over my face for a sec, and I can't see.

But I push the hair out of my face, and there in the side-view, man, I see the ferry behind us in the water getting smaller and smaller, a little plume of black smoke going up from the stacks into the sky.

And then I start thinking about this mass hallucination thing Shane likes to talk about. Like, it feels as though we've entered some other world, you know—the shit going on in the other parts of the world maybe didn't happen—on board the ship, we passed through this mist and this rain and it was like we were going through something—a doorway or some shit like that—but maybe we were just coming out of a kind of collective dream—like we're all nuts and we caught this sickness from Shane and it's just this made up shit that don't make no sense anyway.

And we drive on and on over the road—the sun setting behind us until we come to a lane off the side of the highway.

Shane's like, This is it, we're here, and the lane winds through the woods, the branches hanging low over the roof of the car and scraping the sides of the car, you know? And I'm thinking of these like skeleton hands reaching out for us and I can't tell if they're like trying to murder us or keep us safe, right?

Sometimes, things that seem like a bad omen at first really ain't bad at all, but you never can tell.

And when we pull up to the house I see the white face of the house isn't a face at all but more like a skull—some shitty skull drawing Shane might do when he's stoned—and in one of the eyes I see, like, some man standing there looking out at us.

So the four of us get out of the car, and we're shivering, man.

Shane with the eight pack of Wild Cat dangling from his fingers.

The wind cuts through me like a fucking fang or some shit.

I'm looking up at that eye in the skull but there's nothing—it's blackness.

It ain't a house, it's a fucking castle, man, legit.

It's stone, and even in the dark you can see that the place is just crumbling into the ground, and I'm like, Welcome to some shitty 80s horror movie, right?

It's, like, classic cheesy shit, but here we are, right? And if there's one thing that's true it's that people who maybe think they're about to die never really do—it's too cliché, know what I mean? Unless they're sick or committing suicide, I mean. Unless they've just found out their, like, cute boyfriend is a serial killer, and they're like chained in some sex and torture and murder dungeon and next thing you know, you're in the chili the boyfriend sells out the side window of his gas station.

Like, the world is one shitty-ass writer, but even the world doesn't set you up so obviously as this, right?

Then the door opens, and we hear the sound of, like, a bolt-action getting loaded, and out comes this bigger version of Shane—a kind of horse face with a tuft of grey hair like wire—and I know just seeing him there like that—his smiling eyes are the worst things I've ever seen, man, like legit—I'm thinking this is one crazy-ass mother.

And I'm right.

I'll have one of those beers, he says.

Later, after we eat a dinner of tinned beans—mother-fucker's been waiting for this end-of-the-world shit forever—he's like happy about it, he leers at me and Brit in the lantern light—there's a metric shit-ton of canned food in his pantry, like seriously, right—he's saying to Shane like, Good thing for

you your father is prepared, or whatever—like fuck you, man—
he wants us to see his Radio Room, and I can see Shane is like
scared about it because he knows that we know that his dad's
like bat-shit, right? Like totally bat-shit.

Legit—see the aforementioned dungeon, right?—and
Shane's dad is saying like, I know how to show these ladies a
good time. Like, ugh, kill me, know what I mean?

The whole time, Carter is burrowing into me—kids are
super intuitive, man.

He's got his head right in between my boobs.

The one toy the poor guy has had this whole time is that
chess piece Brit gave him, and it ain't much good for cuddling
but he's clutching it so hard in his little paw I think he might
shatter the thing, right?

Shane's like, Okay, Dad, they'd love to see it.

Shane kinda looks over at me and his eyebrows are raised,
right? Like maybe he's embarrassed—fuck knows I'd be—and
his face is like pleading with me or whatever. His big nostrils
kinda flare.

Carter gets his face in there a little deeper.

His soft sweet little head smells dirty.

Like I said, Shane's dad is bat-shit, man.

For real.

So he takes us down into the basement. The stairs are wooden
and rotting away. You put your foot down and maybe it won't
hold you, you know? It's dark and it's musty of course, but
there's something else in the air too—it's like this radio static
that gets louder and louder the further down we get, and Carter
is so freaked out it's like he crawls right up into my arms and,
for a sec there, he pushes his face into my neck, I think the step
really will fall away, but it don't.

The wood and the stonework, I like to think sometimes of the people who build things like this, right? Like houses and shit like that—but also everything else—nice big houses like this one, even if it's about to fall apart—and how a hundred years ago a group of people built it and some rich dude like Shane's dad buys it and shows it off or whatever—it's like some ego trip—and the work that went into it—like, proof of what a lame-ass the rich guy is—is alive in the very walls and the floors and the roof and the windows and the everything.

I'm thinking of that, and feeling Carter in my arms so heavily—before I had him, people I knew always talked about how, like, it changed your life forever, and of how like profound it was, right?—and I was always like, Sure man, whatever—but then once it happens to you, you know what they mean—it's like some secret book of knowledge or something, right?—like something Shane might talk about—which sounds ludicrous but it's also True with a capital T—it's like a painting that you are making only you can't control it.

And that's what the world's like—like it's history or some shit—but it's also the present and the future, and as we are going down those steps into whatever's down there under the ground—like it would be dumb of me to be thinking about, like, a crypt or something, but I am—I'm thinking of Shane's dad and of Shane, right?—like how for me Carter is a beautiful painting being made every day right before my eyes, but for other people the future is something they wanna own or some shit like that—like, they want everything—the house the car the kid the lover—to just be an extension of themselves and that's it and that's, like, fucked or whatever.

It's dark like I said, but there's also this light I can see as we descend, and that static sound is loud, man, like legit loud—and usually I think of light as this good thing, like, the sun or life, right? But whatever it is about this place, that dim light that's flickering down there is making me think of like cancer or some shit—like it's a lame-ass analogy, but the light is like a rifle flare in the dark and the static is the hum of some murderer's bioelectrical system—like the ominous sound of a trillion tiny jaws working away on you—it's the sound of whatever the fuck makes Shane's dad tick tick tick tick tick times forever.

On the last step, Shane and his dad ahead of me, Brit's little footfalls on the steps behind, I start thinking of her—how she came into my life—like I'm closer to her than anyone—how like when Shane would be out beating the streets or whatever, how she'd make fun of him sometimes—like, she'd strut like he does and flare her nostrils because I guess she must know on some level how afraid he was of her—how like sometimes it felt like he only wanted us to talk about him, right? Like, if there was anything else—the most basic thing like getting harassed by some fucking dude on the bus—shit every girl in the universe deals with—he'd like insinuate himself somehow into it, right?—what's your favorite colour? Number? Song? Writer?—we'd end up talking about him almost out of manners, you know?—like it was bad manners for us to talk about anything other than Shane—and anyway, he always said the same shit: his favourite writer was Eminem—but I still felt bad for him, and her too, and me and everyone else in the world.

And I get that now, you know? I know, meeting his dad—it ain't just the looks department, it's the fragile ego department or something I guess and now here we are in the basement, and what do we see?

It's some high-end stereo system but without the million-dollar speakers—just these like old-timey amps, right? Like, off of a gramophone or some ancient record player—like they kinda look like big brass horns or flowers or some shit like that, if you know what I'm saying. They look like the business end of a tuba or whatever where the notes come out and not the end you blow into, right?

And they're connected to some very impressive looking radio—like a bunch of knobs and little digital displays of wavelengths are on there and there's a desktop computer hooked up to it somehow and like a million pounds of cable on the floor.

It's very scary, and like kinda total beauty, you know? Because there's a cement floor, and I'm looking down at it, and then underneath the cement floor there's something else, right? Like maybe a bomb shelter or some shit that Shane's dad made—like right down there with the bones there's a heart full of canned goods and like life or whatever—but maybe not, I dunno.

And as I'm looking at the floor, I see Shane's feet—he's wearing these steel-toe work-boot jobbies, and I'm like thinking to myself, like, I've been looking at these feet for the last several years and God I'm like kinda in love with them—like, I'll miss seeing them, right?—and right now I'm kinda frightened for my life a little bit—like Shane and his dad are maybe both psychos—maybe all of us are—and it's not like I'm into foot-play or something even though I am down with anything—but there's something just then like totally sad and lovely about seeing his feet there on the floor like that—it's the same kinda thing as when I would hear him brush his teeth before bed at night sometimes—I'm laying in bed waiting for him and hear him brush his teeth and maybe cough or some shit like that—maybe he takes a piss or whatever—and my heart is kinda crushed or something.

It happened here.

Back in ancient-history times, like a hundred years ago or some shit, this motherfucker was trying to send a wireless message right across the Atlantic.

And he did it—like he sent the letter S right across that motherfucker—I remember that because of my name, know what I mean?—the first wireless transmission in history—and the place he sent that shit was Cornwall, where my dad's from—so this whole Radio Room shit my dad does—it's like his hobby or whatever—this shit is connected to us.

But it's deeper than that yo—deep as the ocean—because what my dad's at in that basement is straight up outta the Marconi playbook—that's dude's name BTW: Marconi—that guy believed if you had the right kinda shit—like, sound equipment or whatever—you could theoretically and like literally listen to the past—fucked up—and he was like the real deal kinda scientist thing or whatever—and he thought this shit was possible.

That's because sound waves don't die—the particles continue to vibrate, like forever—same deal with light—it's like thermodynamics, know what I mean?—and that's what my dad wants because he wants to time travel, for real—or open a portal to some other world—he's obsessed with the past, yo, seriously—he's like a monarchist you know—fucker'd be happy if no one ever voted ever again.

It's fucked up, G, because like, with his taxidermy and his drug smuggling and his gun running and his Radio Room, you know motherfucker thinks shit is more valuable dead than alive, know what I mean? Like no one made any money from some tarantula if it's just been hanging out in the jungle all its life—like guns and bombs and drugs kill people—and that's cream—that's straight-up profit all the way—and that's my dad, yo—that's the motherfucker who made this world and then brought me into it.

So here's the shit—the old man set up these big-ass fucking microphones up there where Marconi sent off that letter S, know what I mean? And there's a live feed that comes into his Radio Room and that fucker spends ten hours a day just listening for voices in the static—he's insane, but maybe he's onto something—but if you twist your mind in the right way sometimes, you can trick yourself into hearing some weird shit in the noise and in the nothingness, because all you hear from the mics is like straight-up mist man—smoke, fog—it's nothing, but it's also not nothing, know what I mean by that?— and if you go up there and look out you see the very same shit—like just that dark ocean and the mist and it just goes on that way forever and ever.

So we're standing in the Radio Room, and Dad's watching us.

And for one sec, Dad totally looks like that homeless dude I spoke with outside the McD's back in T Dot, you know?

I try to make my face still—dad's eyes are warm and fierce— his face splits open with a smile—he's still got the Lee-Enfield in his hands—fucker hasn't put it down since we got here—ate his canned beans with it across his lap.

Ghosts, static, and a flickering bulb—no one says shit.

Dad taught me about the world—raised me right and tried to make a man of me.

This is the way the world is, and you got to do what's right, know what I'm saying?

We all gotta do our duty.

Later that night, me in one room, and the girls in another— You're under my roof, and under my rules—because I guess Brit and Nina assumed we'd sleep together like usual except not because that's not how Dad rolls—like, he must think Brit is just our friend—and it's like he don't notice the bruises—he walks right into my room and says to me—Did you bring that skin job?

And I'm like, Yeah, here, and take it out of my bag and hand it over to him.

I can see by the way he's holding it—fucking thing's still wrapped in tinfoil like he asked—it's like some serious shit going on here—like he's holding a baby or some shit like that—and he unwraps it and drops the ball of tinfoil to the floor and is kinda caressing this Pine Marten thing and holding it around its neck—I realize then he ain't caressing that sucker but is really slowly tearing its skin apart and inside that thing is some kinda gadget he fiddles with and he drops the dead thing's skin to the floor.

Fucking Pine Marten just got one eye—and it's looking at me—except not, because that bitch is dead, know what I'm saying?—it's dead, just like all the rest of them are.

I watch his fingers on the gadget and something seems to snap into place—I can see Dad is getting kinda super emotional about it—his jaw keeps clenching and unclenching—and he glares at me—and then there's this soft blue light on his face because the thing he's holding in his hands has come to life and it's a Bug, dawg, except not a bug but a thing by which you blow shit up—a detonator—I've seen this same shit on YouTube videos—and a kind of thrill rushes through me because here's my dad sharing this moment with me—I really am his son.

And that's when we hear the crash and boom coming up from the Radio Room.

Craig,

I get it—the outside world, right?—it's bullshit. Because when the pain comes it's from the inside, from your very own heart, from the ones you love for really real. And you love me almost as much as you do the thoughts you used to have about the life you once had, and how happy you were.

I get it, baby, and it's okay.

We were dumb to think we could be together in that special way.

But it was pure magic for a while, baby—and everything's alright.

We've both got a new life in front of us now, don't we?—and it's really scary what has to happen and the way things have to go—but that's just the way things play out sometimes, right?

I was reaching out for you tonight—it feels like so long since we last talked, you know?

I was laying here in bed—thinking of you and your heart and how cruel you are—I was frightened, baby—I kept thinking of the Radio Room down there in the basement, you know?

The static and the dim light—Shane's dad down there, waiting for a voice from the past or some shit like that—I got so angry and hateful and felt myself smile in the dark.

You're gonna be okay, okay?

You're meeting new people now, and you're getting to do interesting things, and it doesn't seem as bad as it did before and I'm grateful and proud that I was there to help you whenever you needed me, baby.

So I'm gonna get up from the bed.

I'm wearing this old white nightgown I found in the closet—it's like a gift from you, baby— and it smells like mothballs and damp and lavender—and I'm a ghost in this thing, baby. I'm gonna haunt this place even though I haven't died yet, you know?

And maybe that's what makes me do the thing I'm gonna do—because I feel like I don't matter very much—I'm hardly anything—but I do matter, don't I, baby? And that's because of you.

So here I am in a nightgown and bare feet, and I'll take an oil-lamp that's on the bedside table and I'm gonna go down the steps outside my room through the living room where there's all these creepy animal heads mounted on the wall—a raptor with something in its claws behind a pane of glass—and I'll be quiet, baby—I'll be a little sparrow in an eave—holding a little flame in my hand, and weird shadows are up on the walls and I'll go through the door into the basement and down the steps and I'll be thinking of the moon and the constellations out there and up over us all—my world and yours right beside each other and nearly touching each other—and I'll be listening to the static and seeing the light.

The world is so fucked up.

And the fucked-upedness is everywhere.

It's in every particle, you know?

And I'll throw the oil-lamp onto Shane's dad's fucked-up listening equipment and the whole thing will go off like a bomb.

When Shane and I first got together, I couldn't trust him, man, legit—but I loved his cock and the way he fucked me, and his heart—I told him he had hard, cold eyes that were too close together—which was true, and I told him other mean things and lies and some other things that were true too.

And I told him some nice things.

The first time I saw him, he was wearing a red tracksuit with white racing stripes down the arms and legs. Bright white sneakers. The sidewalk around him was kissed with dead leaves and litter—the exhaust from a nearby bus made the air black, toxic, and totally magical. I smelled the burnt fumes coming up to me like a song or an offering or some shit like that.

He'd come around looking for Leo, calling up to our balcony on the second floor and I came out and looked down at him—he wasn't just another waster—a cigarette behind his ear—gold rings, gold chain—and seeing him, down there, I couldn't breathe—he was sexy, man, totally—there was something sad and menacing about him.

He was like, Yo, Rapunzel, Leo around?—and I frowned and felt my pussy tingle and shook my head, No, he ain't, and went back inside and sat on the couch and was like, Fuck, like, who is *that*?

He really gave off this vibe, man, for real—like, second time—it was at this pharma party off Roncesvalles—an apartment above some Portuguese chicken place—I noticed he had this slight lisp that he tried hard to cover up—his voice was kinda soft and whispery and there was something about it that made you feel like he might snap a chair or some shit—like legit—seriously tense.

He was real into me—it was easy to tell. He had his shirt off—he always took it off when I was around—and Leo was super pissed, man, because Leo was sort of chubby or whatever and then here was this like super delicious eight pack in my face—he told me he was gluten free, and I was like, Shit, so that's it, huh, cool.

So I let him know. I just kinda put my fingers on his forearm real gentle like and it was electricity, man, seriously.

We were sitting in a corner of one of the rooms alone—talking shit—and I just wanted to say, like, You're beautiful, you're so beautiful, but I didn't say that—I just said something dumb and sort of trembled or whatever, and anyway he already knew what I was thinking and likewise I knew what he was thinking too—but we pretended we didn't know and just pretended we were friends but we weren't friends at all—we were already something else.

I leaned over and touched his forearm and asked for a light, and when he lit my cigarette, we locked eyes, and anyway, that night Leo must have taken some heavy downer with Viagra or some shit because he slouched in the La-Z-Boy with drool down his chin and a hard on you wouldn't believe pitching a tent while the party went on and everyone was laughing.

Those were the days, man, for sure.

But I couldn't trust Shane at all. I hated that scene but just kinda went along with it for a while—all these little skanks hanging around—and they hated me because I was like the queen of it for real—all the boys wanted me and I could take my pick—and my pick was Shane.

And here I am in bed with Carter snuggled into me—it's totally dark but somehow I know his eyes are open—it's like I can feel them moving around the room, right?—like I said, he's super intuitive, man—and I hear Brit get up from her bed—two single beds for guests in this room, and a window through which you can see the limbs of trees, just, like, swaying in the wind—that storm Shane talked about is beginning to brew.

Back in the day—we were at some other party, me and Shane and a bunch of others—it was some big old house like this one up in the country—all high ceilings and stone floors and one giant-ass fireplace and weird creepy portraits on the walls and all kinds of junky shit everywhere—it was when really all the trouble started with me and Shane.

It was like the summer house of one of Shane's dad's old business partners I think. All these rich kids with the, like, old-school hip hop on bust all night, and I remember feeling freaked out by them—like, I remember thinking: If you kids wanna seem legit you should be listening to the fucking blues.

Everyone was sitting around in the big living room with a fire raging—beautiful, man—the light on everyone's faces—white masks smiling—everyone getting bombed, man, legit—and a thunderstorm came out of nowhere—and the house went black—like power outage sudden as fuck.

The house shook. The windows filled with lightning. Rain pounding down. A thrill went through each of us—the air was alive, man, seriously.

And someone had the idea for everyone to go upstairs to the bedroom that had this big-ass balcony for a better look at the storm—it sounded like the end of the world out there.

So up we all go and out we all go—BOOM—like, we're all going to die—and then the sky lights up and we're all looking out at the trees in the like serious flashes of lightning—it's like a strobe effect—the thunder so big you could feel your bones trembling—and Shane's beside me—his smiling face in a flash of light—and he's holding my hand and we're getting soaked— it feels so good, like money, and everyone screams and beneath the smell of the rain and the air, I can smell Shane's body— when he's scared or nervous he smells like an animal, man, legit—and in the blood darkness between lightning strikes— my eyes burning—he moves in close—like slow motion, man—it's like he's moving through water—he moves in and I feel him kiss my cheek like so sweetly—and I grip his hand—and later, after everyone else has gone to bed and the storm has moved off down the valley, he leads me again by the hand out into the little town that surrounds that big house and to the very door of the primary school—the flags of the North American Zone whipping in the wild wind on the lawn out front of it—and he presses up against me and puts his hand around my throat and kisses me and pulls my hair and pulls my skirt up and it's the hottest shit that had ever happened to me.

But right now, it's a dream, man, legit—Brit in her nightgown—I'm watching her in that nightgown she picked out from the closet—it ain't real, or it don't seem very real to me just then—she's just some little wisp or whatever moving across the room and her bare feet like kinda whisper across the floorboards, man, it's creepy and beautiful, know what I mean?

And I watch her light the oil lamp there on the bedside table—her face suddenly lit up in the wavering light of the flame—her enormous shadow on the wall and up onto the ceiling as she takes the lamp and makes for the door, and I'm like, What the fuck is Brit doing, man, seriously?

And just a few moments later, that's when the world really does come to an end, like legit.

Boots on the floorboards.

A boom, a hiss.

The fire is hot and bright.

My heart.

Before I know it—Shane and his dad are here.

Shane's dad with the Bug in his hand.

Heat at my back. Light on their faces.

I lead with a left feint. Then a right cross.

Left hook.

The Painting Game, right?

Shane's dad takes a step back more from shock, I think.

My fists sting like fuck. There's blood.

He drops the Bug—I've seen that shit in videos Shane showed me.

How this world will end.

Shane backs up—his boots scuff the floor.

That sweet horse face—he's petrified—I think I love him.

I snatch up the Bug.

It's heavier than I thought and it glows.

One button I push—Game Over.

I'm up the steps and out, screaming to Nina.

Smoke, man, seriously—it's everywhere.

Out the front door and into the night.

The dark and the woods—thorns tear my head—my feet on sharp rock.

One button, one button, game over, game over.

An animal dash through branches—it's quiet for a minute and I hear the bolt action of a rifle flick over—Nina's crying out to me and then there's a gunshot—you must hate me so much, baby—there's just one gunshot—it's unreal, man, and too fucked up to think about too much.

The sound echoes off the trees.

I climb up—there's blood and green stems—the smell of dirt and sap and sweetness—my hand grabbing for something—sharp hard leaves—I hear their boots below me snapping branches and look down from the tree—they haven't seen me yet.

I'm sitting here—the thing in my hands.

It's bright and warm as a heart.

I love you, baby.

It's okay, okay?

It's okay.

It's okay.

It's okay.

ACKNOWLEDGEMENTS

Thanks to ArtsNL, The City of St. John's, and The Lemon Tree House for providing financial assistance during the completion of this project.

To Rebecca, James, and Rhonda at Breakwater Books.

To Lauren Hodder, Milan Parab, Mark Callanan, Chad Pelley, Ellen Squires, and Jo Rees.

And to my family.

CRAIG FRANCIS POWER is the author of the critically acclaimed novels *Blood Relatives* (2010), which was shortlisted for the BMO Winterset Award and won the ReLit Award for fiction, and *The. Hope* (2016). He lives in St. John's.